**A DARING STORY,
TOLD WITH PASSIONATE HONESTY**

Once again John Rechy takes us to an unexplored part of our world, a leather and Western bar near the decaying and deserted waterfront of a large American city. It is amid this sexual battle-field that the story of *Rushes* unfolds during a single evening that culminates in one of the most shattering and powerful scenes in recent fiction.

Rechy's compelling, dramatic story is "unexpectedly elegant ...it has a stylishness, a sense of pace and design. Rechy is a writer of genuine gifts and obviously a man of compassion.... At the end of *Rushes* you will better understand pain and pathos." —*The Miami Herald*

Other Works by John Rechy

CITY OF NIGHT
NUMBERS
THIS DAY'S DEATH
THE FOURTH ANGEL
THE VAMPIRES
THE SEXUAL OUTLAW: A DOCUMENTARY

Rushes

A NOVEL BY

John Rechy

Grove Press, Inc./New York

First Black Cat Edition 1981

ISBN: 0-394-17883-1
Library of Congress Catalog Card Number: 79-2302

An excerpt from *Rushes* has previously appeared in *Christopher
Street* magazine.

LIBRARY OF CONGRESS CATALOGING IN PUBLICATION DATA

Rechy, John.
 Rushes.

 I. Title.
PZ4.R297Ru [PS3568.E28] 813'.5'4 79-2302
ISBN: 0-394-50861-0
ISBN 0-394-17883-1 pbk.
Manufactured in the United States of America

GROVE PRESS, INC., 196 West Houston Street, New York, N.Y.
10014

FOR MICHAEL EARL SNYDER

AND FOR THE MEMORY
OF MY MOTHER

A C K N O W L E D G M E N T S

I would like to thank the following:

Russell Barnard, for first suggesting that I deal in full with some of the subjects of this book.

Kent Carroll, for his invaluable encouragement and his illuminating, intelligent, and sensitive perceptions, which have consistently strengthened my work.

Melodie Johnson, for a unique, stimulating relationship.

Marsha Kinder, for her cherished friendship and astute, challenging criticism.

George La Fountaine, for a supportive camaraderie and the generous expression of his views.

Rita La Fountaine, for her special affection.

Claudia Menza, for her patience, help, and kindness.

Zella Riley, for a long-lasting closeness.

Barney Rosset, for his continuing support—and for his courage.

Michael Earl Snyder, for his sustaining love and his creative comments, which, from the first draft to the end of this book, provided a major contribution.

I

In nomine Patris, et Filii,
et Spiritus Sancti.

1

I will go in to the
altar of God.

As OFTEN as he comes to the Rushes,
Endore still feels a clash of excitement and dread in anticipation of the sights, sounds, odors he knows will assault him. The astonishing array of cowboys, motorcyclists, construction workers, policemen, lumberjacks, military-uniformed men will cluster intimately within the red darkness. Muted music will pulse into the rancid smoke. Laughter—that laughter—will crack mysteriously at the point of euphoria. The most shadowed part will churn with bodies increasingly bared as night moves deeper. Mixed with the heated odor of the congregated flesh, the rot-tinged scent of "poppers" will hover like cummy incense.

Endore pauses on the street in the midst of violent-sex turf

near the city's abandoned waterfront. He always does in preparation for entering the Rushes, whether to prolong the expectation or to postpone the actuality. A sexually handsome, dark-haired man in his upper 30s—he appears younger—he wears an individualized adaptation of the requisite "uniform" in the Rushes: boots, jeans, denim shirt open to reveal a triangle of tanned flesh; his chest is muscular, defined.

Behind him, the network of iron that had once been the elevated, stretches unused, a leftover prop, rusted over, scratching its outline against the distant soaring landscape. Shadows of the tangled iron network divide the street into gray and black patches. The night is dusted ashen orange by the lights from the area of the piers. Hot mist rises smokily from the coarse-paved street, moist from an early drizzle. It is the first sweaty night of spring. Summer breathes into the humid breeze.

Near the Rushes, meat trucks are abandoned for the night. During the day they haul denuded carcasses of cattle hanging on savage racks, raw flesh to be cut up later in the wholesale butcher shops across the street. At night, men invade the bloodied floors of the trucks for sex. Before the aisles of trucks, a man licking his lips is signaling with exposed genitals to a naked man at the window in the apartment building across the street.

The walls of that building have been lashed with red and black paint—angry phallic swirls and slashes like enciphered curses. Ripped tile has left gouges in its lobby, Endore knows. A few nights ago he answered the signal of a handsome man motioning from a window to the entrance. Endore walked up the squeezed aged corridor and to an open door, where the man waited. They blew each other on the floor of the desperately chic apartment.

Now beyond the scrim of dark mist, other forms wait within the maze of parked trucks. Shadows within shadows stir the darkness. Feet on discarded beer cans jangle the silence. Nearby, a youngman stands as if undecided whether to

join the sexual field. Seeing Endore, he darts away along the block.

The youngman's dark curly hair. The startled eyes in the beautiful, sculpted face. Where, before? Shadows, too, and— ... Too vague to grasp, the memory slides away from Endore.

He moves toward the waterfront. Two women or transvestites sit on a truck ramp before one of the empty warehouses there. One of the female figures is black and large, the other white and small. Almost leaning on each other, both dangle their legs signaling drivers. Their sequins and colored flesh challenge the dark.

Beyond, shadows prowl the dead warehouses along the piers. Fire and vandalism have battered the abandoned buildings. A wharf juts into the gray water. Barges float dead.

The larger warehouse extends the equivalent of two blocks over the water. Endore knows the muted world beyond its oxidized gates. He has entered it often, knows its various vicissitudes of light—dawn, afternoon, dusk; and night—when even the darkness finds it own illumination, draining it from car lights floating in and from streetlights—ashen umber creating a mist like embers. All is visible, coated in gray.

Within that warehouse, haunted male figures lurk for nightsex in the burnt-out rooms, among the rubble of cinder, wood, clawing cans, broken metal pipes, tangled wires like dry veins. In recurring forays with sticks, slashed bottles, knives, guns, crowbars, packs of gaunt young marauders also prowl those areas, for "queers." The crunch of assaulted flesh—and the filthy floors are bloodied.

Endore sees a light-haired youngman lingering before the maw of one of the warehouses. Endore begins to cross the street. But cars curving in opposing armies, their screeching compressed by the hovering iron network, impede him. He sees the youngman enter the scarred building, stooping under the ripped oxidized gate, its border like the blade of a jagged guillotine lowered midway.

Not crossing the street, Endore tells himself: It wasn't

Michael. But was it? Did I push him there! He backs away from the gutted piers, walking again toward the Rushes. He passes the luring trucks. Forms pulsate, sighs stir the muddy darkness

In the indented lowered entrance to an abandoned building, a man fucks another. The plaster of the wall pulverizes like ashes as the bodies strain.

Endore hears that laughter—and the assertive sound of booted footsteps so familiar in this area. A group of five men swaggers toward the Rushes. All of them carry rings of keys looped through thick belts, colored print handkerchiefs displayed in back pockets. Two of the men are dressed in vitreous black leather—it shines like the oil floating on the puddles of water on the street—and the others are in vaguely military, vaguely Western clothes—consistent with the posted dress code at the entrance to the Rushes. Only the macho men like them and Endore may enter it; a beard-stubbled man at the door nightly discards the "sissies" and other undesirables. Recognizing him as one of their breed, the men nod slightly to Endore—and he nods back almost imperceptibly—the barest hint of a salute among them. Chas will be at the Rushes this hot sensual night, Endore feels certain.

Before they enter the Rushes, again the sound of the men's coarsened laughter is thrust into the humid air.

That forced, toughened laughter. A laughter which recurs. It has no origin in humor. It erupts without object. Endore notices it increasingly in the arenas of the sexhunt, in all the places where the new homosexuals have fled into ghettos. Even in the daytime as they shop perhaps at flower stands, in fashionable boutiques, in chic antique shops, even then that laughter predominates, especially among the doggedly masculine breed. Endore listens for it now. He attempts to define it.

Defiance, yes, it contains that. Pride? A new pride, Endore insists. Yet the sound always pulls back, pauses, jerks toward hysteria. At the point of euphoria it stumbles as if on a raw bruise. Stabbed with despair. Or is there a lonesome hollow at

its center? Is that laughter an uncertain weapon? The sound of unsure survival? A dogged pretending at happiness? Endore feels empty each time he hears it.

Only a few doors before the Rushes is one of the city's most popular orgy rooms. No sign designates its presence next to a wholesale meat company. Beneath the iron bones of an unused fire ladder and a tattered awning, a square concrete mouth opens onto the sidewalk. Now it waits. But in a few hours, in the later evening, squads of homosexual men, most by then in black leather, will ascend the scratched passage into the Rack.

Endore senses it before he sees it—a mechanical presence in the sweating night: A black, chauffeured limousine hardly moves along the street. Its windows are tinted black. The humming motor stops near the Rushes. Endore sees the barest outline of a face peering out from behind the black glass. The more definite outline of a hand presses against the window. The fingers open almost as if to reach out through the glass. The face retreats. The fingers remain, then they slide down. It's her, Endore knows with rage. And Martin. The mechanical purring of the car resumes. The elegant black engine pauses before the trucks and then moves toward the shrouded piers. He actually brought her here, Endore thinks, but he won't dare try to get her into the Rushes.

Almost there now, Endore sees a goodlooking shirtless youngman in his early 20s standing in posed street-toughness—legs spread, head cocked—at the corner of the street. Although this is not a hustling area, he is obviously bartering for sexmoney with an older man. When Endore has already passed them, the youngman follows him with his eyes.

Before the entrance to the Rushes, Endore stops again. Mute graffiti is scrawled on its walls, a ubiquitous wordless language.

He looks back at, and remembers, the vista he has passed through—blocks and blocks populated by men roaming or waiting, only by men, homosexual men; only men, hundreds, more, many more, most in the costumes of leather and West-

ern "masculinity," this night of ambiguous weather; men standing mutely on corners or pressed against buildings darker gray than the sky, or, others, torsos stripped, leaning out of windows, or shoved in clusters against shaded doorways along the crooked streets; men gathered in laughing groups outside tough male-crammed bars, or slouching against motorcycles or on the steps of apartment buildings; men connecting openly or waiting to connect: a vista charged with a dark sexuality which rushes from the streets into the waterfront bars, to the abandoned piers, into the dank warehouses and toward the edge of the water, the end of the land.

As Endore stands near the Rushes, a heated gust of wind shoves loose trash against the curbs, where plastic bags overflow with packed garbage. Piled to be picked up, the bags are like corpses after a deadly plague. New free-form sculptures on the landscape, Endore thinks.

They remind him of the photograph-paintings he saw at an exhibit earlier tonight. The artist had painted on huge blowups of black-and-white photographs. "He attacks violence too lovingly." In his mind he has already written that as the opening sentence for the column he writes on random subjects, for a fashionable heterosexual magazine read by many homosexuals. The artist makes love to the spent violence, he wrote mentally; he freezes the moment after it—shards of bloodied glass like a red kaleidoscope; a lamp shattered into prisms; ripped clothes a blend of colors on a lambent white floor; amid the chaos of a raped room, a lightly hued telephone overturned, its sculpted receiver dangling disconnected, wire stretched into a slender helix. For the artist, the peace after the rush of violence seems beautiful, the aftermath of rage contains a perfect geometry. The source of violence is left undefined. Endore's feelings about the "paintings" continue to shape. An intrinsic ugliness was buried in the beauty. Order—...

Tires of a speeding car screech on the street. Frightened, the older man talking to the shirtless youngman runs away. Tight-squeezed male faces, hate-pocked, stare out of the car's

windows. Clenched fists prepare to thrust bottles. Fury knotting at the fleeting sight of the cowardly young invaders, Endore presses himself against the scrawled wall to escape the inevitable pieces of breaking glass. The youngman thrusts his body next to Endore's.

"Faggots! Queers!"

The words are hurled out of the moving car along with a bottle, another, another. They shatter on the sidewalk.

The youngman next to him looks at Endore. Endore notices that panic has erased the hardness from the youngman's face. The long-lashed eyes are terrified. Against the same wall, the thighs of the two men touch. The younger man does not move. Endore breaks the contact.

As if the severed touch has released his anger, the youngman runs in the direction of the car; it has already disappeared into the electric orange of the summer night. "I ain't a fag! Motherfuckers, I ain't a fag!" he shouts after it.

Endore turns in deeper anger away from him. Before entering the Rushes, he stares at the smashed glass on the moist grimy street: beautiful, like scattered sequins on black velvet.

He walks into the Rushes.

The beard-stubbled man guarding the door of the bar nods him in.

Excitement and dread meld in Endore.

Red lights and smoke create a darkness like dim fire. Within it bodies seem at first to writhe in a dance of slow pleasure, slow pain. Smothered music crushes rancid smoke containing the clinging odor of poppers and sweat. Over it all, the recurring laughter breaks at the point of euphoria. Endore is assaulted by the raw actuality of this bar, the dazzling visual shock of the congregation of machos. Cowboys who don't ride horses, construction workers in plastic helmets, motorcyclists who travel by cab, policemen without authority, lumberjacks who work in the concrete city, military-uniformed men who belong to no corps—they are all here. The Rushes is their headquarters.

It is the most popular of the "heavy cruising" bars that

pock the decaying area. Though it is not strictly a "leather bar," an undercurrent of rough sexuality charges through it. Along the plundered street, there are rougher bars, where all the men are in funereal black leather—handcuffs, chains, boots may dangle as decorations from the ceiling. But men who are lured by the atmosphere of "masculine toughness" without willing to surrender to the total and identifying commitment expected in overt leather bars, prefer the Rushes. For some it is a "macho" bar, for others a "hard-fantasy" bar, a "uniform" bar, a "leather and Western" bar; a bar for finding a masculine companion for "ordinary sex" or for "heavier to heaviest action," without one's mere presence identifying which. For others, it is a bar for courted discovery and expected surprises.

Many muscular, lean, goodlooking—though not all, as appear at first glance, the accumulated masculinity asserting its own collective beauty—men here seem to be in their early 20s to middle 30s. Virtually all wear boots—brown boots, black; calf-length, knee-length boots; polished or scuffed boots; boots adorned with bradded studs or decorated with chains; engineer boots, motorcycle boots, military-style boots. The "uniforms" are often mixed, cowboy hats and silver-studded black belts, gleaming darkly, dissecting bare torsos; construction helmets and vests; military caps over plaid shirts. Like the bartenders, others are shirtless tonight—more will be later—welcoming the heat thrusting into the artificial air; dots of oil or sweat shine like beads on hairy or smooth chests.

All of the men clutch their drinks—usually beer—too tightly, as if in protection against a dreaded effeminate move. To further ward off that curse, they pose slouched against the walls, the bar, on stools, beer crates; thumbs hooked on belts; hips thrust out as if demanding obeisance from a kneeling form; one booted foot braced, another clamped to the floor as if barely to withhold a thrusting motion. Almost all the men standing alone appear at times to see no one. Hunting eyes barely move, connecting only in mysterious synapse.

The former "sissies" have developed a rough, bruised beauty, as clearly homosexual as drag; contrived, studied. Unreal. Increasingly alike. Endore sees; there is a new conformity, a marked sameness among the men of this sexual army—not only in the "uniform," the cut of the hair, the stance—not even in the strange laughter in common, no, it is in a look not yet quite etched into the faces—a new look of defiance and disdain, but aimed at their own; of hurt defiance, terrified disdain. With it there seems to be a vulnerable meanness that charges the sexual arenas with tensile hostility. In groups men remark brutally, coarsely—like buyers at an auction—about others walking by alone, coarsely if approving, brutally if not. Yet in a second an unhealed scar is brushed among them. and angered pain bleeds out.

The new masculinity is damned to bouts with the tenacious vulnerability. At recurrent moments, especially when liquor slackens control, the forced rigidity snaps like the enigmatic break in the laughter. Poised tenuously, the hard pose tilts, falls, shatters. Astonished, the mean look softens. Effeminacy captures the former masculinity. Then the liquor-tinged laughter becomes shrill and the break at its core lasts longer as if discovering itself.

Nightly, often from fashionable bars, stylish parties, elegant openings, expensive restaurants, chic discos, this make-believe working-class comes to the Rushes to connect for sex. They arrive in private cars, taxis, even limousines. Posted notices in the waterfront bars warn them not to walk, especially alone, through the violence-mined area ruled sporadically by tribes of homosexual-hating invaders.

Tonight, as on every other night at the Rushes, wordless promises will be made—kept or withdrawn, Endore knows; lifelong wounds exposed in one cruel moment; and anger will erupt as the hypnotic choreography of the sexhunt continues uninterrupted within the pressurized tension of exiles and the swirls of smoke, bleeding darkness, constant music, jagged conversations. All of that remains constant, as unchanging as

the Ordinary of the Mass. It is only the particular connections, the particular wounds, the particular anger that will differ, he knows.

He looks into the grimy dark enclosure that is the Rushes. Already he feels its possessive power. The popper-tinged smoke encircles him; the collective sexual energy of the roiling bodies, the friction of flesh, pulls him. The dread apprehension drains away.

It is not a physically extraordinary place, this large square bar. It has been allowed to become increasingly trashy to augment the aura of toughness, a welcome to the encroaching decay from the waterfront. Plaster is gouged like the missing pieces of a concrete jigsaw puzzle, calcimined edges blurring the connective pieces. The rubble of crushed beer cans and cellophane wrappings is shoved against corners. The Rushes is divided into partitions visible to each other and defined only by wooden posts connecting the floor to the low ceiling. At the end of the evening, a layer of smoke hangs unmoving. There are few lighted areas—more are just less dark than others, and they further divide the bar into murky pools, but to initiated eyes the Rushes provides its own clear visibility even across its length. Along the posts are scarred circular counters. Black vinyl stools are scattered about the bar, their ripped tops spew dirty hardened cotton. Men sit or lean or prop booted feet on discarded beer kegs, crates. Littered sawdust patches the floor.

A long half oval, the main counter is scratched in formless traceries created by cans, bottles, glasses. A huge American flag hangs behind it and over the low shelves of bottles glazed red by the light. The flag is new. Flanking the entrance are two areas which remain relatively sparse and quiet—protected from the influx of noise—even on jammed weekends. It is there that men collect to talk or to eye and evaluate from the sidelines the sexual combatants.

Toward the back, four steps ascend to a second level; only two areas are violated by light, and even there smoke bled of

its red hues extends grayly into the spill under a pool table, as well as into the dirty glow from a jukebox. An indistinct mothy light floats over the entrance to the toilet. Toward the back wall, this higher level is deeper red to the very point before it is snuffed out by darkness, but—like every other area of the Rushes—still permeable by knowing, practiced eyes. Beyond that penumbral demarcation, shadows fuse periodically in cursory motions of sex, more definite ones as the night moves.

In reverence to the naked hunt, props common to other cruising bars have been discarded. No game machines break the solemn rites with blinking lights and buzzes. Two pool tables, one dark now, are for frozen sexual display. Even the jukebox, its light tainted gray, is silent. The Rushes will not relinquish control of its sounds. In other bars and discos, rhythms blast out in crushing vibrations. At the Rushes, to augment the seriousness of the sexual rites, the same music is muted. The sounds emanate from unseen tapes. A smothered sexual growl burrows subliminally within the waves of smoke. Bass tones pant like an animal in slow heat. At times throughout the carnal hunt the Rushes seems to breathe, whisper, sigh, moan. On rare moments, either by accident or design, the music crashes through in an orgasmic rush.

Other than the flag, the only "decoration" is a series of erotic drawings along the walls, like the undelineated panels of a black-and-white comic strip. All unattainably muscular, raunchy fantasies of impossible masculinity, some bodies naked—cocks huge and engorged, balls like ripe fruit—other bodies exposed through ripped patches of clothes, still others in leather or in unidentifiable uniforms—the large cartoon figures painted without shading or nuance are exalted exaggerations of the real men who often pose before them.

Cheap peeling paint, cracking plaster, sweating bodies rubbing against them, scrawled markings, have distorted many of the drawings, yet others remain sharp. The result is that some of the faces convey vestiges of expressions, but even

those may be delusive, ecstasy transmogrified into pain by one broken line, a slice of shadow, a swirl of smoke. Other visages, square-jawed, obdurate, are blank of any interpretive emotion.

Each panel depicts figures in poses of assault or submission—but which, is often equivocal because of the melding and fading of clarity and ambiguity in the lines; a vague surrendering figure in one panel slides into a bold posture of assault in another. There is no discernible sequential order in this pornography of implied violence, but one or another rudimentary figure may recur, the same man in faint outline perhaps transmuted later into assertive delineation.

The series ends abruptly in a blank panel. The barest trace of an unfinished figure lurks there like a ghost. The remaining area once blank is carved now into an anarchy of male organs, lines, Xs, cruel scratches. There are even some clumsy inked attempts to resurrect the missing figure into an even further bloated parody.

At times Endore has made cursory inquiries about the drawings, but transitory bartenders trying to evoke past invisible owners of the Rushes have merely added to the mystery of their origin.

As Endore penetrates the Rushes farther, he feels he is shedding his past. His whole life compresses into this night. To all but himself and those who know him beyond it, like all the others here he will be what he appears to be or says he is. Lies will be true if believed. Only what is heard or felt or seen—in here—is real. The Rushes demands mysteries; secrets exposed are not necessarily revealed. People not present are phantoms in unsolved mysteries whose solutions lie in the abandoned past. Even the allowed splinters and fragments of memories—clues—are hued by the red subdued light. The past is the moment of walking into the Rushes, the future is in making out. In between are the entrances and exits of others intersecting the trajectories of constant glances.

A shirtless man, wrists bound, faces another man, in a

uniform. Endore is staring at the painted panel depicting those two figures.

In the strip next to that one a leathered man is holding another's arms—...

Endore's attention is pulled from the drawn figures on the walls to a familiar form facing them. Back to him, the slender, tautly muscular body is arched. The man wears a black leather vest, no shirt, a tilted leather cap hugged by a small-linked chain. Tight black leather chaps embrace his legs. Studded leather straps encircle his biceps. His belt is formed by large, silver motorcycle-chain links. He is talking to one or more men, but forms passing now before Endore cut them from his sight. Despite the many others here similarly dressed, Endore recognizes the expertly choreographed leathered figure.

Rising simultaneously from different parts of the Rushes, laughter detonates above the voices and the moaning music. Endore listens. Is the laughter attempting to smother the cries of the enemy screaming outside for blood? he pursues its origin. But the hollow in the haunting laughter is passed.

Moving farther in, he feels the clawing eyes that reach out to whoever enters the bar. He has already become a cool, handsome, desirable—pastless—man among other cool, handsome, desirable, pastless men. Eyes connect with eyes. But it is too early for firm commitment. This is the time of messages of possibility only, like the message he exchanges with a handsome man staring at him.

The blond man wears a low white tank top to exhibit a magnificently sculpted muscular body. Endore does not move away too quickly, no, knowing that to do so may sever the possible connection irrevocably rather than extend it; and he extends it by holding the look, then just allowing his eyes to slide—not pull—away.

As always, he will wait, alone or with friends, in the "safety zone"—one of the quieter enclaves near the entrance. He will collect glances, and he will send them out, careful

never to extend too overtly. As successful a sexcruiser as he is, he that way thwarts possible rejection, a knife poised to stab the most beautiful as well as the ugliest. Rejection without later redemption is death in that night's life at the Rushes.

"Endore! Endore!"

2

O Lord, I love the house in
which You dwell.

As OFTEN as he comes to the Rushes,
Chas is still rocked by its rampant sexuality—a sexual ban-
quet, he calls it. A part of all this sensuality and rough male
beauty, he experiences a sense of communion with other like
men. Only homosexual men can be truly masculine, he be-
lieves, because they have had to battle to be that, to thrust
away the effeminacy shoved on them by those who now, in
late justice, imitate his new breed. He is revolted by "sissies."
When, as the tired evening wanes he sees the leathered mascu-
linity often wilt about him, he is outraged. That never hap-
pens to him, no; he remains the tough man of his own
pornographic fantasies.

Chas prefers the Rushes to the more overt leather bars. A
bar for sexual adventure and discovery, it is ripe for converts.

That tempers the fact that, for Chas, many of the men here are looking for—he sneers—"just plain fuckin and suckin"—and even, far, far too many, for an illusive, single "lover."

For Chas the Rushes is alive. It inhales the odor of sweet male sweat and exhales the odor of poppers. Music pumps its pulse. The red-tinged currents of smoke course like blood into the veins of this huge body which contains the individual sex warriors united in sensuality, and banded against the hated invaders—the "straight" punk hustlers, the "queer-haters," and the effeminate men, the transvestites.

Chas loves this enclosed world and lives almost for his incursions into it. It is the first "faggot bar" he ever entered—"faggot" is a word he uses with earned pride, the way some black people use "nigger." Often he tries to evoke that first startling time; but just beyond the memory of a series of mental "orgasms," he pulls back—that night's greatest excitement is wafted by fear.

There is a rough masculinity about Chas. Goodlooking, dark, 27 years old—more imposing than tall—he conveys a simmering brooding sexuality. His open vest reveals the field of dark hair on his chest. Occasionally his hand cuddles his large cock, which he attempts to keep in a semi-erectile stage by wearing a metallic cockring about the base of his balls, forcing a steady flush of blood. The dark-print handkerchief displayed like a banner in his back pocket, the heavy ring of keys, the tiny silver earring—all worn on his left side—proclaim his role as a dominant man in "heavy sex," a good "top-man," one of the best. His "bottom-men" must be equally masculine.

Proud, he has strutted in full regalia to chic fashion shows to which he is invited.

He adds embellishments—silver chains, straps, even handcuffs—like earned medals. He has a collection of cockrings fitted to his scrotum. First, years ago, came the brown boots and jeans—brown, he would learn later, is the signal color of the curious, black of the initiated. For a time he even wore a cowboy hat. Then came the black boots. One propped on a

low stool, the other planted on the floor, he stared at them in the mirror. The black leather jacket followed, in winter; the black leather vest, in summer. When he tried on his new tailored chaps, as black and shiny and tight as the sleek skin of a panther, his cock grew hard and full. The look complete now, he ground the heels of his boots onto the floor as if to stomp on something discarded. The tailor blew him. Chas's hand pushed the head down his leathered thighs, to his glassy-black boots.

Although he is not beyond "plain fuckin and suckin," he is openly dedicated to S & M.

During one of his periodic excursions to other cities in search of new "heavy scenes"—and his reputation as a topman precedes his forays—Chas was asked to play an auctioneer at a simulated "slave auction" in which attractive and eager men agreed to be "sold" into "a day of service" to the "highest bidder." Only theater of pain, the auction was held in the enclosed patio of a private unkempt mansion in a now-shabby part of the city. It was a late afternoon lacerated by a desert-seared wind. Dead palmtree leaves scratched, angered, at their own shadows. Dozens of invited leathered men gathered for the charade. Onto an improvised platform, the "slaves" were led out naked in loose shackles, miming pain.

Caught in the crashing waves of rushing amyl power, Chas strutted on the platform. He held a heavy chain wrapped about one fist, its loose end dangling in makebelieve menace. He vaunted the "prime meat" of the willing "slaves," pinching their nipples, slapping their buttocks, "forcing" their avid heads to his groin, his boots; his heels clamped assertively to the floor. He was "binding" one of the "sold slaves" with imitation handcuffs when almost a hundred black-leathered policemen yelling, "Cocksuckers!" "Fags!" "Fuckin queers!" rushed in to arrest both posturing "masters" and "slaves."

Chas remained on the platform while the two uniformed factions—one pretending, the other real—fused, then collided within the heated wind. The real cops attacked with clubs. The spilled blood of the assaulted actors was real. One youn-

ger cop looked up at Chas. Choosing him, clearly choosing him, he jumped onto the platform. In a long stopped moment, the cop faced the similarly attired man only inches away. At the second before which, Chas knows, their lips would have connected—and then I would have pushed his head easily down to lick my boots, Chas is sure—the cop swung him around and handcuffs clanked.

Chas felt the cold clasping iron bracelets on his own wrists. The cop led him next to the naked "slave" Chas had just "handcuffed," the play handcuffs now replaced by real ones. Chas still held the chain in his hand. He dropped it.

All charges were dismissed as spurious after the men at the auction were jailed for the night. When Chas remembers the incident now, it stops at the point at which he handcuffed the willing "slave."

He no longer rides a motorcycle. He sold his "Harley" when he was in an accident which left him with a "sexy scar" from his ear to his cheek—and he points out that the scar is on the *left* side. But Chas is no coward. On the piers one frozen afternoon which hardened the sound of footsteps on the rubble, he disarmed a "queer-basher" ready to lash with a chain at a cowering man. The attacker fled. Chas looked down in confusion at the heavy dangling chain in his hand and at the man still cowering there. Chas flung the chain into the water. He watched it moodily as it sank, only momentarily tearing the layer of stagnation, which quickly sealed itself in oily grime.

Chas is often aroused by the impossible bodies drawn on the walls of the Rushes, though he wishes a new artist would restore the faded ones. Sometimes, leaning against one of the panels, he feels he becomes one of those exaggerated men. In the drawing he's now facing, a leathered man is holding another's arms pinioned behind him, a third man, in uniform, is about to—. . . Often Chas tries to imagine what the expressions were in each before they became blurred.

"Is he here?" he asks in a husky voice.

"Yes," Don answers. One of the two men talking to Chas,

Don calls out again toward the entrance: "Endore!" In his middle 40s, Don looks older. He cannot bring himself to wear "the uniform"—knowing he would look wrong; he tries to get away with traces, subdued plaid shirt, wide belt, ankle-length brown boots; even so, he feels uncomfortable. He will not come alone to the Rushes, afraid of being refused entry. He uses his friends' attractiveness as admission.

Standing next to Don, Bill waves to Endore. Almost 24, Bill is blond, slenderly athletic—more like a runner than a gymnast—boyishly goodlooking. He wears expensive, tailored Western-oriented clothes. Brown boots. "Endore!" he calls too. Then he feels a stab of trepidation. He hasn't seen Endore for tense weeks.

"That aloof bastard," Chas says.

"Aloof means can't have," Bill thrusts at him.

Chas touches the ring of keys on his left side. "Bullshit—I've known Endore for years and there's never been that between us." His stance hardens.

"We've all wanted Endore," Don says. He is particularly fond of Endore, quoting from his columns as if they were gospel, quite often soliciting his opinions.

"Too bad he doesn't have sex with friends," Bill says. But did he with Luke, that night? he wonders. No.

"I've never wanted him," Chas asserts. He spreads his booted feet farther apart.

The three men stand in one of the islands of space near the entrance. This quieter, sparser area provides a vista of the bar, the forms roiling within the muddy redness.

Chas turns his body away from the panels on the wall—and from Endore's approach.

At the elevated back of the bar, the only lighted pool table floats in a cleared dome. From where Chas stands it looks like a small lighted stage. He knows it well: Outlines are leaning toward the table. they sway—playing pool. The game is not important—only the poses it allows. A shirtless. arched body tilts. tenses: a sinewy arm thrusts the cue stick against the balls—when he plays. Chas always freezes that pose as long as

possible, then rams the balls. The collision of the stick against the racked balls scatters a round of fading reports. Another body stretches to slide the scoring beads strung on a wire like a giant rosary over the table. Buttocks propped on the edge of the table—when he plays, Chas always angles one leg—now the body leans back, pole extended erect, held by fingers tinged mascara-blue by smoothing chalk. The blade of light truncates a bare torso as it leans on the pole, flexed pectorals bisected by it, obscured chin propped on its tip, tightened thighs pressing the stick's heavier end—when Chas assumes that pose, he slides the stick slowly up and down, up and down. In the perimeter of the severed light, other men pretend to wait their turn while their eyes—Chas always feels them first on his crotch—study the slow dancers in this interlude of the sexual ballet.

That's for later, Chas thinks, if I want it. Now, from this distance, all he can see is the illumined flesh—"meat, prime meat," he loves to call it. From here, the amassed bodies seem to be involved in an arcane ritual. Yes, he may join them soon—and then the denser darkness beyond. His cockring squeezes his balls tighter. Aware of Endore's nearing presence, his body girds.

Endore is there.

Bill flashes his most boyish—dazzling—smile at him, wiping away the apprehension. Have they talked since Luke left the city?

Touching his leather cap in a hint of a salute, Chas nods but does not face Endore. His eyes are still on the slabs of flesh under the pool-table light.

Don slides into a heavier shadow. "It was a dreadful exhibit, wasn't it, Endore?" He raises his drink to his face; the glass is empty, but he continues to hold it there. The remaining ice looks glassy, broken. "Were they paintings or photographs?"

"The artist painted on blowups of photographs," Endore says. It's the first time he's seen Don since his abrupt telephone call, and the older man seems uncommonly anxious.

Endore's feelings about Bill are in suspension. Bill changed his life, or was it Luke? Endore was once attracted to Bill, and still is intermittently. But none of the four men here has ever had sex with any of the others. They met outside the area of the sexhunt—through mutual friends, at exhibits, parties. That can create a sexual barrier between men used to hunting in bars. If sex is not immediate, it may never happen. Still, there are undercurrents, stirrings among them.

"We walked out," Don is rushing. He insisted on leaving when he saw Endore. In the bath-of light at the exhibit, and already jangled by the benign violence of the paintings, he had unsuccessfully tried to avoid even Bill and Chas. But then, they hardly really ever look at me, he reminded himself; still, each glance from them made him pull back. But Endore would notice. Outside, Don invited himself to the Rushes; Bill and Chas were already in their bar clothes. When Don called out to Endore just now, he did so automatically, responding to the kinetic pull of their close friendship. The red shadows shelter me, he assures himself. "What *did* you think of the paintings—or whatever they were."

"I thought the artist rendered violence too lovingly," Endore answers.

A key word spoken, Chas pushes his leather cap forward and raises his chin, preparing to confront Endore.

With pain, knowing that it is not he who is being looked at, Don notices the muscular man in the white tank top staring in their direction. Don feels the evening's third lunge of terror. The first was when he avoided Endore earlier—and a hint occurred when he saw the paintings; the second was when he noticed the hustler lurking outside the Rushes. Don averted his look, to thwart any sign that the youngman might consider him a potential client—he has never paid for sex—but also because the young shirtless body reminded him of one he longs to expunge.

"Violence! Is that what they were about?" Bill says. "I had enough of that when Luke left," he releases. "Oh, you know he left the city, don't you, Endore?" Endore is so handsome,

Bill thinks, but he and Luke were too alike, both dominant; they couldn't have got together.

"Luke's gone." It is not a question. Endore remembers the frantic man who crumpled crying in his arms.

"Yes. It's my first night out, really, since he left." The memory of Luke's face—always so desperate and sexual at the same time—brushes Bill's mind like the touch of a ghost. "Here, Endore," he tries to erase the memory, "take my beer— it'll give me an excuse to check out the bar again. You know, I actually hate beer, but I can't bring myself—even after all these years!—to call out for a 7-Up in a gay bar." Well, his humor has survived, he congratulates himself. Beyond the smoke, one of the panels on the walls depicts a man on the ground, fallen or thrown. Others crouch about him. The fallen man looks like Luke. The blocked memory thrusts forward to Luke shouting, "No, it is not perfect!" Bill pulls his eyes away from the drawing. They rake the area.

When homosexuals who do not expect to make out with each other, for whatever reason, gather in a bar, there is a scattering of visual attention at regular intervals.

Before them, the cowboys and motorcyclists, construction workers, cops, lumberjacks, telephone linemen, soldiers grind within the main pit of meshed flesh. The artificial air pants only intermittent coolness. Gleaming as they insinuate in and out of the shadows, nude torsos twist toward each other as if to fuse into a huge single body. A match suddenly held to a dangling cigarette strikes blotted features into life. Eyes search, discard, search again. The sound of laughter and voices achieves its own level of silence over the swallowed music.

Along the walls and against the garish malebodies painted there, men pose in studied aloofness, their drinks a further subterfuge during these moments of exhibitionistic separation in the trenches. But unceasing glances traverse.

Endore accepts Bill's beer.

Chas faces him. "Hi!" he fires.

Each time the two meet, there are moments of tense ad-

justment, as if in the interim since they last saw each other, even if only a few days, they have become estranged. This was so even before Endore wrote a column attacking what he interpreted as the ubiquitous signs of fascination with sado-masochism rampant among masculine homosexuals. He admitted his former participation in "violent sex"—for him, as for most others, a charade that quivers at the tenuous edge of reality; he had worn its leather uniform, felt the rush at humiliating a willing other.

Even when the two men agree—and they often seem to—nuances of differences abound. Both feel that abundant sex—what others but not they call "promiscuity"—is—Endore says "can be" and "should be"—an enriching, unique experience not to be denied or surrendered to conventionality posing as liberation; and both agree that sex need not occur with love—Chas says "does not." When Chas was arrested at the "slave auction" and the sensational raid was reported luridly across the country, Endore wrote a column upholding the right of the men to hold the auction, no matter how repugnant, as long as there was no force.

All that, and the fact that in flailing against S & M, Endore did so not from a rarefied distance but from within, against what Chas holds is the ultimate in male trust and "male-love"—he encloses that in quotation marks—arouses a sense of intimate alienation between the two men—like that existing between two generals of opposing factions in an internecine war. Its battlefield seems at times to become the Rushes.

"You just returned from your trip?" Endore asks, as if, this once, they will allow that to explain the uncomfortable distance.

"Yeah. Whew! I found a real heavy scene, man, one leather bar after another. And a private place called the Catacombs! Wow! At one time you would've loved it, Endore," Chas does not accept Endore's offer of a truce. He holds out his beer as if to toast that part of Endore's past.

"At one time," Endore says.

"Oh, Chas would still be away, but he had to come back to

tend his antique 'shoppe'; you *do* spell it with a *'ppe,'* don't you, Chas?" Bill likes to needle Chas—and Chas, him—but they are careful that a ribbing tone blunt the hostile words.

"You think my owning an antique store makes me less a man?" Chas demands.

"I don't—but it seems you might. Luke was very sensitive about being a hairdresser, and we know now, since that movie told us, that they *all* think they're straight," Bill says. Luke would hide his hands—which were long and deeply veined, beautiful—when he caught himself moving them a certain delicate way.

Chas's voice is tight. "Well, hey, I'm not ashamed, man. I can bring it all together. Fuck, man, I go to my store in leather, and—. . . It's no stranger than your being a goddamn clerk—. . ." He sees a familiar body moving toward the deepest pool of shadows at the back of the bar. It's Michael! Chas looks at Endore. Endore does not register awareness of the presence. Chas's tongue brushes his lips hungrily.

"A clerk! I beg to inform you that I am responsible for one of the chicest—. . ." Bill starts frostily; but realizing that Chas has succeeded in piquing him back, he says, "I'm not against antiques; if it wasn't for us, there wouldn't be any!"

Endore laughs. He stops himself. He has begun in certain places to attempt to listen to his own laughter as if it emanated from someone else; to search out that tone, or hollow, that pause, that break. But he knows the mysterious stasis occurs only when the laughter erupts without object, released as if by the barest touch of a nerve.

"I don't think that reference to antiques is funny," Don says. He is forcing himself not to go to the bar for his third drink; he has drunk the melted ice. Is Endore looking at him too closely? he wonders. And why hasn't he mentioned his being gone since he telephoned to tell Endore he'd been called away unexpectedly? Touching his forehead—a slight swelling there?—Don lowers his head and moves into a buried shadow. "Getting old, especially in our world, isn't—. . ."

"Bill didn't mean that," Endore says. Don is hiding his face. His voice was so frantic when he called to tell him he was out of town that Endore won't stir his obvious anxiety with questions now.

"Really, Don!" Bill protests. "You're not that old, and I didn't mean you. You think every reference to time is aimed at you. That's what makes it so difficult for you to—..." He backs away from Don's pain.

"To make out? That's what you were going to say, isn't it?" Don demands. He sucks at the empty glass. As they stand there, groups of men mill in this zone. Don is increasingly aware of the stares his three attractive friends are getting, returning, even rejecting. It is always so, but tonight each glance denied him chafes his raw nerves. "But that's not why. It's because I'm ... plain; and here—..."

"And a brilliant lawyer in real life," Endore reminds him. But that doesn't matter in the Rushes, he knows.

"Real life?" Chas says. "What's real right now is this sex paradise, and that's all!"

"A disturbed paradise," Endore hears himself say.

"You can't get off that S & M thing," Chas says. He breaks the locked stare between him and Endore. He looks beyond the massed bodies in the main portion of the bar, beyond, toward the shrouded back. He knows that area well, as he knows every inch of the Rushes. Often after posing at the pool table, he will join the bodies beyond it; he will have glanced back to invite others. The sex there is not usually what Chas calls "heavy": more a preparation for the late-night orgy rooms. Two marines kiss, a cowboy gropes the firm pouch of a construction worker, a biker slides to his knees before the waiting erection of a lumberjack, a cock may slide into a lubricated ass. When he is in the dense jungle of shadows there, Chas can usually direct the sex at least to the outskirts of "heavy." His growled commands, muted consistent with the quiet dance, ignite the darkness with sex.

"What?" The broken moment between him and Endore

was so intense that only now is Chas aware that Bill said something to him.

"I said," Bill repeats, "that if you wear anything more on the left side to prove you're a 'top-man,' you'll fall sideways." Curving his body slightly, he dares to mock the rigid masculine stance.

Prove! Chas charges at Bill: "I saw you on that contraption at the Rack—. . ."

"Not me!" Bill denies.

". . .—and the guy had his fist all the way into your asshole." Chas is floundering—it was dark, ambiguous, and he knows Bill—who believes in "fidelity"—was still involved with Luke.

"That's a lie!" Bill says. "If you—. . ." He retreats. Chas is raging too ferociously. "What's the matter with you, Chas? Ever since you went to the piers before we came in, you've been wanting to fight." On their way to the Rushes, Chas separated himself from the two other men—to go, he said, fondling it, "charge up" his cock in one of the warehouses where men were lingering. There were two female figures—obvious hookers, one black, one white—on one of the nearby ramps. As Chas approached, the white one, in a black vinyl dress sprayed with sequins, stood up. The black one remained swinging her legs. Bill couldn't hear the words. Chas stomped back angrily.

Chas crushes the evoked memory of the encounter. I should have punched "her" when "she" spoke to me, he thinks. On this hot, turbulent night he has already begun to threaten the tacitly respected boundaries between him and the others.

Endore felt Chas's spiraling tension, and he pulled away from it. He studies the field they will all be moving into. He recognizes a famous ballet dancer—a motorcyclist draped in chains—talking to an architect—a construction worker. A chic working class, Endore often thinks.

"A sleeping beauty." Don says aloud. Realizing he's verbalized his thoughts, he tries to laugh; a nervous laughter. "I

meant that muscular man over there." Tension squeezes his words. He's not sure now whether he meant the man in the white tank top or Endore; the accusation swells: So aloof! Endore sometimes chooses to leave the bar alone. "He looks like a sleeping beauty waiting for his prince." Don laughs again.

In Don's laughter there has always been pain, Endore knows. That's not the sound he tries to locate. And the look in Don's eyes—that's clearly the look inherited by so many homosexuals who drink heavily and are past a certain age; it burrows in the eyes. That's not the look that Endore sees in the new men. Its progenitor?

"A prince who'll never show up," Bill says, looking at the muscular man. Luke waited like that, he remembers. It's a miracle I approached him, gorgeous as he was—nobody else would. Live pornography. He explores his feelings. He misses Luke. Very clearly. Yes. Yes. He tries to catch the eyes of the muscular man.

Chas crushes a cloth ampule of amyl nitrite—the precious "poppers" he loves and is never without; when he can't get the real ones, he settles for one of the liquid substitutes of butyl nitrite more readily available—Rush, Bullet. The aphrodisiac vaporescence rushes blood to his brain, clasping a vagrant sexual moment. Now sensual images of the Rushes compress inside his mind, then resile, framed by a throbbing blackness. Again, he feels his cockring squeeze his growing cock. He holds the cracked ampule to Endore. "I got the real, powerful stuff, tonight," Chas coaxes.

"Not now," Endore rejects.

Chas withdraws it, as if to erase the gesture. Fumbling, he holds the ampule unexpectedly toward Don.

"I like my sex straight," Don says. Tonight his need to connect is screaming. The last time was—... He bolts the memory shut.

"That's not all you like straight," Chas seizes the double meaning.

Bill recoils from the chemical odor. But already it brushed

over the memory of the crucifix Luke insisted on keeping over their bed. Sometimes in the isolated reality of the chemical sexmoments, Bill would look at it while he licked Luke's body. The long limbs of the nude figure over the bed seemed to strain.

The disturbing tension growing in him—Don wants to verbalize it in order to dissipate it; but he can't locate its definite origin, it has too many components. "That hustler outside looked normal," he tries.

"Normal!" Bill is indignant. "I didn't think anybody used that word any more."

"Fuck, Don," Chas shoots, "you think the guys you're attracted to are heteros"—he often refuses to say "straight," as Endore also does—"just because they rob you."

Don winces. "I'm not at all attracted to norm—. . . hetero—. . . straight men. And no one has ever—. . ." The pain knotting under his ear stops his words. His hand is trembling about the empty glass.

"That's cruel, Chas," Endore says.

"Sorry, Don," Chas whispers. Outside the Rushes, he likes Don. But the bar changes everything. The Rushes is for the fit warriors. Chas's sense of communion with the others is compromised by Don's implied judgment. As if to wipe away his attack on Don, he looks at the panel to his left. Two men are tearing the clothes off another. The blurred expressions in the drawing bother him tonight.

"I know I don't make out the way I used to," Don won't let go, and knows he never made out well.

Chas waits for another chemical buzz from the popper. It comes. "I always make out," he says, feeling his cock throb in a series of rushes. "And *I* go after what I want. That's dominant. Waiting to be approached is passive, and nothing to brag about." He looks at Endore. "Like that muscular sleeping beauty over there," he diffuses his meaning.

But he means Endore's method of aloof cruising.

"Definitions blur," Endore tries to dissipate the implied charge. Chas is rampaging.

38 ·

"Only yours," Chas thrusts. He grinds his boots on the sawdusted floor; by now that has become a familiar gesture from the first time he forced the man to lick them. "In S & M there's a top-man and there's a bottom-man. It's all clear and honest."

"Is it?" Endore asks him.

Again, Chas licks his lips, this time to release his trump: "Mike is here."

"Michael," Endore corrects him coolly. "He never liked to be called Mike." He remembers the blond head nestled under his chin. The *reddish* blond hair. The beautiful face fresh even on awakening. And the laughter—unscarred; his laughter was unscarred. He does not look in the direction toward which the three other men turn to see the blond youngman cruising the crimson forest of shadows.

"I said, we don't allow—..."

The words rise clearly from the entrance.

All four men—and the others in this enclave—turn in that direction. The man guarding the door is blocking the entrance to a smallish figure. A tall shadow looms next to it.

"My God," Don utters, "is it really—...?"

"Oh, God," Bill echoes.

"Fuck," Chas spits.

He did bring her here, Endore thinks. The outline of her hand pressed against the black-tinted window of her limousine. The hand pantomiming touching was blocked by the glass.

3

Send forth Your light and
Your fidelity.

AS OFTEN as he comes to the Rushes—
"between affairs"—Bill still experiences the same collision of
fantasy and reality. He knows that the cowboys, construction
workers, and telephone linemen here are not that, and he
wants them to be; yet the real ones would not match his fan-
tasies, which only full consciousness of their specialness can
fulfill. He adjusts by creating his own "unreal reality."

As always when he's here, his clothes are only "oriented"
toward this bar; the styled "Western" shirt, the indigo Italian
jeans display his own mode. With his blond hair and lithe
body, he looks just as good in any of the city's stylish discos,
which he frequents—for dancing. His body is sinuous within
the rainbow-dyed vortex of lights. For sex he almost invaria-

bly ends up at the Rushes among the men whom he jabs for their rigorous machismo—and whom he needs because of it.

Within the firm knowledge of his own boyish masculinity, he challenges that machismo. Sometimes he will even lunge into campiness, flirt with outlawed poses—limp wrist, thrust hip—daring incursions into the macho psyche. Others in the bar shed their masculinity in jarring, shocking accidents—but Bill gets away with it all because it is deliberate. Then in one magical movement all the sinews of his body, magnetized, come to almost military attention at once, and he assumes the macho stance. A mysterious Southern accent tinges his voice then.

Bill came out early, in his teens—and easily. First came the muscle-building magazines. When he saw the cover of one on a newsrack, his heart gasped at the shiny colored photograph of the almost naked man. His outstretched arms were flexed so that each sinew was carved on the tense muscles. The abdominals were etched over tiny white trunks which barely concealed the groin. The thighs were strained in full striated bulges. The stunning body gleamed with oil or sweat. The face stared enrapt, at nothing, or perhaps toward the flooding light of the sun.

Bill boasts he never felt guilt about his next love, written pornography. And why should he? To him as well as to others his age, it was easily there, to be used creatively. He made his choices contingent on a tacit promise of definite sexual roles and players. A jacket photograph or drawing of a gorgeous muscular body being "adored" by a man equally masculine but slender, younger—even "prettier"—would get his money order.

He tried photographic pornography but was appalled by the skinny bodies of so many "tacky kids with nothing but large dongs." When he did locate a photograph of a muscular body being "worshiped" by an attractive younger man, Bill's hard fantasy would deflate if he turned the page to find the muscular man licking the slender boy—or both going down on each other. Even more of an enraging "waste" for Bill would

be two gloriously muscled men of like age responding mutually.

Bill's attractiveness allowed him to be just as selective about his lovers when he shifted from fantasy to reality. He began a series of brief affairs—which he ended the way he had traded a favorite sex book for another more exciting one.

He met Luke. That was Bill's deepest and longest affair; "the first person I ever really loved." With Luke he did not need pornography.

True, Luke still had sporadic bouts with the "spooky religious" stuff Bill had long abandoned. Once, after "insignificant quarrels" about it, he went so far as to get Bill to go with him to church. Bill agreed—if Luke would go dressed as a cowboy. He did. Bill entertained himself through the interminable service by looking at the men in the paintings on the walls of the elaborate church, the faces so handsome, the bodies so strong. He tried to point out his favorite to Luke. who became furious. Attempting to give the unreal figures "motion," Bill's eyes shifted from the 14 stations on the walls to the pages of Luke's cherished old prayer book. The same handsome men were depicted in the reproductions of gaudy religious paintings in the book.

Many of the figures in the gaudy paintings—familiar from Bill's childhood—were actually sexy, handsome muscular men straining—much exposed flesh. A painting in front of the book revealed the crucified figure almost naked. Each muscle of his outstretched arms tensed into sharp definition. The beautiful body—sculpted abdominals, sinewy straining thighs—gleamed with sweat. The brief white loincloth hardly covered the groin. The figure did not seem pained but seemed, instead, to bask ecstatically in the flood of light. Oh, was it the same painting? A similar one, then?—the one from which as a child Bill had blotted out the disquieting too-red blood in order to stare in fascination at the beautiful stripped shiny body. Did it have the same inscription under it? "Greater Love Than This No One Has."

Between Luke and Bill all was perfect. Then it ended.

Bill prefers to hunt rather than be hunted. A recurrent paradox in the homosexual world, the hunters, aggressive in their approach, like Bill, are often sexually "passive"; the hunted, waiting to be solicited, courted, like Luke and Endore, are often sexually "dominant." Of course, the definitions do not hold—Chas is a "dominant aggressor," but sadomasochism, which eludes Bill, has its own exotic rules. Then there are the many men—most?—who prefer mutuality, and those who shift roles. Did Luke? Of course not!

Because Bill is very desirable, men often attempt to respond to him the way he wants to respond to them. Then he will either ease his partner away or—quickly, before the other can—he will part his long blond legs and offer his slim, tight, down-brushed ass for fucking.

He is attracted to Endore, who reminds him of Luke; whether or not Endore is attracted to him, he is not certain, sometimes feeling yes, others no. He finds Chas sexual but pulls back from the postures of violence—and from the overtness of his "costume." For Bill it is that, a costume, unreal, with no context in reality; it *is* itself, stands for nothing else. "Realness" is very important to Bill; "unreal reality." Outside the Rushes, he likes Don as a good friend. Inside, Don brings too much unwelcome "real reality."

For Bill, the Rushes is a fantasy bar, the best. At certain times in the evening, and with the expert eye of a stalking cat, he can locate in a sweeping arc of the bar—and collect visually like a stack of photographs—the most attractive men in the room, and he can do it through dense smoke and red shadows.

Although the drawings, which show the same figures shifting roles in subsequent panels, naturally displease him, Bill has a few favorites among them: especially one in which a "gorgeous hunk"—magnificently exaggerated beyond any possibility of reality—stares ahead as if at an invisible object. Bill disagrees with Chas, who said once that the man was cruising an even more exaggerated image of himself. In the drawing, two men denude the main figure and another hovers at his feet. The possible implied violence, Bill erases facilely.

Bill has many friends, including women, who respond to his easy masculinity. He likes—respects—transvestites. Often, in the area of the piers—which he does not cruise, aware of the pillaging raids of violence—he will see the tawdry figures. He will go out of his way to greet them. He would have done so earlier if there hadn't been that encounter between Chas and the vinyled transvestite on the ramp. She seemed to be waiting like a sequined panther for Chas.

Bill looks toward the entrance to the Rushes. I hope they won't let her in, he thinks. There is only one breed of woman he dislikes, and Lyndy is its epitome.

"We don't allow women," the voice of the man at the door is raised.

The woman's voice says: "I know, darling."

"But you will allow her, won't you?" the voice of the tall man with her says to the beard-stubbled man at the door.

"And you're not properly dressed for this bar," the man at the door tells the man.

The four men look away from Martin and Lyndy, to block the pulling knowledge of their presence. But the awareness encloses these moments in sudden silence among them. Fusillades of voices and laughter rush to kill the hollow.

Endore turns in the direction where Chas indicated Michael was. He waited long enough to look; the youngman has disappeared.

Holding his beer between his legs like a surrogate hardon, Chas lights a cigarette, cocking it in his mouth so the smoke causes him to squint. The bar is distorted through the smoke, wavy, like dark-red water in which sexual bodies sway.

Bill's gaze sifts the bar, then moves toward the back, the farthest area, as if that way to abandon the disturbing presences at the door.

From that back elevated portion of the bar, a squat unused jukebox sends out a sullied halo of light; that is its purpose. Like the affusion of light over the pool table, its vague circumference provides exhibitionistic highlights for bodies on display. Often Bill will stand near it, just stand, for long

moments, outside the boundaries of the dirty light. The men within it seem at times not to move, as if at last they have captured a perfect pose. Bill wishes the muscular man in the white tank top would stand there.

Endore looks again at the magnetizing figures at the entrance. The raised voices are becoming more subdued but firmer.

"Do you know who she is?" Martin asks the beard-stubbled man at the door.

"Ask him if he knows who *you* are, darling," Lyndy's voice is almost joyous.

Endore forces his attention away. Don is so nervous. There is something different about his face.

In the compressed moments created by the intruding presences at the door, Don feels Endore's look on him. Why the hell doesn't he ask me why I was gone so long? Does he suspect? Both Chas and Bill wouldn't remember he'd been away, and they were "gone" too part of that time. He will force Endore's attention away from him in any way: "Luke and Billy were together four months, so you see it can work," he flounders.

"Three," Bill corrects. "Then he couldn't get hard, and he blamed me." Bill removed the crucifix after Luke left—that was all of his own Luke didn't smash. Bill remembers Luke's body—smooth; he had almost no hair on his chest, just the shocking heavy nests under his arms. Bill loved to lick them.

"Be glad you're rid of him," Don says abruptly. Will they notice it's his fourth drink if he gets another?

Bill erupts: "You never liked him, Don. He used to tell me no one did. Except you, Endore." His look flings an accusation based on a question. "You don't understand that I loved him. But Endore does."

Endore nods.

Chas studies Bill. He and Luke despised each other, and Bill seemed to enjoy that. Chas wouldn't mind having Bill, fucking the slim blond ass, holding—. . .

Luke. Endore remembers. The handsome man, yes, but he

remembers more than that the pained eyes. Not unlike the eyes of the youngman outside when he pressed against the wall next to him and their bodies touched. Another face is superimposed on the memory, like a double-exposure, the face of the other boy lurking near the trucks. Again a memory flickers—but is it now of the shirtless youngman or the curly-haired one? Has he confused one with the other? He cannot recognize even the nuance of the memory—pleasant or unwelcome? It reflickers, is snuffed. He glances at the faces of the men drawn on the walls. A slice of a shadow converts the look on one into anger; curling red smoke reinterprets it.

The presences at the door pull again. The smallish figure of Lyndy has moved to the side of the man guarding the door. Martin is talking to him in flinty tones. The woman faces the smoky haze before her.

Don't let her in! Chas is glancing at the two figures. He touches the dark close stubble of his beard, a mere dark shading, its roughness feels good. He eyes a goodlooking man passing by, keys on his right side. "Cologne!" Desire smashes. To drown the offensive odor, he retrieves another cloth ampule of amyl. A slight pop—he cracks it, inhales. He waits for the sexual synapse. It comes with a silent burst. The sealing blackness has blocked the woman out. Through the throbbing black frame sealing the moment, he glances at Endore, but this time he does not hold the crushed ampule to him.

Don says, "Maybe, Chas, you should protest to the management that that man dared to wear cologne. He obviously got by because the man's attention is distracted." His voice is traced with anger. "Clearly the Rushes doesn't allow sissies, or ladies—. . ." There's no respect for ladies now, he thinks, none. He's aware that the smallish figure of the woman has retreated somewhat, the men's voices are hardly audible.

"Or older guys," Chas aims.

Even Chas spoke those words softly, but their mere evocation is always a curse, Endore knows. Age. Even as desirable as he is, knowing his body is more muscular—with much

younger men, yes, he notices the velvet softness of the creaseless flesh. The velvet feel of Michael's ridged stomach.

Chas holds out the ampule, like incense, letting the sexual fumes pervade the smoke.

"I hate that stuff," Don pulls away from the clutching odor. "It smells like dirty socks."

Allowing the chemical to stir his memories, Bill leans over to inhale it this time. "Whew! That *is* powerful!" He has not sniffed any since one night with Luke. "God, was Luke into that stuff. Sometimes he'd pass out on it." But Bill would go on. Now he tries to think of Luke, to enhance the sexuality; instead, he thinks of the naked figure over their bed.

At the door, the voices are muted.

An impasse? Is she retreating? Endore's look rivets to the entrance.

The woman is obscured now by the two men. She walks slightly past them. The man at the door seems about to block any further move. Then he stops next to her. Martin speaks to him again.

Deceptively petite, pretty, in her 30s, slim, Lyndy stares boldly into the Rushes. She wears a tailored dark velvet tuxedo without a blouse. She holds a string of pearls in a loop before her. She bites one but only with her lips—dark like the outline of her eyes. Stark eyes, stark lips are the only features of her face revealed by this light. A second strand of pearls rests on the velvet.

Chas feels his temples throb. He looks at the glorious maleflesh meshed about the bar. There are more bodies now. The amyl recoils. The bodies vibrate with the accelerated beating of his heart, as if the chemical throbs control them. Then the receding rushes strip his anger at the woman's presence. She mustn't come in!

The man at the door abdicates to Martin's new words.

Lyndy slides past the man at the door. "I'm in!"

Beside her, Martin, tall, slender—in his late 40s—is dressed in fashionable evening wear—an affront here. Even in the tor-

pid light and smoke the man and the woman radiate the aura of power. The beard-stubbled man surrendered to it. The woman enters the red caverns of the Rushes.

So easily. She came in so easily—but riding on Martin's power, Endore thinks. Endore himself has close friendships with women, perhaps closer than with men—he has been accused of preferring the company of women. There are women he loves—without posing at desire or bisexuality; he considers that a subterfuge, disdains it. He has written against the hostility burgeoning in the macho ghettos against women. But would he support another woman's entrance into this bar? Yes. Perhaps. No. He is astonished by the possessiveness the Rushes has aroused in him.

Seeing the woman enter, Don's mind clicks: Good!

Chas squeezes the ampule of amyl between his fingers. He would be affronted by any woman's presence in the sacred domain of the Rushes, any violation of this macho font. But Lyndy—and with Martin! She has come to challenge all he worships; she will do so with her slashing smile, her devouring eyes, her soft purled curses. Chas lets the expired ampule of amyl fall to the floor, where it squirms in the sawdust like a dying worm. He grinds his black heel on it.

Bill looks at the crushed ampule. There are times when the flux of the amyl is not pleasurable. The clasping moment, refusing to release, can be violent. It twists him into darkness, he hears his heart beat. Bill's body jerks. A wing of sadness slides over him. In fragmented fascination, he's still looking at the squashed ampule. A memory of Luke—no, of the aftermath of his last time with Luke, possessions strewn, broken—lies beached and dead in the wake of the unwelcome rush. "When Luke left, he smashed everything," he hears himself remember.

Endore looks at him, in surprise at his abrupt words.

In accusation; he's looking at me in accusation, Bill knows. "It wasn't my fault! I did everything!" he shoots at Endore, releasing the tension he had merely allowed to burrow. "The three-ways, the four-ways—not enough! I picked up tricks for

him—did you know that, Endore?—because—can you believe it?—he said he was shy! Shy! I even let myself be—..." The jarring rush passes.

They're all looking at him. He's grateful for the distraction at the door. It obviated whatever Chas was about to say.

Groups of men are recognizing Lyndy and Martin. Powerful themselves in that other world outside this night, this bar, many of these men are accepting them—pretending to accept them—now that they've passed the barricade, Endore thinks with irony.

Bill looks away from the woman and Martin. Often he goes to discos with pretty women, heterosexual or Lesbian; and he knows—feels—he would have—might have—applauded the invasion of this macho fortress by a woman—if only to watch the outraged machismo tested—but not by Lyndy. She's here for cheap titillation; a spurt of adrenalin for boredom. But perhaps there's more. Still, have his feelings toward the Rushes been always this tight? To avoid seeking an answer, he searches out another of his favorite drawings on the walls. Where is the man alone, clothes ripped, and the—... He didn't locate it; his glance was intercepted by that of a construction worker. Clutching at the look, keeping it steady, he tries to erase his earlier outburst: "I'm here for sex, just sex—not love," he says lightly. "But I don't want to go to the back part of the bar for it." A touch of anxiety edges in. He looks at the pulling shadows in back, not even shadows; there the bodies mesh in blotted darkness. "Have you noticed that hardly anybody wants to go home and have sex any more?" he thwarts the attention threatening to rush toward the entering figures. "Or anyhow not with only one person. People just want to make out in back rooms." I won't go to the Rack, he thinks.

It wasn't him at the Rack, Chas thinks with some disappointment. "You're always looking for a new lover," he accuses. Bill looks particularly "hot" tonight.

"And why shouldn't we look for one person?" Bill asks. Chas would be so attractive without all that sinister black

leather. A cowhand—he'd make a good cowhand, so lean and hairy, yes.

"Why not many?" Chas asks.

"Or one and many," Endore says.

Don looks puzzled. "That doesn't sound like you, Endore." he chastises. He doesn't know now exactly how he feels about Lyndy's presence; a brush of resentment. "I remember your column in which you wrote love is an unnatural state for queers. 'Learned in heterosexual imitation,' you said; I remember the phrase very well." Especially when I'm alone, he thinks, when I'm alone, it's good to think that being with someone else is unnatural. "I was reading it the night I called you—I keep my favorites of your columns in my desk—..." He catches himself too late. "I took it with me to read," he revises.

And so he called me from his apartment, pretending to be out of town, Endore knows.

Bill sighs in frustration. "Did you actually say queers, Don? I'm sure Endore didn't." Soon he will raid the arena of the bar, but first he'll collect more interested glances. Where is the muscular man? I hope he moves near the jukebox; his muscles would make shadows on his body.

Endore answers Don: "I didn't say love was an unnatural state." Did I feel it? Or something I call that? And the icy pain. *That* is unnatural, yes. If I could, would I blot out the memories, quell the intrusive feelings? "I was writing about the insistence that we *must* have a lover—so many always looking for one impossible person."

"Not all," Chas reminds.

"Too many," Endore says. "We even claim to have lovers when we don't, as if alone we're incomplete; that's sad—and unnatural—whether you're homosexual or not. And I was talking about the selfish possession of bodies we call 'faithful love.'"

"Amen," Chas intones—and thrusts: "But was it unnatural, what you had with Mike?" He mocks Endore's insistence: "'Scuse me, I mean, Michael." The knowledge that Endore

was involved with the youngman—if he was—affronts him, as a deserter affronts a staunch soldier.

When Endore doesn't answer—and Chas waited—Chas drawls: "Your archangel is real popular·in the back part of the bar, and you wanna know why?"

"Chas, if you—. . ." Endore stops. Has Michael, with Chas? No. Michael's not there yet. Yet. Was I right? And was that him at the piers? I would have crossed the street into the warehouse. The traffic kept me, he thinks, trying to remember what kept him other times, on the street, at parties, even— once—here when they both left, alone.

Nearer them, Lyndy pauses with Martin to greet a familiar face, perhaps someone they have worked with. Her titled claim to wealthy—archaic—aristocracy is unquestioned, as is her status as a top designer of women's fashions; bold, defiant, scornful clashes of the expensive and the cheap, the real and the plastic proclaim her designs—cashmere and vinyl, crepe de chine and dacron, voile and mylar, moiré and orlon.

Martin is even more famous; a painter whose vast canvases render in minute detail the perfect angles and shapes of modern architecture; buildings, bridges, avenues, as if unused, never· to be used—a tectonic order unmarred by even the shadow of a human form. He is also a photographer and the escort of other famous women, the ex-wife of a powerful senator, the wife of a rock star, a drifting princess—obsolete women who feel safe with him.

"And so the Mona Lisa of the chic gay bars has come to the Rushes with her consort," Endore releases the postponed announcement. Often he's seen her—surrounded by dazzling creatures of all sexes—holding surrogate court, usually with Martin at the disco restricted to the rich, the famous, the gorgeous—and ruled paradoxically or appropriately by a squat ugly man on whom they have bestowed the papal power of excommunication from glitter. Tonight Lyndy is attempting to extend her boundaries. Other men knot about her and Martin.

"I hate that fag hag." Chas spits on the floor.

"That's like calling Caesar a soldier," Endore says.

"That sounded like me," Bill says, but he can't laugh. He has sat with her and other beautiful youngmen and women, yes, at other bars. Now she's here. Why? "How did Martin manage it?" he asks.

"He owns things," Endore says. "Property and people."

"Not the Rushes!" Chas asserts.

"I heard a Catholic family owns it," Bill says half-seriously.

"Jewish," Don says.

"The fuckin Protestant Mafia!" Chas derides them all.

Bill pretends to take him seriously: "You heard that too?"

"Shit!" Chas hates any intimation of ownership of the Rushes. "I think I'll go to the back of the bar and charge up; man, my big cock needs a good macho mouth wrapped around it," he says. Lyndy. Her presence floods him with disgust. He went in full leather to her recent showing. He has always hated her, her assuming looks, her doubting smile. Why the fuck is she *here?* Why did Martin bring her? Chas begins to move away.

"You're running from them, Chas," Don pays him back.

"From that cunt?" Chas is indignant. "I just want a little back-bar action, two heads on my—. . ."

Lyndy glances toward them.

"Always bragging, bragging," Don says.

"Just because *I* make out, man." She's here, Chas faces. Actually inside the Rushes! His turf, his bar for communion. She's here. Now Chas remembers the transvestite on the piers. Her words to him resound. "Tonight I'm gonna conquer me a real macho stud for some rough sex, man," he tries to rub out both the presence and the memory.

"Do you feel, Chas, that by saying 'man' after each sentence and holding your beer to guard against a broken wrist, do you think your masculinity is increased?" Bill jabs. "Luke was like that," the memory touches him. "Every now and then he'd slip up on the wrist."

"But you'd remind him," Endore's voice is steely.

"Did he tell you that?"

"No," Endore answers. He looks at the scrawled panel where the drawings should end. Did the artist just walk away from the unfinished "series?" Endore has tried counting the number of scenes depicted—14, 15, more, less—the panels meld into confusing permutations, figures connecting one to another.

Lyndy whispers to Martin. Both look toward the four men. Lyndy waves.

Endore nods. Looking away, he asks Don gently: "And our respected lawyer, what are you looking for?" He wants only to remind him of the identity he left at the door, to sustain him with the knowledge that he may regain it by leaving—although he knows how difficult it is to shed the iron spell of the Rushes. Why did he tell me he was out of town? Was he? Again, he searches the scratched panel. This time it's as if at the edge of violence the series tangled on its implied nihilism. Did the artist die before finishing the drawings? Was he in the process of restoring them?—and that is the reason why some are bolder than others? Yet there seems to be a selectivity in the boldness.

"Oh, I'm just looking for a drink," Don sighs. Strange to see a black man at the Rushes. Don is staring at a handsome black man who just walked by. "Or for a new friend to add to my beloved small knot of friends. Or just for someone to talk with into the night. Actually I'm looking for someone to fall madly in love with forever—if you'll forgive me my trespasses, Endore, for being 'unnatural.'" He tries to laugh, but the laughter hurts. "My forever is getting shorter." Again he glances at the black man. He's standing against one of the panels—nude men grappling over some intimate object of clothes. Tonight the drawings disturb Don particularly.

"No love for me anymore," Bill reiterates. "But look at this feast of studs," he says spiritedly. "They don't all wear too well, though, you notice? First you think everyone's so gorgeous, and then—. . ." He shrugs.

It's true. The visual assault of flesh and sensuality does not

hold entirely. When the throbbing collective corpus of the bar releases the individual bodies, earlier-extinguished flaws emerge even in the smoothing red lights. Several of the men are wrong—starkly—in the uniforms, others expose bodies not in the right mold for exhibition, still others offer up their masculinity early, some faces age in minutes. The sensual assault recedes, somewhat, somewhat, even more, yes, but not totally, never nearly totally. There is always the insistent macho beauty asserting itself everywhere.

"Still," Bill reassesses the situation, which may shift with his mood, "it's not bad at all. That construction worker is pretty humpy—he's looking over here, I hope it's at me. I think I'll go get a—..." He stops. Don is ready to release the accusation of attempting to avoid Lyndy and Martin.

Chas has intercepted the looks from Don to the black man. "You like niggers, Don?" Especially now, he wishes he could drive Don away. Now with Lyndy and Martin here. And drive away the memory of the transvestite.

"I am not a racist," Don is indignant. "How can you, a queer, call anyone names?"

"He said 'queer' again," Bill marvels.

"Maybe that black dude is as proud of being a nigger as I am of being a faggot," Chas says. "You thought of that? Hey, how about it, Don, you hot for a big black hung stud? He'd stumble on your antiques—..."

"Which he bought from your shop-pee," Bill forces Chas back.

"I was just glancing at him—..." Don begins.

Feeling the presence of the approaching woman like light doom, and the tension of the remembered encounter with the transvestite like an invisible knife, Chas goes on relentlessly: "You want black cock, Don, and fuckin Bill wants another lover—..."

"Oh, no," Bill protests.

"... —and Endore." Chas lunges. "Endore is looking for—..." He suspends the words. He allows them to dredge into Endore.

Endore looks into the depths of the shadows, as if to separate them. When the veils of red smoke part, he faces the abandoned panel of scrawls. Did the artist leave it deliberately blank?

"What are you looking for in the Rushes, Endore?" Chas asks softly. His booted feet are planted so hard that the muscles of his thighs knot.

4

Deign to grant some part
and fellowship.

As OFTEN as he comes to the Rushes,
Don still feels an outsider in it, and is. In the homosexual
world of the bars there are avenging ghosts who refuse exorcism: the relentlessly effeminate among the relentlessly—even
when unsuccessfully—macho men; the faded "beauties"
changing into "queens" and clinging to shadows and the
shadows of memories; and the older men—often near-alcoholics—who refuse to disappear from the sexual arenas or to
surrender to the isolation of tight dinner groupings of men
their age and older, gatherings brightened or rendered even
more desolating by an occasional, quite often discreetly
bought, "boy."

Don is one of the avengers.

Men his age—or men who look his age and are not "sexy"—are not welcome here nor in many of the other bars, orgy rooms, baths; increasingly, posted notices bar the entrance to "over 35s"—or those who look over 35. Even where there are no restrictive signs, such men may be banned from entering the "private clubs" because they are not "properly dressed" or because of a fire ordinance limiting the number of clients; yet others pass by. There are men, even older, who manage miraculously to continue surviving in that world, sacrificing their bodies to sweaty rituals at the gym, the male "beauty shops," Don calls them. But those smashing survivors are very, very few.

Masculine, yes, but not sexually so, Don was never attractive; plain even in his youth. So he became a "good friend," a devoted listener, a good sympathizer when love affairs collapsed. He gave grand parties and made a point of introducing interested people—discreetly—to each other. In return, infrequently, someone desirable might accept his offer of a hungry blowjob. Or at a party Don might meet a friend of a friend, no place to stay; such a man would be welcome as Don's guest, and then again Don might—or might not—be rewarded.

Each time he comes to the Rushes—using his attractive friends as his passport, hoping people will think he's involved with them—he tells himself he will not plunge into the fray, not now, not later. He comes here to "visit with friends and learn the gossip"—and "queer bars" are where that happens.

Happened.

He knows that that reason is subterfuge, exists only in memories of an increasingly real past—the 50s—hued in ambers and pinks, the tints of naughty romance, when gossip was endemic—not really mean, no, at worst slightly nasty; how else did one learn about others "who were"?—what star went in drag?—who—who else—had been busted? You came to the bars to interpret it all, give it meaning. Camp. Have fun. Don could be coaxed to do an impersonation of Tallulah—which

friends said sounded more like Ethel; but he would do it only for his best friends, dalling; and he wasn't sure he liked it but they loved it and that mattered.

No, he has not forgotten the harrowing "interludes." The bars were raided periodically—he himself was arrested once for "disorderly conduct"—entrapped by enticing vice cops, charges dropped after many court appearances and thousands of dollars. "Just the usual harassment." If the same bars raided didn't reopen, others did. Nor has he forgotten friends who committed suicide in quiet shame at having been "discovered," usually after an arrest. But in his mind those times were less complicated because everything was clearer: To be a "queer"—a word he cannot expunge from his vocabulary—meant to accept being an outcast, and to hide at least half one's life.

The openness now! Magazines everywhere full of organs like slabs of meat. Books full of fucking and sucking! Men in the macho ghettos like sexual armies trampling out love. Sex on the open streets! Ugly marching demonstrations! "Queers" shrieking slogans for God knows what new rights. Oh, they still languish, look at them, but in macho costumes.

When did it change? The death of Judy and the Stonewall Inn riot, when the "queens" fought the cops. For Don, a troubling death, a troubling birth.

Why do I come to the Rushes? He reminds himself that there have been those nights—rare, rare, rare, but he hugs them in his memories as if there had been many such nights—when he has connected with a gorgeous someone so shaken by a rejection that he will turn to Don for urgent immediate affirmation of his power to attract. Don will bestow that affirmation. Other times—he reminds himself of this too—if it's the exact moment and he dares to approach someone being avoided as "unapproachable—too conceited," he may fill the other's astonished emptiness, hurt narcissism—and he will connect.

Don has always longed for "a beautiful lover." Each time he comes to the Rushes, he screams for a miracle he knows

will not occur but waits for: An extraordinarily attractive man will see into his soul and find what his plain face and body do not have. But no one looks that deeply—"any more"—and he continues searching, only in the most attractive and disdainful men.

He detests hustlers. When they look at him "that knowing, mercenary way"—the way the shirtless boy outside might have stared at him if he'd given him an opportunity—but he looked away—he is hurt for hours, even days.

He used to cruise the piers. If he saw any of his friends, he would usually abdicate the arena to them. Even the darkness has its light, and most often he faced brutal rejection there. Still, there were times—again he hoards these—when he would wait until he saw several attractive men, and he made sure they were attractive, gliding into one of the gutted rooms. Moving in surreptitiously—when the bodies tangled and the origin of one more groping hand might not matter or might go unnoticed—he would insinuate himself into the tangle.

He has not been back since one lacerating night. The moon was so bright that the metal bones of the cadaverous warehouse cast black shadows. The water exhaled a cummy stench as it licked at the decomposing edges of the pier. Don attempted to join a clutch of sex. He was pushed away violently. He ran deeper into the lit darkness, stumbling.

His mind careens from the horror of that night.

Now, the drink in his hand gone, he discovers again that he has swallowed the melted ice. He has begun to perspire, longing for another drink, but he doesn't want to touch his face to wipe the perspiration, afraid to summon Endore's close scrutiny again, afraid to arouse the dormant pain. Instead, he glances at the drawings on the wall. Men about to shove another as if to pinion him against a tree. Ugly. The gross exaggerations repel him, the menace. The men in the drawings would resemble Chas except that he's too wiry. Still—. . . Bill? Much too boyish and cleancut. Endore. Yes, they resemble Endore.

Tilting the empty glass again, Don looks at the handsome

man—his friend, his good friend, his good friend Endore. And Chas. So wound up tonight since he saw that "drag queen." And now confronting Endore with that brusque question about what he's looking for in the Rushes. So rude. But why *does* Endore come so often to the Rushes? Too often, it seems to Don this moment. Endore comes here just to be with, not in, the Rushes.

"I'm prowling our jungle," Endore answers Chas.

Chas allows the answer, for now. "A hot jungle, and we're hot animals." He holds a cigarette between his lips, the match in his fingers, ready to strike.

Don leans away from it. "At times the Rushes is somewhat more like a cathedral," he says. About the bar, rows of men stand in solemn outline against the walls.

Chas misunderstands. "Where we worship or are worshipped, yeah, and that's righteous, man." He cracks the match.

Don recoils from its flicker.

"If Luke hadn't been a Catholic," Bill says, catching the interested eye of a cowboy walking in—he's increasing his prospects for tonight, "maybe he wouldn't have got hung up on all that spooky stuff." The cowboy looks back. "That crucifix—Luke kept one over our bed, did I ever tell you?" He looks at Endore.

"Small wonder he couldn't get hard," Don says.

"Actually it was sort of sexy," Bill thinks aloud. "The blood was too fake to be a turnoff." It glistened like red wax. The white body was stark and sensual. Oh, oh, the cowboy is slightly femme already and he hasn't even had a drink. The loincloth concealed but clearly suggested the genitals between the straining thighs. Bill retrieves his invitation from the fake cowboy.

"I'll have to tell you about that place called the Catacombs," Chas tells Endore. Bill's words have evoked it.

Lyndy's laughter tugs at their attention. She and Martin are lingering with a group of men in assorted macho uniforms.

In her laughter there is nothing. a hollow sound she

makes, Endore thinks. Did Martin take her to the piers? The limousine paused before the trucks. When the black engine returned and stopped, did the rough-stanced youngman hustling outside think the wealthy car had stopped for him? Endore remembers the scared face. If the youngman ran to the car, did Martin discard him without a glance?

"That cunt'll be here soon." Chas hears Lyndy's laughter.

"She'd call you a prick," Bill responds automatically; he is used to "defending" women from contemptuous remarks in homosexual bars.

"I'm not ashamed of my cock," Chas says.

Bill simulates an endless yawn: "We know, it's huge, enormous, proud, erect, pulsing, pounding, a long shaft, throbbing—..." Retracting—he saw Chas's head snap toward him like that of a rearing colt—Bill asks Endore: "Does Lyndy really design her clothes right on her black models?"

Endore knows the woman and the man best. As a popular columnist, he moves at times—as they all do—in her orbit, their circumferences intersect in mutual arcs—but, until tonight, not here.

"And Martin photographs them like upright corpses," Endore says. He has seen them in her black-and-white studio. She and Martin stood like ruling pieces in a three-dimensional chessboard. The black female models before them hardly moved. Eyes closed, their eyelids were painted shiny white, mascara-thickened false eyelashes like straight bristles. Behind the unmoving women and to the pulsatory beat of disco music, tight-clothed white male bodies chosen and easily discarded by Martin shifted from pose to pose into jagged geometric tangles. The men's urgent fluid motion and the women's lifeless stasis were seized, but aloofly, by Martin's ticking camera.

"I've never believed that Martin doesn't have sex with those beautiful men he photographs; they're all so anxious to be chosen," Don says. "Is it true, Endore?" he solicits.

"Perhaps, yes," Endore says.

Who? The question is asked and quickly answered as the

woman and the tall man are increasingly noticed farther into the bar. Many of the men turn hostilely from her, many spit their defiance onto the dirty floor, turn unyielding backs to her—and to the man for bringing her here. But even more—and soon several of the previously recalcitrant, informed of their identities—nod, accepting their power perhaps so theirs may be extended outside. A few of the men may be Martin's models, others may want to be seduced by his famous camera. The black-outlined smile on the woman defies the pursuing—but waning, waning—hostility. Her large eyes blink, as if recording the astonishing visuals—the leathered manikin-stiff presences, the barechested posing bodies, the sexual soldiers in expensive working-class uniforms.

One pearl still kissing her lips, Lyndy fingers one of the two strands, rubious in this dyed light. Now she releases the strand. The pearls fall on the black velvet of her tuxedo.

About the bar, the overt expressions of hostility have all but faded, at least on the surface.

"Darling!" Lyndy greets Endore and turns her cheek for him to kiss.

"Darling," he says flatly to her and rejects the cheek.

"Darling." She extends it to Don.

"Darling!" Don obeys.

"Darling," she calls to Bill.

"Darling," Bill says frostily.

"Darling."

"Hiyuh!" Chas spits.

Lyndy eyes him with amusement. "Darling," she tries to extort from Chas.

Chas stares at her. Lyndy laughs, a tiny laughter. Martin nods to the men. They acknowedge him back. Lyndy says to Chas, "I didn't recognize you for a moment, darling Chas. Of course, I've seen you in leather before—*mais sans tous les accoutrements!*"

"That means without your chains." Bill isn't sure whether his hostility then is aimed at Lyndy or Chas.

Chas stretches his body before Lyndy. The vest opens far-

ther to exhibit his hairy chest. He clenches his hands behind his neck, revealing the dark tufts of sweat-curled hair under his arms.

Lyndy's black lips tilt at the edges, stretching the smile.

"And so you've raided the Rushes," Endore hears himself say to her.

"I do so like to be first into forbidden territory," Lyndy says.

"But you aren't," Endore says. "Martin's been here before."

Martin does not react; there is not even the tremble of a reaction. "I promised Lyndy that our romantic cynic would be here," Martin says to Endore.

"Why did you come here?" Endore asks Lyndy; his voice is controlled, but he feels a burgeoning anger which he would prefer were not there.

Rude, Don thinks. And Endore *likes* women! Those columns he's written in their defense. Rude. Men aren't gentlemen any more. His lips are parched, he'll *have* to have a drink soon.

Lyndy says, "To be with friends. Though I must admit I didn't know *how* many! We were at Andy's earlier, and some of the same faces are here now."

"The faces are somewhat less tired here," Endore pursues. He will have to explore the disturbing rage, this sense of—... outraged possessiveness?

Chas laughs. "Amen!" he approves.

The looks of the two men connect, this time in alliance. Against the woman for invading their domain, Chas knows. Against the woman *and* the man, Endore knows, for invading their domain, however differently he and Chas may view that violated territory and the nature of the violation, however different their reasons for outrage—no, Chas's reasons will not be his, their look has signaled only the pact of cobelligerents, who may yet confront each other.

In posed annoyance, the petite woman pouts. "I'll be the first at the Rack," she announces slyly.

Chas's eyes assault her. "No, you won't!"

"I doubt that even Martin can get you into the Rack, darling," Endore says. He pursues his feelings, to make sure that no demon lurks in his antagonism toward this woman. Is he affronted only by her, her presence here, affronted only by the breed she represents of smiling, despising infiltrators into a world they have neither earned nor been shoved into? Yes, he insists, it is *her* and her breed because Martin's presence affronts him as powerfully. But does it? Yes, Martin equally. But differently? He hopes the evening will answer.

Martin shrugs.

"One can try," Lyndy says.

"They. Won't. Let. You. In," Chas asserts.

"But, darling. look!" She spreads her arms and looks at herself. "I'm here in the Rushes!" she says triumphantly. "And the Rack is just next door."

Now Endore accepts their presences at the Rushes. There is a retrospective inevitability to that. Throughout the years of cold intimacy between Lyndy and Martin, and Endore—and, yes, Chas—there has always been a fascinated hostility, a hostile fascination as if the discovery of a vulnerable secret in one will—may—prove there is none to find in the other; a plenary justification which only the other's weakness may provide. Or is it so only for him? No, that has always been there, hints coalescing during the recurring bouts disguised in endearments, branded with "darlings." Yes, it was inevitable that the entangled fascination would be extended into the battlefield of the Rushes.

"Let's get a drink, darling, and you can see more," Martin says to her; then like a tourist guide: "In the back the serious sex is happening—beyond the pool table where they pose; here it's just a preliminary evaluation of possibilities that occurs. And conversations between 'friends' before they move into the arena as enemies battling for the same body."

"No *serious* sex at the Rushes." Chas resents Martin's arrogation of his beloved world.

"Ciao," Martin tosses back without turning as he moves away with Lyndy.

"Oh, do wait for us!" Lyndy flings back like a curse at the four men.

Disbelief. Anger. Acceptance. Anger. Acceptance. Acceptance of power. Lyndy moves like a delicate conqueror through the tide of reacting flesh.

Chas spits.

Endore knows that between his obeisances to the rituals of this night's cruising—and now he wants sex, very much—he will return throughout the night to this island, staked as an arena, to confront the man and the woman; yes, both. He feels it will be so with Chas—the four lured to each other like detectives to uncover a mystery. And Bill? Perhaps, perhaps not; he's too caught up in the splendors of the Rushes. And Don? Tonight he's troubled, patched wounds are being bared.

Don wipes his forehead and feels the puffiness. But Endore is studying the reactions in Lyndy's wake. "Drinks?" Don asks the three men. His words pull at the clinging spell, but they don't expel it.

Chas wants a beer. He was going to cruise the bar in his first sortie of the evening—feeling "hot"—but now he'll wait until Lyndy and Martin move away from it.

"A 7-Up," Bill pretends to whisper.

Endore's hands are cold on the warm bottle of beer. He nods yes to Don.

Don goes to the bar. This time he will get a double shot. He likes to buy drinks for his friends—to fuss on his way back as if he were just about to spill the drinks—anything for good friends.

At the bar—away from Lyndy and Martin, Lyndy facing the red maw of bodies, Martin's back to it—Don sees the black man he noticed earlier. He's handsomer than he appeared at first. Is it his imagination, or did the man look at him? Yes. Even in this bar, with its miasma of prejudice, like that of so many other homosexual bars, especially the "leather and

Western bars" like the Rushes, the black man is eliciting much attention. *Is* he looking at me? Don glances to both sides of him, to see whether someone attractive is next to him. Yes, on his right, a blond youngman who averts Don's glance, angling his body away. Don gets the drinks, asks for a tray to carry them on. Again, he's sure the eyes of the black man are on him. Is he a hustler? the thought pounds. No, nobody hustles in the Rushes. The black man has pulled back into more darkness. Expecting me to follow, later?.A pinprick of pain pierces his temple. He rushes back toward his friends.

Moments of silence enclosed the three.

Endore listens to the shooting laughter about the bar, the break challenging definition. Again the laughter explodes, this time out of a man near them. Endore turns to look at the man. Drunk already, he leans his head wearily on the shoulder of a man with him as if the laughter wounded him.

Bill's eyes are choosing. Another cowboy is glancing their way; the construction worker over there; a—... What the hell is he? Oh, yes, an aviator.

Chas breaks the tensive spell. "Fuckin cunt!" he growls. He grinds the sawdust on the floor. He despises women increasingly. When he thinks of soft flesh—... He loathes weak heterosexual men, too; and weak homosexuals. All weakness! He touches the coarse stubble on his chin. Especially Lyndy—that type. He touches his leather chaps—they feel soft, but it's a rough softness. To purge his thoughts, he looks at the walls, seeking out the panel in which a man is pointing authoritatively to another, ordering him. Stretching again, he can smell his own clean male sweat. "She wanted me to call her darling—but I didn't!"

Don returns juggling the drinks ostentatiously.

"A major victory for us, Chas," Endore jibes, "ranking at least with the resistance at the Stonewall." He is referring to the first homosexual riots against the police during a raid of the Stonewall Inn one sweating summer night.

"Stonewall!" Don cringes from the memory. Not long ago,

he stumbled on a demonstration commemorating that day—thousands of homosexuals marching and chanting down the streets with raised fists. He ran to avoid it, but the chanting pursued him. He could hear it badgering into his apartment, and he closed the windows.

"She kept wanting me to call her darling," Chas persists.

"Poor Chas," Bill ribs. "She should have seen from your keys that you're a master in search of a slave.... I can't picture *her* licking boots."

"You fruity shit, lay off!" Chas focuses his rage.

Bill looks away. Whatever was stirred on the piers has been exacerbated by Lyndy. There's that goodlooking marine over there—but often that type is interested in all that silly bondage and discipline. However, he's been known to change people's minds. Where's the aviator now?

They have accepted Lyndy about the bar. Because she has the kind of power they admire—she's rich and famous, and chic. Endore thinks, watching the diminutive figure of the woman and the looming figure of the man conquering more of the machos at the bar. Yes, he admires Chas's resistance, and that of others, too—to *her*, to *this* woman.

"The only demonstration I ever joined," Don is musing, "was when we flew our flags half-mast for Judy." He tilts his drink, to swallow; he stops himself, holds it in both his hands, as if to force them to keep it away from his lips for longer moments. He remembers: Judy is dead! a man on the telephone screamed at him. It can't be, Don insisted. It can't be! But it was. She sang about the defeated, and he loved it. We all loved it then, he thinks wistfully. Oh, it was a ritual for them. When she performed in the city they vied for seats on the front row—and waited eagerly each time. Would she turn up? If she did, would she be drunk or sober, fat or slender? Don felt an empathic triumph either way. And each time, he brought roses, blood-red roses which he then flung in offering at her feet. Judy is dead.

"Nobody listens to her anymore." Chas tosses. "The

Stones still say it, cause they sing from where it counts." He gropes his groin harshly. The cockring feels good to his touch. His fingers outline it.

'I prefer Barbra Streisand," Bill dares deliberately, and in further defiance curls his body.

"Puccini," Don sniffs. "And Judy, of course," he adds loyally. The ice soothes his lips. He wishes he could fish a piece out and apply it to the smarting area of his face, but that would call attention.

"Actually all that's changed since then is that costumes have come out of the closet," Bill says. The macho pose jumps back. He knows Chas hates his leather referred to as a "costume." "Now *that* was a funny remark," he congratulates himself.

Endore smiles, complimenting Bill's valorous camping—yet he remains attractive even here. The earlier tension between them has eased, but it's a deliberate easing on both their parts. "But that's not all that's changed," Endore says.

"Listen!" Chas flings. And waits. As if not sure what he will say, merely wanting to protest Endore's tone. He gulps his beer, then brings the bottle to his chest, feeling its coldness there. He doesn't know what he wants to protest, Endore's words were ambiguous. "At that place I told you about—the Catacombs." he speaks in a deceptively soft tone. "they tied this beautiful dude upside down, naked, bound by the ankles from the ceiling. For thrashing. I don't know why, but at first no one wanted to go first although the dude was begging for a good whipping. I got my belt out and—. . ." He flails his arm like a whip. "That's all it took, then everyone—. . ."

"That's hateful," Endore stops him. By softening his voice, Chas seduced them into listening.

Sick, Don thinks. Sick.

Bill turns his head away, belatedly rejecting Chas's story.

A cold blackness rushes Chas. He erupts: "So fuckin superior to it all. Endore. Looking down on me because I'm into S & M." He pulls at the memory of the "slave auction" he conducted. "Openly." he says. He made the willingly shackled

slaves kneel. "Man. remember that." He threw the chain into the filthy water. No. Not that memory. "And proudly." The upturned man—his mind pulls that back; his whip cracked like a gun against the bared flesh. "Openly and proudly, man." Another memory crowds the last: The memory lunges to a tall figure in black, and then to another—and then those are shoved away by an image of the transvestite in vinyl looming on the ramp at the piers. "You deny it, Endore," he tries to blank his mind. "but to sacrifice yourself to another—to accept that sacrifice—that's the greatest . . . 'love,' if you wanna call it that. How much will you do for it—for . . . 'love,' huh? And how much will you demand of it?" His voice is passionate. The hair mats on his chest, wet from perspiration and the cold sweat of the beer bottle.

Endore turns away from the passionate anger, and from the tight muscles knotted in urgency. Their encounters have hinted before of matches. Tonight's pressures are defining a clearer contest; those of other nights, preliminaries. But Endore is not certain he wants to accept the challenge tonight. "That's a new definition of . . . love. that includes pain and humiliation." he says.

"There's no real pain. and no real humiliation, *you* know that." Chas pauses. His voice is insidiously soft again. "I still hear what a good top-man you are." The cold beer, the cold bottle—he welcomes the coolness breathing on him.

"Were." Endore says. The image of himself of years ago has been evoked. Booted feet straddling whoever was his beautiful willing "slave," Endore looked into the other's eyes —always that unwelcome moment beyond his control—and he would feel awash in—. . . Pity. Anger at himself. Then the surge of power would wipe those away. "No more." he says.

"Here at the Rushes all that counts is sexual power." Chas asserts. "and it radiates from between the legs. raw naked cock and sex: that's what rules here. And what the fuck? Outside it's another kind of power that reigns. Why should it be different here?"

Don waits for Endore to answer. Tell him! When Endore

says nothing. Don sighs. "And that's why at the Rushes, I'm not worth a damn. This moment I'd give all that I am outside to be—..."

"No, Don!" Endore tries to stop him.

"... —to be desired by someone beautiful." Don finishes. He looks from Endore to the black man: has he followed me here? he wonders. No. Don looks at the bar through his glass, empty again: The bodies trapped in the red smoke seem to be grappling with each other.

It *is* another world, the Rushes, Bill thinks. I forget, whenever I'm away: we all change, and even more as the evening goes on. He adds a man in a Western and brown-leather combination to his possibilities. Visually right. But when Bill moves in, who of the men he's signaled will hold up? Will they reject him! the doubt pushes. "Sometimes Luke and I would stay at home," he remembers a time when he was away from the Rushes. "All I really asked was to give myself totally to him."

"And that's all." Endore's words are tense.

Bill frowns. "Luke made the rules, he was the dominant one." Even when he stopped getting hard. Yes, he would lie there, Luke, eyes staring; pulling at his own cock which would lie relentlessly limp, his naked body wiped with the oil Bill rubbed on it. "I don't mind, baby," he would tell Luke, and it was true. He would lick the prone body: "Just lie there." Bill says aloud now: "I know Luke blamed me for God knows what sometimes, but it wasn't me who was weird. One time he kept insisting I tell him I loved him, between my sucking—..." He stops. "It was spooky."

"We have to find love." Don wonders whether he slurred any word.

"Not every night, not every moment. Not even ever!" Endore says. "Then when—if—we find it—..." He is surprised by his overt anger. He searches the growing mass of bodies: has it thrust Michael out? He can't locate the familiar body.

At the entrance the red darkness parts. Gauzy in the smoke, a figure stands there. As always, the attention shifts to

the door when the darkness separates allowing a fresh warrior into the arena. As the waves of smoke melt, the figure forms into that of a handsome youngman, not tall, quite young. He is bringing out some identification to show the man at the door.

"You sure this is your age?" he asks the youngman.

"Yeah," the youngman says. "Bobby—I mean, Robert. See? Legal age plus three days. I've been legal three days, man."

The man at the door says hostilely, "If you're here to hustle or—..."

"What?"

"Hustle. Sell it, sell your body. If you're here for that, you're in the wrong place. Stay outside with the other punks, or go uptown where—..."

"I'm not here to hustle."

The man allows him in. The youngman is sucked into the field of attention. He advances. Apprehensively. Cockily. Shyly. Not wearing any hint of a uniform, he looks out of place in a loose ordinary shirt and unselfconscious jeans, scuffed tennis shoes. Only his young beauty provided him entry. His hair is dark, curly; the face is lean, bones already asserting beautiful angles. The loose clothes do not disguise the coltish body.

The four men are looking at the youngman. They heard scattered words which told them this is his first time in a bar.

Endore tries to remember his first entrance into the Rushes. But too many subsequent memories, of entrances—and exits—have absorbed the first one. There was a choking excitement, yes, but there always is.

Looking at Robert, Chas's mind bolts back. His own first time at the Rushes. Behind the black shroud that threatens to snuff the memory of excitement lurks a dark figure. Chas watched. Now he looks at the youngman. Was I that obviously new my first time?

Robert moves into the sparser area where the four men stand, lean against the post there, sit on stools.

"Too bad his first time is in the Rushes," Endore says.

"He came looking for it," Chas says ominously.

Don looks in horror at the youngman. For a moment he thought it was the hustler from outside, but it isn't. Still, memories scratch at him, of other faces, another face. No, it can't be!"What is he doing here?" he says aloud. It can't be him! "He looks too—. . ." He touches his neck; the pain burrows more deeply.

"Normal, huh?" Chas confronts him.

"He looks wrong, that's all," Don revises nervously. "Like a hustler."

"You think you see them everywhere," Chas says. His eyes study the youngman intently.

"Or like those boys that raid the piers; they look alike, you know, those and the hustlers." For the first time tonight Don feels the origin of a scream.

From a closer distance, Endore's and Robert's eyes connect.

"What is he doing here?" Don demands.

Endore recognizes the youngman. He was standing near the trucks earlier tonight; he seemed to hide from him. Again there's the tip of another memory. Of crushed glass and rubble.

5

Show us, O Lord, Your
kindness.

As OFTEN as he has imagined coming
to the Rushes, Bobby—Robert—feels a different excitement
now. Sexual arousement—his cock hardened—is flailed by
fear. These moments are rushing to sum up his life. His body
exudes cold heat. His vision blurs perspiration gathers in
tremulant beads on his long eyelashes. It's as if he's viewing
the bar through shifting dark red water. The next moment he
feels tossed into the smoky ocean in which exposed pieces of
flesh swim. Nothing he has glimpsed in surreptitious forays
into livid-white sex-magazine stores, nothing he has imagined
lying in bed alone remembering the men he saw after one of
his exploratory incursions into their world, no, nothing his
brother has warned him about—nothing matches the sensual
reality of these men, all hunting sex. Reality has swallowed

the fantasies. After prowling outside it for three nights, he is in the Rushes.

The visual tide recedes, leaving individual figures like sexual jetsam. His eyes recoil from one to another: the muscular man in the white tank top, the tall cowboy, the blond biker, several men in plaid shirts, a shirtless man, another. His eyes float away. The hairy-chested man in the open vest, and next to him the handsome man in the tight open denim shirt—. . . It's him! Robert turns to flee as he did earlier when he encountered him by the trucks. And before that, that hypnotized afternoon of bodies and haunted decay. Orange waves licked at the hollow sound.

He wishes the music were louder—it's like a growled hum—so that it would smother the loud pulsing of his own body. *Is* it his body's? Or the music's? The bar's?

Eyes. He feels them. He's dressed wrong. Do they see the bulge growing between his legs? The man in the denim shirt. The man in the vest. When he glanced at them, they were staring at him.

Look away from them!

But his eyes are nailed to the two men. Bare chest covered with hair. Tanned muscles stretching the tight shirt. The black leather on the one. Did he notice it only now? Does it repel, frighten him? Excite him? No, it's the naked chest, the arched sexual body. When he looks at the other man, in the denim shirt, he feels uncluttered desire.

A chemical odor raids him. Near him a man sniffs from a small dark bottle. Even the wafting scent made Robert edgy.

Run out!

He doesn't move.

"What?"

"What are you drinking?"

How did he get to the bar? Until the bartender—and his chest is bare too—repeated the question, he didn't realize he was there. Now he remembers the rising heat as the bodies pressed his on his way here; he kept his eyes lowered. Hands brushed him—. . .

74 •

"A beer." He stares at the bartender's wrists. He's wearing split handcuffs like bracelets. The compressed present is so overwhelming that reality is occurring in spurts of sensations and sights. Cold. He's clutching the beer, an anchor in the waves of sexuality. Hot. A bare arm slides against his elbow.

"Huh?"

"I said, you gotta pay."

He digs into his pockets. Change falls but he will not bend to pick it up. A cool wetness on his chest. He blows on it. The beer has slid out of his lips and onto his chest. These men. So masculine. You'd never know they were—. . . He blocks his brother's word. If he knew I was here! He shoves away that part of his life.

Blotted darkness. He's staring at the curtain of shadows beyond the pool table. Figures bend under a shaded light. The smothered darkness leads to a deeper one. Figures twist the smoky shadows. Sex.

He's back near the entrance. The man in the denim shirt. The handsome face, the body he remembers. I followed him. A shaft of sunlight pierced the tangled darkness within which forms bunched.

The black leather vest, the exposed arched body.

Leave now!

He looks away from anyone who seems about to approach him. Would he if it was either of—. . . ?

Several men are about to tie up another. They've ripped most of his clothes. Robert is looking at one of the panels on the wall. The sexual figures resemble some of the men in the Rushes. His eyes glide over the panels—some faded, others blurred by the smoke, the shattered plaster. The figures seem almost to move. One of the men, jacketed, holds a whip. Robert pulls his eyes away. To the last panel, swallowed by slashes and swirls.

He's looking at the man in the denim shirt, and the man is looking back at him.

Endore continues staring at the youngman. A splinter of the insistent memory bruises his mind. The boy ran away.

That was earlier, by the trucks. No, another time. There was the crunch of glass. No, the glass was earlier beside that other youngman outside.

"He's a hot little dude." Chas raises his beer in a toast to the youngman.

"He's beautiful, all right," Bill says. "But not my type. Too innocent."

Innocent! The word affronts Don. " 'Youth is no guarantee of innocence, and age no affirmation of corruption'—you wrote that in one of your columns, Endore, it's one of those I saved," Don says eagerly. His words are precise, to control any quivering. He read the column over and over. Each time he walked the areas of the city where surly malehustlers lurked, the memorized words gave him sustenance.

It was a column about the young boys who attack the old in the ghettos, Endore remembers, and about the ones who pillage cruising areas like the piers, luring, then beating, even killing homosexuals. "But neither is the opposite true," he reminds Don. Endore continues looking at Robert. "He feels ugly, guilty," he says aloud. The youngman is trying so hard to look cocky as he moves about the bar; trying so hard to camouflage his fear, and he's so unsure; Endore is studying him.

"He keeps lookin at me," Chas says.

"Oh, I'm not so sure it's *you* he's looking at," Don says. Pain needles his temples. A drink would cool them. I shouldn't have come out yet, he tells himself. A few more days.

"At you then, huh, Don?" Chas derides.

"I'm sure not," Don says. "But at Endore. Or Bill." Is it the same boy? No, he wouldn't dare be here. Would he even recognize me?

The presence of the boy has diffused their attention from Lyndy and Martin. But her recurrent laughter reaches them in soft puffs of assertive sound. She will keep her promise to return. Eager as he is now to join the sexual feast, Chas will wait until he can declare his war against her.

Two men walk by. Both are dressed in black motorcycle

cop uniforms. They wear helmets, handcuffs, empty holsters, gloves. It is a uniform popular in these bars. The uniform overtaking the body, the men stand like rigid manikins.

"Ugh." Bill turns away from the two men. He dislikes that uniform very much.

"My God, how can they dress like the men who arrest us and hate us!" Don says.

Endore, too, loathes that uniform, for the same reasons. He rejects the looks of the two men.

Chas feels confused now by that uniform. He used to be attracted to it, to wearing it, although he never has. The memory of the cop who handcuffed him has blurred his reactions. But he nods toward the men. He touches his groin automatically—no, the sides of it, feeling for a certain spot there. He pulls his burning hand away. He looks at it, a sudden fist, crushing memories; he opens it, releasing others. He remembers the chain he held at the slave auction; he dropped it from handcuffed hands; he dropped it into the water. The two memories interlock. He looks away from the uniformed men.

They strut away.

"The little dude's ripe for pickin, go any way at all!" Chas looks at Robert. Bolting past the protective darkness in which his mind imprisons him in ambiguity, the submerged tenebrous figure from a past time stands silhouetted on the screen of his memory. Chas lets himself remember: He stood like this. He adjusts his booted stance, feet wider, hips tossed out. "The kid's first time." His voice is almost soft. "What's he feeling, huh? Fuck! When I first came here—. . ." The hand of the remembered black figure, gloved, drops to his own groin. "I'll never feel like that again, the excitement, the heat." He chops the fragment of laughter rising. "The—. . ."

"Fear," Endore finishes.

Fear? Chas frowns. "No." He pushes the word away. He studies Robert. He remembers the makebelieve slave auction, the youngman willingly posing as a slave. He crouched. No, it was the man on the pier. The chain—he flung it at the cop. No, he tossed it into the water, which swallowed it.

"My first time here," he says. "I saw this guy. I'd recognize him even now, that's how well I remember him." His eyes idle about the bar. He laughs, and stops before apprehension pushes into the sound.

Endore detects a tautened strain in it. But why is it so difficult for him to hear Chas's laughter, almost as difficult as to hear his own?

"I got hot looking at the dude," Chas continues, to ease the memory away. His laughter begins again, is chopped again. "He actually pulled out his—. . ." He strangles the laughter by tilting the last of his beer to his mouth and allowing the liquor to spill over. Then he looks down where it moistened his groin. His hand touches the wetness. The interrupted laughter is finished. There was no middle.

"Is that all?" Bill says. The marine hanging around looks very hot.

"Yes." Chas is solemn.

"Well, that's a let-down. 'Pulled out his—. . .' What kind of a story is that?" Bill says. Hot, yes, but the cowboy isn't bad. Bill can't remember, though: Was that the cowboy who turned femme so quickly? *Was* he a cowboy? "Really, Chas, what kind of a story—. . . ?"

"Shut up!" Chas shouts at him.

Silent tension winds about them.

In the trenches to the sides of the entrance, the knots of men are beginning to untangle. The individual hunt for connection, lonelier than any other, is pushing at the serious part of the hunt. Friends turn into strangers, even enemies. Some men are leaving the bar together, ending the hot-night's hunt. Two of them walk out, arms about each other. Two others leave, kissing.

That doesn't mean they'll make it, Don assures himself. His hungry eyes follow them. Outside, they might see each other more clearly and then—. . . He smears his vision of them by holding the empty glass to his mouth.

Bass tones of the stifled music beat like a heart.

Bill feels the bar's rhythms luring into the sexual vortex.

He has filed the general locations of the marine, the construction worker, and two cowboys—an extra one to offset the one who may be femme. All those have answered more-or-less definite signals. The biker is too leathery. But maybe not. And the aviator—is he an aviator? And there's the man in the army fatigue cap and combat boots. Most of those gave vague signals. Soon he'll move in. But not into the wrestling shadows in back.

"It's the highest group high—the Rushes," Chas says aloud.

"Suicidal when it fails," Don says. Why is it hurting so much more now than in the last few days?

"It's not for everyone," Chas says.

Anger dulls Don's pain. "Because I'm over forty, I'm supposed to stop living?"

Endore says gently: "At the Rushes anyone can be old when the night ends." He knows the feeling of desolation when all connections fail and last night's successes are wiped away. All the men here know it—he, Chas, Bill—no one escapes it—some just more than others. When tonight's sexual battles end here, there will be those—so many—still glaringly alone, the strain of unsuccessful hunting nursing the faces, beautiful men, unattractive men, all playing roulette with desolation, each night. Will this night slaughter them?

"To be a good faggot," Chas pronounces, "you gotta be strong. Otherwise, get out." He directs his words at Don but cannot look at him. "One sex rush after another—that's the reward."

"Not enough!" Bill protests.

"Fuck if it isn't," Chas says.

"Only if there's nothing more, or when more has ended," Bill says. Luke. Luke.

All three men wait for Endore's comment. None.

Jabbing at Endore's silence, Chas pushes into a new round: "Those rushes have been your life, Endore. You hate that one exception when you betrayed it with Michael," he says with passion and shoves the combat beyond sparring.

"Betrayed! You speak as if the Rushes is alive," Don says.

The black man. There he is again. Oh, God, is it possible he's looking for me?

"Yeah, and *I'm* loyal to it!" Chas hurls at Endore.

In the sudden quiet among them, Lyndy's laughter floats toward them.

Robert looks at the men again.

At Endore? Chas is an expert at locating sexual attention. Yes, at Endore. He relocates his booted feet. Exactly like that, that first time in the Rushes. He'll break the kid's look on Endore—ending this round now. "I think I'll go look the jungle over." Before Don can accuse him of decamping, he says, "I'll be back." He hasn't broken his promise to himself to confront Lyndy; he's merely made another one.

Don wants to ask for a drink, but he doesn't like to impose on friends—except in inviting himself along. The handsome black man is lurking nearby.

Chas swaggers past Robert. He pauses. Vest open, beer to his lips—held to them for seconds—eyes dark on Robert. Snap! The look between the youngman and Endore breaks. Robert's eyes transfer to the figure of Chas. Clasping the look—a promise of more—Chas moves toward the bar, glancing back to hold the invitation.

A familiar figure here, Chas is still the object of much attention. The bartenders greet him—he's made it with most of them. At the opposite end of the long bruised counter, Lyndy still sits, her pearls about her wrist, black lips pulled, eyes hungry. Martin stands beside her like an effete king. The leathered courtiers have paid their tribute—and moved away. Leaning against the bar, Chas surveys the area. No one who really gives him a sure hardon—his test.

A man sidles up to him. "You look real hot, stud. Can you get heavy?"

"Yeah, but not with you," Chas discards him with a bark. As the evening moves the hunt into the sexual quicksands, Chas slurs his speech into a sensual growl, low, guttural; his grammar loosens deliberately. He hates to be approached by those he does not desire.

Avoiding Lyndy and Martin—for now; the confrontation

must be exact—Chas moves up the four steps at the back of the bar. Forms crouch over the pool table. Beyond the heavy darkness at the back, bodies toss. Some action there. Like other times, he'd "force" an eager head between his legs, grope another's heavy cock and balls; an interlude, a charge. But tonight he's not sure he wants to join there. As long as the woman and that man are here, they inhibit him; he has to push them away, to purify his turf. Then he can move like a proud animal in it again.

He walks up the stairs. Many hot studs here—but he has not had even that preliminary signal his cock gives him, like an electric stab. He feels a hand grope him. A goodlooking stud, yeah; Chas squeezes the other's cock and balls, tightly. The other does not resist. Then Chas moves away. His own cock didn't harden.

Tantalizing, inviting, he pauses under the stained aura of its bleak light before he enters the toilet, a truncated tunnel redolent of urine. Sexual exhortations usually for humiliation tinged with violence pock the peeling walls. Outlines of swallowing mouths and engorged cocks are carved like scars there. The light is filthy yellow. Four men stand before the aged urinal, like a trough, sediment smooth as velvet on the stained porcelain. A man sits on a toilet. A round hole in its gashed partition gapes into the next cubicle, where a man in leather stands. The odor of poppers further taints the air.

No one moves, it is as if all have been trapped in a dream of squalor. Now Chas locates himself in the middle of the men at the yellow trough. He opens his pants, exhibiting his cock. Then he begins to piss, an unsteady stream at first—that disturbs him—then a gathering flow, finally a full gush—that pleases him. He looks down at his liquid discharge splashing on the soiled porcelain. In a glance, he's determined there's nobody here he's attracted to.

Leaning back, pulling at eyes, he does not squeeze out the last drops. He shoves his cock into his pants. His fingers touch the moist spot there. Warm. His memory darkens as if the dim yellow lights had inhaled.

Outside, he makes his way through the packed bodies. He

stands at the top of the steps, watching the Rushes. His groin stirs, yes, but at the collective sexuality, like at other times. He feels a rushing joy. His! His world, his beautiful sexual banquet, yes. A reedy darkness stabs through the joy.

From here he can see Endore. Don. Bill. Robert.

And Lyndy. She stands up. She edges away a new group of men who have come to acknowledge her power. Her hand on Martin's arm, she moves away from the bar. Other men still turn their backs to her invasion.

Down the four stairs, Chas makes his way through the twisting flesh. Robert. The kid is standing before one of Chas's favorite drawings. Two men face each other as if at a standoff; sometimes, in Chas's heated mind, one "wins," other times the other does. Very close to the youngman, Chas tilts his beer to his lips again. His torso stretches, the leather chaps inch down. Now he loops a finger through his thick chain-linked belt. He lowers the pants and chaps until the tip of the triangle of thick hair about his groin shows glistening. From behind the tilted bottle, he eyes the boy, trapping him in the tinted gaze. He holds that stance, hips thrust in challenge and invitation. Now he brings the beer down, down, toward his legs. His eyes are clamped on Robert—on the careless hair, the lean sensual young face, the lithe body—and then Chas feels it, the first real rush of a hardon.

Robert looks away. He's afraid, yes, and excited.

Don't move too fast, he's new, remember, remember, Chas warns himself. Turning sharply, he joins Endore and the others. "The jungle is hot tonight," he says. His growl imitates the roar of a lion.

"Here they hunt with their eyes, only their eyes at first. The movements are slow, like those of a dance," Martin describes the rites. "Sometimes like a funereal dance," he judges.

Don begins looking for a stool for the woman. Chas is sitting on one, but he doesn't get up. There's one near the black man—but Don can't bring himself to go there now. He finds another stool. "For the lady," he explains to the man near it.

"I'm back!" Lyndy announces, her hands open.

"So we see," Endore says. "And so is Martin."

"So he is. It hasn't happened yet," Lyndy pouts.

I won't ask her what, Endore thinks.

She wants to be asked what, Bill knows.

Fuck if I ask her what, Chas thinks.

"What hasn't happened, darling?" Don returns with the stool.

"Astonishment! Like Gide—I want to be astonished! You told me about that, Endore."

"It was Cocteau who said that to young artists," Endore corrects.

"*Plus que chic,*" Lyndy approves. "*Je l'adore!* But no, I haven't been astonished yet. Amused but not astonished."

"We'll try harder," Bill says. He glances at the Rushes, a flashing look, as if to snatch it away from her.

Lyndy's head jerks, but her lips pull farther at the edges as if welcoming the implied confrontation. Thanking him, darling, she sits on the stool Don brought her. She gazes at the drawings on the wall. Her lips open, the tongue touches them. The lips close. Her look slices away. "Of course, there's still much more to the hot jungle," she says. "Is that what Chas just called it?"

"Oh, he can," Endore says. "His credentials are intact. He's fought in the wars." Only the casual tone veils the anger. She—and Martin?—have not earned the right to experience either the joy or terror of the Rushes.

Chas nods approval.

"You speak as if one needs a passport into the battle zone," she says.

"You do." How quickly she perceived the arena, Endore realizes.

Martin's eyes slice at Chas's keys. "The placement of the keys indicates general position, darling," he announces to her, "a 'top-man' or a 'bottom-man' in the quaint vernacular of the natives. Dominant or otherwise. The color of the handkerchief indicates sexual activity, mild to, as they say, I think, heavy. A

silent language like that of the eyes. And often confusing."

"How much did your clothes cost, darling? All that leather is expensive," Lyndy asks Chas.

"Lots, custom-made, all of it." Proud, Chas looks down at his sleek chaps and then he glances at the leather straps encircling his biceps. The studs imbedded there are tiny silver pyramids.

"I'll use keys in my new designs—the new femininity!" Lyndy announces.

Chas winces.

About to rebut, too swiftly, too overtly, too clumsily, Endore knows. He interrupts. "The keys—left for sadist or right for masochist?" She loathes women more than any of the men here, even Chas, Endore purifies his campaign against her presence.

"Guess, darling," she purrs.

"Then we should know whom you hate more, men or women." For years the close antagonism between Endore and the woman and the man with her has hovered on the brink, the three—and Chas—poised in despised closeness and fascination. He may push it over tonight.

"Do guess again, Endore!"

"Women adore her," Martin's lips move.

"They loathe me," Lyndy says flatly.

"Darling, I'll get you a drink," Don offers. Such unbelievable rudeness! And he needs another drink. Despite the often overt racism at the Rushes, several men are hovering about the goodlooking black man nearby, Don notices. How many more would cruise him if others wouldn't see them?

"No, thank you, darling." Lyndy indicates an almost-full glass and makes a face.

Don takes a deep breath, holds it. Fear tightens. Then anger. Just stay here, with Endore. Or leave. A whisper of relief touches him. Then he looks at the massed flesh ahead of him. Where is the black man now? Leave the Rushes! "I think I'll venture into—... the chasm," he says and laughs to soothe the last word.

Endore reaches out to touch him. Don brushes back En-

dore's hand. Excusing himself elaborately from Lyndy, Don moves away. Good luck, Endore thinks. His eyes follow Don— but his look is intercepted by the figure of Robert, so out-of-place yet so beautiful in his unselfconscious clothes. Men glide about him, but he continues to thwart any advance by studying the bottle in his hand.

Oh, another one! A lumberjack in a peaked cap has answered Bill's signals. How many has he lined up? He takes inventory. The cowboy—two of them, one femme though; he can locate only one. The aviator is silly, actually. The marine—yes, but that tacky leather guy is talking to him and should keep his shirt on with *that* waist. There's the gorgeous muscular man in the tank top—of course, who could miss him? He would be Bill's first choice. But he seems to be here just to be seen by many.

"I'll go to the Rack tonight," Lyndy's voice is casual as she tantalizes again.

"We'll see!" Chas says.

"Don't count on it, darling," Endore tells her.

"Oh, allies?" Lyndy glances from Chas to Endore.

"No, Lyndy, they won't let you into the Rack," Bill says. His mind shoots out memories. "Those ugly contraptions and straps. I went there with Luke the only time. He'd point out who he wanted me to blow, and he'd watch, then I'd suck him, and then in that one large room where they—. . . I did everything to get him hard." Bill looks at Endore. Although the memory pushed out the words, Bill deliberately coarsened them, to assault the woman. But now the memory is filtered. "I fell in love with Luke moments after I met him."

So quickly, so easily. Endore remembers Michael's lips brushing the words against his cheek. The gentle opening of the secret wound, with a mere breath.

"Ah! Since we're confessing—. . ." Lyndy kisses a pearl. "We drove to the piers."

"You didn't go in?" Endore asks her.

"Not then, darling. No passport, remember? And, you see, my pearls—. . ."

"You're not wearing the real ones, darling," Martin says.

"Ah, non?" She frowns. *"Vous êtes sûr?"* She holds them out to Martin. "Can you tell, darling?"

"Of course not—there's no difference," Martin says. "There were two whores in garish colors on the ramps." He looks at Lyndy.

Chas spits on the sawdust, rubs the spit into it.

"You remember them, don't you, darling?" Martin asks.

"Yes," Lyndy dismisses.

Oh, no! Now the marine is talking to the fake cowboy—and he is definitely the femme one, Bill sees. Where's the construction worker? The muscular man in the tank top *is* superb. But he just stares straight ahead—although—... although he actually did seem to glance at Endore. Wait! The marine is alone again. Time to move in. "Excuse me."

Bill weaves his body expertly between other bodies: he creates spaces where there are none. He stands next to the marine. He has short-cropped hair, he's square-jawed.

Don sees Bill. I hope he doesn't make out. No, I hope he does. The black man—... Just as well he's gone. But his eyes strain. He sees the blond youngman who angled away from him at the bar. At least he and the black man haven't connected, Don feels a slight victory. Bill's talking to that man already, he's so forward.

"Hi, stud," Bill thickens a Southern accent for the marine.

The "marine's" posture thaws. "Huh-*I*" he drools.

"Oh, excuse me." The Southern tone evaporates. "I think I see a dear friend." Bill flees. To an outlaw biker, yes: no keys, no heavy leather—not a Chas.

"Hi, stud," the "outlaw biker" says to Bill.

"I think we're looking for the same thing, hon," Bill slips away.

He retreats to where the others are. From here he'll scout the territory again. He has learned that when two assaults in a row don't work, it's better to retrench and start again.

Endore sees the blond, slender form of Michael walking toward the bar from the shadows in back. Beer in hand, he makes his way to the border of the area where Endore is.

Michael stops. He holds his beer to Endore, as if in a toast.

He was so gentle, so vulnerable. Is he still? So eager to please me. Even that way. But he was wrong—I didn't want that, Endore insists, he was wrong. What are the implications of that hinted toast?

Michael turns away. His shoulder brushes Robert's as the two youngmen move in opposite directions.

Chas has remained silent, surly. His eyes stake the bar, returning always to Robert, each time verifying the recharging excitement between his own legs.

The youngman passes by them. Don't look at them! He pauses. Eyes. Moves away. A step. He stops. Another step. He waits. What does he want? Why *exactly* is he here? Careful to stay within the sight of the men, he moves farther away.

Lyndy has captured the slow dance of their eyes. "What a beautiful youngman," she says. Then she lunges. "Why don't you be his guide past the jungle, Endore?" But she looks at Chas.

"He's already here," Endore contains his voice.

"Perhaps he can lead *you* out then. They say a child shall lead them," she laughs.

"Not in the Rushes," Endore says.

"That's where they found Moses," Martin derides.

"Is the boy looking at—. . . Endore? Chas?" Lyndy goads.

Chas's voice is becoming a deeper growl. "A kid like that, man, lookin, and he don't know yet for what—. . ."

Lyndy's glance at Martin signals his attention. She licks her lips, as if the pearl she bit earlier were still there to taste. "Why don't you go show him your hairy chest? You're always telling us how successful you are, Chas—and how well you're . . . hanged."

"Hung," Bill corrects her.

"She means hanged," Endore says.

Lyndy forms a precious noose from one strand of pearls, the long one, and dangles it from her chin toward Endore.

She's sensed the tenuous alliance between him and Chas against her, Endore thinks, and she's moving to wedge them

apart, but he will not allow it. He waits, not risking a wrong move. He pulls his eyes away from her tiny noose. Don is nearing the black man, he sees.

Leave right now, Don tells himself, never come back. He stands in the midst of the hunting men, all ignoring him. He looks back to see whether Endore is looking at him. Yes.

Endore closes his eyes for a few moments, to blot out Don's painful presence.

Chas is quiet, pensive.

Bill edges away from the crosscurrents of tension. He'll scout the bar again. He motions a vague wave as he returns to the funnels of flesh. Then he feels—yes, feels—the memory of Luke—and he glances back at the others, as if to thrust it back. He sees the outline of Lyndy's eyes and mouth, black in the red light. The black lips part. He looks away, moving, and he sees Don standing next to the black man. Don is touching his temples again. Was he doing that at the exhibition? Yes, Bill remembers. Does he hurt there? His face looks a bit—. . .

Don removes his fingers from his forehead. The pain has eased. The black man is handsomer than he thought. Light, light eyes. Amber, Don decides. Even in this light they couldn't be that clear and not be amber. And the muscular arms. Don sees the thick carved veins on them, the broad forearms, and his throat tightens with desire.

Endore looks away from Don.

"That kid'd be easy," Chas brags. He studies Endore for a reaction. None. He knows Endore never advances first in the sexhunt. "I like them real masculine," Chas seems to withdraw.

"The boy is *very* masculine—even without props," Lyndy pursues.

"Yeah—. . ." Chas still studies Endore.

As if to break Endore's silence, to push him against Chas, now, Lyndy asks Martin: "What is it slaves do, darling, in S & M?" Her tone is flippant, cruel.

"Oh, darling, I don't really know. I think they kneel before

the master. lick his boots, they're called queers or cocksuckers in return, something or other, and they get to—. . ."

"Why the fuck don't you leave the Rushes?" Chas counterattacks, looking from Martin to Lyndy.

The pulled smile on Lyndy's face almost breaks.

Martin's icy hauteur is unthawed.

Chas turns his back on them. Robert. Yes. Yet if he advances and it goes wrong—. . . An expert at thwarting rejection by swimming only when he has established that the sexual currents are favorable, Chas will test them.

Endore looks away from Robert. The confrontation he anticipated with Lyndy—and Martin—he did not know its shape; now, revealing itself, it is unexpected. A quick convolution of words has tangled him and Chas. She has split their silent alliance swiftly, for now. Endore does not look toward the youngman. Don—has he approached the black man?

Don opens his lips, to speak to the black man. The words don't come. He glances down at the man's brown arms, the veins playing there. Then he searches out Endore, for distant comfort, but Chas's dark leathered form intercepts his view of him. Chas is with that boy!

Robert looks at Chas about to approach him. The black leather gleams red.

Don feels a tremor of doubt again. But. It's not the same boy, it's not, it's not. Yet if it is and Chas—. . . He pushes words out at the black man. "You've run out of beer, can I get you another?" He actually spoke that.

The clear eyes look at Don.

He'll reject me, he'll—. . . Don's words of invitation reverberate, pursuing him. Again Don searches out Endore, for borrowed strength. But Endore is facing Lyndy.

"What game are you playing?" Endore asks her. His voice is very controlled.

"I don't play," Lyndy says. "Do I, Martin?"

"Always," he says.

"Are you playing, too?" Endore turns to Martin.

"I've seen it, and it bores me."

"Does it, Martin?" Endore asks.

"Yes," Martin hisses. Then: "Look at Chas and the young-man, Endore. You're avoiding it."

Chas's eyes insist Robert look at him. He and the young-man are only inches apart. Chas's hand floats over his own groin. The warm moisture there still lingers from the moments in the toilet. His hand searches it out. Robert is looking—yes, he's sure. Then the blurred figure his mind avoids stands blackly before him. Chas removes his hand from his groin.

Robert turns away. Fear. But he doesn't move. Desire.

Chas looks back at the others. Did they see the kid turn away? He feels the cold edge of rejection. He turns his own back to the kid. An ambiguity—the kid is still there. It's not over.

"Chas is afraid. All his bravado and he is afraid," Lyndy says.

"Here, we all are," Endore says. "Except you, Lyndy. You're safe here." He glances at Martin.

"I did go to the piers, you know, I went into the ware-houses," she releases. "Last week? Rot, decay, sex." Her eyes hold Chas and Robert.

"Where you think it belongs," Endore says.

"And some of you too, apparently," Lyndy says.

"Why did you take her there, Martin?" Endore confronts the cold man.

"They're our monuments," Martin says.

Endore looks again toward Robert and Chas. Their backs are to each other. But neither has moved apart. And Don. He seems to be waiting for the black man to speak; answer.

"It was a warm late afternoon on the piers," Lyndy re-members. "There was rubble everywhere. Rot. Silence. De-bris. Sex."

She saw it—the gutted collapsing warehouse. She walked under the gate, which is like a rusted knife.

"I bent to touch the spotted decay," Lyndy says. "It was as

soft as ermine." Her hand rises as it did behind the dark window of her limousine. It remains there as if demanding more. Then the fingers clench over the pearls on her velvet suit. "Shall I tell him what we saw by the trucks?" she asks Martin.

6

O God, Who established
the nature of man
in wondrous dignity . . .

As OFTEN as he comes to the Rushes,
Endore still wonders why he is pulled to it—and he is. True,
the men he is physically attracted to come here, but they are
the men whose attitudes he often questions. And so at times
he tells himself that he returns to find out why he comes to the
Rushes. For him, the bar contains a central mystery, and the
identification of that mystery might be its solution. Some
nights, he feels on the brink of discovering it, when the collec-
tive laughter in the middle of the evening—before the hunt
turns solemn—seems to him to threaten to bleed from a
pierced central wound.

The Rushes was one of the first of the rough bars that
emerged along the waterfront several years ago. Most had

names which evoked, fear, threat, filth—the Hole, Pure Garbage, the Pit, Trash, the Shaft, the Toilet. There had always been "leather and Western" bars throughout the city, but their concentration along the waterfront revealed a toughness inchoate in the others. The bars here were born old, the ragged stores taken over and left unkempt, as if the spoiling piers had shaped them out of the spilling dross.

Entering the Rushes the first times—he cannot remember *a* first time—Endore felt a sensation different from that of other times in other bars, so many other times, in so many other bars. In retrospect, he feels, at times, that the drawings on the wall alerted him, and he felt apprehension. Something kept in hibernation throughout the more overtly repressive years had awakened here—and in the orgy rooms which came soon after, bearing similar names. It seeped out of those places and into the troubled "paradisiacal" ghettos—Sunday mornings the determinedly masculine men lounged along the streets like triumphant casualties of the night; others wandered like deserters in neutral turf.

It was in those bars that Endore began attempting to grasp the message of the split laughter. A new threat apprehended as inevitable and therefore only to be staved off by leaving it unacknowledged; an unwelcome awareness of a temporary troubled peace, a temporary peace to be seized?—the dichotomy would account for the break. Was anger coagulating?

Soon, other questions battered him.

Why, after the bursts of "liberation"—why, now, the courtship of filth, even when sterilized filth? Within the safe, enclosed bars and orgy rooms, why the imitation of the dank tenebrous places into which others had been shoved by oppression—toilets, crumbling buildings, prison cells? Props from those real places were exhumed and brought, advertised as such, into the bars and orgy rooms—urinals, prison doors, rotted wood—like artifacts and relics to be preserved.

Violence spiraled on two fronts. "Queer-haters" still plundered, as always before, cruising areas outside bars, robbing,

slaughtering, murdering. And now homosexuals mimed, and increasingly executed, sexual violence on their own. Pantomimed "slave auctions" became popular games.

It was then that Endore pulled himself away—and, soon after, that Michael seized his life and he Michael's—from that segment of his world; he felt a dark fury at himself. He explored his own blurring boundaries and moral confusions. When did abundant sex—which he extolled—become a soulless reduction, a sacrifice of, all human contact? It didn't have to! Where did the sexual power endemic to all sexual contacts trespass into oppression, even when willing? It didn't have to! But at the point where such a soulless reduction occurred as absolute, and sex, benumbed, insensate, pushed into pain for mere sensation, he would, he knew, warn against it, oppose it, while, always, supporting its right to be—and supporting, too, the intrinsic enrichment of abundant sex with one or many.

The hardened practiced looks, the mirthless laughter, the ravaging alcoholism which began so much earlier now, the reliance on sexual drugs—these came with uniforms of policemen, of storm troopers, of fascist militarists, even of hooded executioners. Black leather draped the body in sexual mourning. Along with implements for pain, labeled "toys"—clamps, handcuffs, pincers—these uniforms became ordinary in store windows in the ghettos: the manikins were as rigid as the men who wore them in the bars and orgy rooms. The clothes and the stances became as obvious as those of the old effeminacy; a new drag—but now effeminacy was despised, forbidden, outlawed. The masculine homosexuals had become the new sissy-haters, like the bullies who had taunted them as children.

Along with the sissy-hating there came to these ghettos a contempt for women among many of the macho men. Endore despised that.

Now, in the Rushes, he knows he must isolate his disturbing feelings toward Lyndy's presence, yes, and Martin's—and Martin's, he keeps reaffirming; feelings always before in suspension, awaiting definition. If he can find that definition now, he will exorcise the taunting demons resurrecting buried

questions, dredging doubts about his previously uncluttered attitudes toward women. And his emergent feelings toward the Rushes as impenetrable territory except by the masculine men. Like him.

"I went farther into the warehouse," Lyndy continues to evoke the haunted piers, pulling away her question to Martin about the undefined occurrence by the trucks.

And she walked into the midst of violent sexturf, a world Endore knows well. Within the enormous room, its ceiling higher than two stories, are the charred bones of other rooms. Holes are seared into the wooden floor. An erect iron column thrust out of the shaft in the middle of the room is strangled by oxidized pipes. Inside a gutted inner room, wires dangle from a lower ceiling like severed veins.

Stopping the evoked images—they flow easily into the Rushes—Endore searches out Robert and Chas; they still stand close, but their backs are to each other, in the deep redness which licks at them like smoking fireless flames.

Lyndy's lips part; she speaks, a breath. "The free-form shapes of debris and silhouetted bodies—..."

Cinder, scorched wood, torn cans, broken metal pipes. Rubble accumulates against the corners of the fire-blasted rooms. Splinters of glass shine. In the reevoked images, a familiar figure, luminous even in the decay, moved into Endore's mind. And faded.

"There was a hollow sound," Lyndy pulls at Endore's attention.

Disembodied footsteps are realer in the isolated caverns of the warehouse than the now alien mechanical roar of traffic outside. Sexshadows push against knots of darkness. This time Endore evokes the images, as if to pull out the faded figure which glided through them.

"Men moved silently into the abandoned rooms," Lyndy breathes.

Past the bolted darkness of a stairway is another huge room. Slabs of dimmed sun cut the shadows. Within the frames of smaller wall-less rooms, shards of cold glass clinging

to gouged windows, bodies entwine, sucking, kissing, fucking.

"I saw it all." Lyndy's hand rises in the slow gesture.

Like a mangled benediction. And it always ends on the strands of pearls. Endore turns away from her. His eyes scan the red battlefield, avoiding Robert and Chas, but in a sliding glance he saw them still standing like intimate strangers. Endore sees Don and the black man.

Don flashes an alert in the direction of Endore—that he will flee to him for comfort. The black man has not answered his offer of a drink.

"Why not?" the black man says.

Feeling a warmth he has not felt all night, not since that ugly, ugly exhibit, Don still can't keep anxiety out of his voice. "Please wait here, I'll get it, please wait, please."

"Not going anywhere," the black man says.

He wishes Endore had heard; and Bill; and Chas. He moves nervously to the bar. The warmth is chilled by distrust. Will the black man wait for him? Please! He wends his way. Hurry! He hardly nods to Bill, standing looking around as if wondering which area to assault next. So selective all the time because he's so pretty—well, the black man is waiting for me. Is he! Hurry! Don pushes at the men at the bar.

When he returns, the black man is still there. Don hands him the beer.

A trace of a smile graces the hard look like that of the white men here. Then the black man looks away. Don can hear the words of brutal false apology, I see someone I know, I—... And so all he wanted was a cheap beer. But the black man looks again at Don.

"Thanks."

Distrust drains out of the warmth. Gulping his drink, exhaling so that his voice will not break with excitement, Don says, "I haven't seen you here before. Not too many Negroes—oh, I'm sorry—black men—come here. You new here?"

The clear eyes study him—yes, they've got to be amber, Don decides.

"Uh, no, yeah, uh, whattaya mean?"

Does the puffiness show! Don brings the cold glass to his face, as much to soothe it as to hide that part of it. But the black man has never seen him before; so he wouldn't notice, he assures himself. Secretly he stares at the chocolate muscles. Sudden implosions of desire ricochet in shots of pain. He hears his own voice. "Sometimes people come to the Rushes because they've heard it's, well, strange, not really because they ... belong. I mean, I've met some normal—uh—straight—men, in queer—uh—gay—bars." I'll tell him I'm a well-known lawyer, that I'm respected by—... That doesn't count here, he knows.

There's a slight change in the black man's voice. "Just came cause I heard lots about this place. Didn't know much about it."

He's norm—... straight! Don feels urgent desire. Please, let it work. He looks around, trying to locate Chas. He taunted me, thinking I couldn't make out with this handsome man. Well, look now! And there he is—still trying to entice that boy—but he hasn't the nerve to approach him. Don wants Endore to see him, too. But from here all he can make out is part of Lyndy's face.

Lyndy moves farther into a shadow created by the post near which she sits. "There was another empty warehouse," she continues the account of her excursion.

Inside, its original function a mystery now like that of other lingering props in the warehouse, thick grilled wire creates a large cage. Did she see the men mold into one form, and others fusing in smaller pockets? Did she smell the dried urine and dying cum? Or did she arm herself with an expensively perfumed wrist?

"It was slashed with yellow, green, red paint." Lyndy is now describing the aluminum wall that blocks the wharf from the lot.

Colors assault the grayness as if someone tried to coat the ugliness. Oh, and was she aware that beyond that wall, female and transvestite prostitutes fuck their clients among the glued male bodies. Would she look at them?

"Someone had written the word 'Visions.' *Très amusant!*"

The ambiguous word is a giant scrawl on the wall. Did she notice on the same scorched wall a warning against killers?

"The water had an orange sheen, quite splendid really, like moiré!"

Rubble floats in the periphery of the water rejected by the ocean, thrust back at the city.

"Ah! Chas seems ready to spring on the beautiful boy," Lyndy slices off her narrative.

"To extol the virtues and splendors of slavehood, no doubt," Martin almost-laughs.

In Martin's laughter there is only contempt. Endore does not turn to look at the youngman. He remembers the thick eyelashes when he saw him near the trucks. But then he must have had only the impression of long eyelashes, the boy was not that near. Endore feels a sadness that contains Michael.

"Chas has retreated. Oh, just slightly," Lyndy announces.

If he wasn't interested, he would have walked away. Chas has eased his body to one side, only to gauge the youngman's reaction. Robert doesn't move.

A brown-haired man in abbreviated leather approaches Chas. "You're quite a stud," the man appraises him.

Chas hopes Robert heard that. It will increase his interest. But while not dismissing the man, he is careful to hold Robert with a firm look.

"I bet you could give a guy a rough time," the man says in a low voice.

"The right guy at the right time, yeah," Chas tantalizes. He's not sure how much he wants Robert to hear now; he can't be too overt yet.

"You get heavy?"

Chas lowers his voice. "Been known to." He still has Robert's eyes. It's working—and the kid hasn't looked toward Endore in a significant time.

The man's voice drops to a hoarse whisper. "I like your boots."

Chas muffles the growled words. "You a bootshiner? Boot-

licker?" His voice is hardly audible. His look is tied to Robert's.

"Tongue-shine, sir." the man offers.

Fuck! A goodlooking man is cruising the kid now. He'd better dismiss this man. "Well, maybe I'll catch you another time." He raised his voice on those words. He turns his back to the man and now he smiles crookedly at Robert.

Robert smiles back.

Chas moves closer to the boy. So beautiful—a certain softness all mixed with toughness; no, not softness, just newness. What is he feeling? His first time here. A cold wave of heat engulfs Chas. He looks down at his boots. To make sure he is in the exact stance he remembers. The crooked smile is held. From under thick, dark, lowered brows, his eyes capture Robert.

Robert stares at Chas's dark clothes.

Chas is aware of the intense stare on the leather. His own image bounces back at him. For a moment, it is as if he were viewing himself through the kid's eyes, seeing the black chaps, the black vest, the black gloves. No, he's not wearing gloves. His mind reels. The man's gloved hand unbuttoned his own pants, so slowly. Chase touches his own groin. The moisture is gone. Bewildered, he looks at Robert. Then Chas turns away, to leave, to leave the kid alone.

"Looking for a good top-man? I could give you a rough time."

Chas whirls to face the man talking; an unattractive man in solid leather. Chas's forehead creases as if to wring the man's words from his mind. "What the fuck!" he says. "You see these keys, man?" He touches them, jangles them. "*Left* side! You see the earring? *Left* side! And the handkerchief? All on the *left* side, man! That means *top*-man, man. *Top!*"

The man backs off from the pouring rage. "Some guys go both ways, stud. No offense." He retreats.

"*I* don't!" Chas yells. Blackness trembles at the edge of his sight. *I'll have the fuckin little dude!*

Feet spread, crotch forward, Chas drawls at Robert.

"Haw-ya, man? I'm Chas." The coldness recedes, leaving a hot surface.

"I'm Robert," the youngman says.

Chas checks his own stance. Yes, like that. Has Endore moved? He can't see him.

"First time in a bar?" he asks Robert.

It shows then. Through the moisture stinging Robert's eyes, the bodies blur in fluid red. "Yeah"—but he tries to sound tough.

Has Endore advanced? No, and he's looking away. Endore doesn't approach anyone, Chas reminds himself. Then why the apprehension? Chas sees the outlined face of the woman.

"Ah, darling Chas has sprung on the boy!" Lyndy tells Endore. "Oh, you don't care, Endore," she poses at concern. Her voice resumes in fascination. "That same night, Martin showed me the trucks."

The threat of the lurking gangs, the sudden intrusions into the sexual turf, the shouts and curses waking the sexual sleep-walkers—did Martin tell her about that? Did he withhold it? Endore forces his eyes not to slide toward Robert, Chas. He looks at the enigmatic man, Martin. Behind that mask, what?

Endore's voice is calm. "In the daytime those trucks haul meat on bloodied spikes. For the city's meat shops. And for the restaurants you eat in, darling." What was she looking for? What is she looking for?

"Ah, oui?"

At least for the moment Endore's words have blocked her recitation.

"Did the rot inspire you?" he flings at her, detecting the slightest pinprick in her composure. He saw Chas stretch his feline body before the boy—before he could pull his gaze away from them.

"All of it meshed into erotic forms," Lyndy breathes.

"She said it was like modern art," Martin interjects.

Yes. To force his glance not to slip again toward Robert, Endore looks at the muscular man in the tank top. Again, the man nods an invitation, Endore nods a contingent acceptance.

Lyndy's voice is hard. "One must pay homage to decay. One must celebrate the new deities."

Endore studies the pretty face, the enormous eyes, the darkened mouth. It is blank of expression, so blank that he has to turn away from it. Don–. . .

Don says in welcome surprise to the black man, "You just heard about the Rushes?"

"Yeah," the black man says, "just heard that . . . queers come here."

At the black man's ugly words, Don feels a spreading sexual heat. "Black people—even when they're normal—black men, they–. . ."

The black man drinks his beer slowly. "You're wondering if I go with queers? And I bet you're wonderin' if I got a big cock." A trace of an accent seeps into the voice.

"Do you?" Don forms words.

"Sure—cause I'm a straight black stud, hung like a fuckin horse." His tone has become that of a Southern Negro's. "Yuh suck good, boy?"

"Yes! Will you come home with me?"

"And then you'd feel good an dirty."

Did he say that? Don frowns. Leave now. Yes, good and dirty!

"Good and dirty thinkin, black nigger cock, big black nigguh cock, big black duhty nigguh cock." The accent thickens into a parody. The black man's lips tighten. "But so fucking superior because it's only for a short time." The accent disappears. "And after that, I'll be shit and you'll be the big white man, right? Well, what the fuck's wrong with you, man? You with your talk about queers and strange and normal and shit. You listen, I'm as gay as you are, and you know what I'm looking for? Cock, just like you. I want big, white, dirty, *young* cock!" He fires the fatal word again. "*Young!* Now fuck off!"

The cruel words seem to peel at the raw skin on Don's face. He led me on just to be brutal; why? He remains isolated in the midst of the Rushes. He turns toward Endore, for sustenance, but he can't see across the pressed bodies now. In

panic, he turns to one side, another. He was just toying with me! He looks at the shadows toward the back of the bar. And I didn't do anything to him except want him! Anger tangles. He starts to move toward the heavy shadows up the stairs—and remembers the horrible night when he was pushed onto the filthy floor of the piers. The muscular man in the white tank top—still alone. He feels himself moving toward the beautiful man. Don't do it, he screams to himself. Don't! But he is already nearing the man. Before he can approach him, the man in the tank top walks away.

Cascading laughter about the bar crashes on Don. The music is more quietly sinister and moaning than he remembers. He can almost hear the churning of flesh. He sees Bill talking to a man in a plaid shirt. Don't let him make out! Chas—with that boy! Stop it! And don't let Endore make out, dammit. Especially not Endore! His thoughts shove out like curses. I didn't mean that, he soothes himself, and the terrible moment passes. But unscreamed words remain bunched waiting.

From the distance, Endore sees Don. Rejected. And tonight Don is in a particular panic.

"Then it happened," Lyndy says. She turns to Martin. "Shall I tell him now?" she enlists him again.

"Oh, whenever." But: "Do you know who that is?" he nods toward a man moving into the red battlefield. Even in this light deep strain scars the man's face. "It's Steve. Remember him? I discovered him. The great beauty of only a few years back. Look at him now. Drained by lust," Martin says.

"How terrifyingly dramatic!" Lyndy shivers.

"You sound triumphant, Martin," Endore says. "As if you had something to do with it. Steve just looks tired tonight. I don't think it was his own lust which drained him."

"I had nothing to do with anything," Martin pronounces. "Look at the hollow eyes."

"Perhaps he's tired of straining to see himself the way you and others saw him," Endore says.

"You hear that about the eyes." Bill is back with a fresh

7-Up—and a beer for Endore, like a token of truce before there is any battle. Nothing worked in the field for Bill during this sortie. Those who looked good either turned awful or were cruising someone else. And the ones who wanted him, he didn't want. The beauty in the tank top—yes! Gladly! And he keeps coming back. But he does seem interested in Endore. "I don't think it's true, that our eyes show, that way," his voice is sad. Luke and he discussed it. Sometimes at night Luke would wake and turn on the light. Bill would catch him staring into the mirror. Do I have that look? he'd demand crazily. We have hollow eyes because we need more to fill them, they've carved too much out of us with their hatred, he would tell Bill. Often he spoke silly that way. By the tone of his words, Bill knew when it was coming and he stopped listening. Luke would say, I have that look, I have it already. Sometimes he sounded glad.

"Sometimes when we grow very tired of fighting—if only with bitter wit—for our very lives, then I think it shows," Endore says and hears laughter bursting about the bar.

"But that bitchy wit saves us," Bill is pensive.

"At times," Endore says. "But that's not enough!" Urgency charges his voice.

That's *my* way of fighting back, Bill thinks. With my wit. More powerful, for me, than those demonstrations and things. Luke insisted they march in one once. But enough was enough! Luke went alone. Bill catches sight of a trucker. Cute. He glances at Endore. Endore's words reverberate. So often he sounds like Luke. Did they see something of themselves in each other? Who is he staring at? The muscular man? Yes. No. He's looking at that kid with Chas.

"How'd you choose the Rushes for your first time, Robert?" Chas asks the youngman.

"My brother told me about it," Robert says. He doesn't want to think about him.

His brother? A faggot too? Chas is suspicious. He knows of the various shapes of violence in the area. Decoys in bars, you walk out, you're jumped, the skull cracks. Chas has never

been attacked—too tough-looking, he tells himself. What is this kid really doing here? He does look out of place. Just newness? Can he be mistaken about the look in the kid's eyes? No, it's arousal. And the crotch; no mistake about that, it's bunched hard.

Feeling Chas's eyes on his groin, Robert glances away. The man in the denim shirt is not looking at him.

"See it all, man," Chas grabs Robert's attention boldly. "You're in the Rushes, and it's your first time! You'll never forget it. Look at all the proud macho faggots!"

Faggots? That's the word his brother uses. Fags.

"All proud to be men," Chas goes on. He stares at the murals, to find himself there. His eyes fall on one of the few drawings he dislikes. The man in it just lies there, his groin barely covered with torn briefs: beautiful, yes, and macho, but passive, surrendered. "Some are top-men here, some bottom-men," Chas pushes. At each word, he studies Robert's reaction, determining how far to go now. "The keys on the left, like I wear, that means I'm a top-man, looking for someone to—..." Careful.

Robert frowned.

"The top-man's no better than the bottom-man," Chas says. "Just more experienced, the bottom dude's as much of a man, of course—gotta be, no one's a sissy. The top, he tells him ... what to do. Macho sex," he retreats slightly. Then he hears his words but they seem to be spoken by another voice. "It's like—... an initiation." He waits. Waits. "Like a—..." Then he releases the word. "...—baptism."

Chas's words swirl about Robert, sucking him in. He feels dirty. His brother told him, not exactly, but: "The way I got to know about the Rushes," Robert blurts, "is because my brother was bragging about how him and his friends beat up on fags outside here." He turns toward Endore. This time the looks connect. He wishes he could force that man to come over, talk to him, stop Chas's tumbling words.

What the fuck! Chas feels ambushed. But he can't define the trap.

Robert wipes the moisture from his forehead. "Who's the man you were with over there—in the denim shirt, the good-looking dark one?" He wants to cancel his excitement at Chas's body and the evocation of his brother.

Rejection. Chas feels cold. The ambiguity about the kid's presence disturbs him. Chas turns to move away.

"You goin?" Robert's not sure which man he's more attracted to. The man in the denim shirt has grown in his memories so long. Chas has just sprung into them.

It's not over. I just moved too fast. "Naw, I ain't going, just gonna get another beer." His eyes rake the boy's body, the lithe contours. "I'll be back," he promises.

"All right," Robert says. Now he's glad Chas is gone. Again he searches out the look of the man in the denim shirt. It is the woman's eyes he feels on him.

"Do you suppose the boy rejected Chas, Endore?" Lyndy asks.

"There's more," Endore says. A sexual tactician, Chas works in stages. He tantalizes, withdraws, leaving desire to recalesce. "He'll come back to him," Endore says.

Rejection. "Luke accused *me* of rejecting him!" Bill says aloud. So untrue, so strange.

That's what Luke said, that night. Endore remembers. He waits for Bill to say more.

Bill tosses away the memory. From this neutral trench, he scouts the venatic zone. He knows that in the battlefield anyone can be bloodied. As good a sexcruisier as he is, he's decamped several times tonight. If he weren't sure that the muscular man preferred Endore, he'd move in, yes. He remembers Luke acted that unapproachable, and so does Endore sometimes. But maybe it isn't Endore the muscular man wants. Bill's arcking eyes catch Don wandering as if lost.

Don holds his breath, like a swimmer hoarding it for greatest need. He moves toward an attractive man he just saw; was there a spark of interest when someone turned away from him? The man drifts away. Don looks in the direction of Endore. Help me!

Endore wishes he could send out a message to Don, to come back; to soothe his wounds from the bloody battle; to leave. But Don is about to approach another attractive man.

"The youngman seems interested in you. Again," Lyndy taunts Endore. She is still facing Robert. "Are you attracted to him?"

"He's beautiful," Endore says.

"You could offer the boy so much more," Lyndy persists. "You've written about the importance of first experiences. And with you it would be–... loving. One still hears about Michael. Wouldn't it be loving, Endore? Was it?" she claws at the memory.

I didn't want that, Endore says silently to Michael.

Lyndy's purling voice, soft, detached—all night it has floated in and out of Bill's hearing. Now—tense—he's aware of it, oppressive. "Why did you come here?" he asks her.

"For inspiration," she thrusts out, as if she had held the answer ready.

"That's all?" Endore asks her.

"Art for art's sake won't work, then?" Lyndy pouts. "Then let's try this. I want to see the true shape of liberation—and see it where there is no pretense–..." She pauses in mock thoughtfulness. "But, no, that won't do. It is *all* pretense here—the artists, the writers, the lawyers, the dancers, the clerks, the businessmen—they're all here under the working-class drag! So that won't do."

"No." Endore is determined not to show his rage. He will attack only at the exact time.

"You're lured by the scent of sexual blood, perhaps," Martin tosses offhandedly. But then there is the slightest hint of a frown, as if at the echo of his words. He looks away from the woman.

"Oppression," Lyndy pushes the single word at Endore. "I'm here because of my concern for the oppressed minority of homosexuals." Her fingers clasp the necklace. Her lips clutch their smile. "But unlike you, Endore—the elitist social-ist—unlike you, I'm not interested in *all* the oppressed. Poverty

bores. I choose the *chic* oppressed." She hurls the words like a malediction into the Rushes. She turns to Martin. "Shall I tell him now?"

She's threatening him. Endore knows.

"Whenever." Martin shrugs.

"We saw a man beaten that night," she tells Endore.

"My God, look who's trying to come into the Rushes!" Bill gasps.

"How cheap you are." Endore tells Lyndy.

7

Bless this sacrifice
prepared for the glory
of Your holy name.

As OFTEN as he comes to the Rushes,
Chas is still amazed by the sense of continuity it asserts. Even
when he stays away for days, "storing up energy," even when
he has to be gone longer, he feels on returning that he has
never left. That moment connects to all the others past in a
strong chain.

Within that synergetic continuity of the Rushes, each eve-
ning has its identity. Some nights Chas comes here only "to
breathe in the bar"; other times he leaves early with someone.
At times he'll stay until the bar closes. Those nights especially,
he makes several incursive moves beyond the shroud of
shadows at the back of the bar, "charging" his cock up, being
groped and groping; pushing an eager head down. There are

other times when the Rushes itself seems to command the night. Like now.

Chas has what is admired as a warrior's instinct—he seems "always" to make out. The instinct is, more exactly, cunning. When his quarry has flashed premature surrender, Chas sends out his sure questions. Then he moves in—"aggressively."

With Robert, signals clash. A hint of withdrawing—and then he called Chas back. The kid is very aroused by him, but he's attracted also to Endore. Yet Endore never advances; it's unlikely the kid would make the initial move, his first time in a bar. And there's the boy's brother—that is troubling. Still, the kid gave him the only sure hardon of the night.

For now, Chas will retreat from the boy. He will leave a sexual promise to dredge at the kid's desire.

Like a general surveying the field, Chas leans against the bar. Soon, when the evening rushes toward Last Call, his favorite time will occur. The hunt will be unmasked, no more the excuse of being here with friends or for a drink. Sex reigns. The animal stretches, and the Rushes assumes its full life.

A few stools away, Michael is talking to a man. Chas has always been attracted to him. Staring, he tries to force the handsome youngman to look at him. He does. Chas nods. Michael does not answer. Chas nods again. He isn't sure whether Michael answered that time, because waves of anger are flooding the bar, voices are conveying an unspecified message of turbulence. When Lyndy entered, there were stirrings; but now increasing portions of the bar seem electrified, in a state of alert.

Chas maneuvers his way to the trenches. He sees Bill turn away as if in rejection of the sight at the door.

Bill sees Chas standing against the wall, his back to the panel depicting the stripped figure about to be bound by another; from here, it is almost as if it is Chas who is being menaced, Bill thinks. The unwelcome reaction he felt toward the two presences at the door fluctuates, and now he feels an

anticipatory excitement at the thought of Chas's outrage when he discovers them. And what is Lyndy's reaction? Bill looks at the inscrutable outlined mask.

All vinyl and sequins, two incongruous figures stand at the entrance to the Rushes. The smoke swirling toward the open door creates a nebulous red outline against the dying night.

" 'They had terrible strength and force and great were their ambitions; they attacked the gods. They tried to climb into heaven intending to make war upon the gods,' " Endore recites.

"Something from one of your columns?" Lyndy asks.

"No, one of Plato's; he attributed that to Aristophanes; he was talking about what we would call transvestites." And so now he can either free himself of the doubts which Lyndy's presence stirred or face his own hypocrisy. In his columns he has reminded that the Stonewall Inn was what would now be known as a "sissy bar." The "sissies" and "queens," not the masculine men here, were the heroic revolutionaries who fought the cops that first heated night. Rough bars like the Rushes sprang up soon after and ostracized them. Endore upheld the courage of the "queens." Not parodies of women, they were their own creations, assaulting, daring, defiant figures abrading entrenched sexual postures. . . . Now a "queen" in full drag is actually standing at the entrance to the Rushes.

A black woman. And a white transvestite. Are attempting. To enter. The Rushes. Bill forms each careful phrase in his mind, to force the reality. Why is he so tense? He's always "liked" transvestites and women. The Rushes changes everything.

The avenging figures are rubicund silhouettes against the door. Standing there like unwelcome messengers, they threaten the men here much more than Lyndy's full foray. The two have the power of psychic assault.

"You'll get the shit kicked out of you if you come in," the man at the door tells the transvestite.

"Let us in and let's see," the transvestite says. Small, she is

dressed in vitreous black vinyl; needling sequins flash on the slit skirt. Like Lyndy's, her eyes are enlarged by the outlined black; eyes as defiant as the cheap sheen of her skirt.

"We'll just keep standin right here!" the black woman promises. She crosses her spangled arms. She is a ferocious presence. Warring colors—turned into zebra stripes in this light—intercept the exposed brown flesh of her shoulders, legs mounted on spiked brilliant shoes.

How differently the man at the door spoke even at first to Lyndy. "They're as adamant as you, darling," Endore tells her. After her narrative earlier and his lashing at her, hostile silence bound them. "Do you suppose *they'll* come in, Martin?"

Martin's glaciated face is turned toward the door. "Perhaps." He drops the word.

Lyndy's head snaps toward Martin. "Perhaps—... Perhaps you can use this in one of your columns, Endore—what we saw by the trucks that other night. I. And Martin."

She is pulling attention from the two figures—she's enlisting Martin by warning him; reminding him of what? Collusion in some voyeuristic horror perhaps. Martin is the only one who can bring the two in, Endore thinks—and Lyndy knows it.

Her eyes on Martin, holding him, Lyndy says. "I walked right up to one of the trucks," she drops the diversionary words, she has implied them before. "Martin waited. In the Jaguar." She touches his arm; then her fingers shoot back to the strands of pearls. "I saw the shadows of men—limbs intertwined—on the floor of the trucks." She is speaking very slowly, allowing Martin to stop her. "There was no frenzy ... until—..." she studies Martin; his reaction will determine whether she will continue. She tantalizes the core of her story again. "... —until some boys ... attacked ... one of ... the men."

Martin looks away from the door. Lyndy's hand releases the pearls.

The subtle blackmail shaped. But Endore could not grasp its meandering direction. At the trucks, did she raise her hand, the way she does?

She saw a mugging, Bill knows. He and Luke saw a man assaulted once. Luke ran. Bill watched. Later Luke cried. Bill explodes: "Maybe someday you'll be slumming, Lyndy, and someone will mistake *you* for—..." One of us? No!

The two avenging figures at the door have not budged. The shockwaves created by their presence lap farther into the bar, roiling waves of anger.

"What?"

"Two fuckin queens are trying to come into the Rushes!"

That bitch Lyndy's fault! Chas looks in her direction. Her presence festers in the Rushes.

"The day after my tour of the piers, I designed my boldest creations," Lyndy's voice turns gay.

She has skipped a crucial part of her narrative, Endore realizes. "I draped swatches of moiré and slashes of red, I wanted the brightness that only plastic has ... and blood ... but so briefly ... before it turns black." She stares at Martin. "Oh, look, our macho stud is back, our darling Chas," she greets him back.

Fury digs into Chas's face, gaunt with anxious sweat. He stares toward the reddened gauzy figures at the entrance. How dare they? Christ! It's not *her!* No. The queen on the piers was much larger, looming on the truck ramp.

"Macho stud is redundant, darling," Martin tells Lyndy.

"That's it, Martin!" Bill announces. "I've always wondered who or what exactly you remind me of, and I just saw it. You remind me of a depraved pope."

"Depraved pope is redundant too," Martin utters.

"Always standing there—judging but not joining," Bill refuses to let go.

"I judge nothing," Martin's lips pronounce, "and I see nothing to join."

"Looking, then; just looking?" Bill stalks him. "Is that

what you like, to watch? There are so many rumors about you." He allows silence to dredge up interpretations.

"No, that's not what I like," Martin says.

Bill's tone is tripped by memory. "Sometimes it *is* better, just watching. Like jerking off with your favorite photograph, nothing can go wrong then, no broken wrist at the wrong time, no fuck-me when you want to get fucked. One time I pretended Luke was asleep, my live photograph; whatever I wanted him to be. We played games like that; he loved it."

Chas turns away from the tawdry figures at the door. "They won't get in!" he shoves the words at Martin; a note of entreaty impinges. It can't be her! But he remembers lustrous black and stabbing beads. And then he sees the man entering the Rushes past the two punishing presences at the door, and it is as if electricity has replaced the blood in his veins.

Tall, slender—stark, stark—with broken rough features, short-cropped dark hair, the man is dressed—enclosed—in black leather—pants, jacket, cap. Gloves. He wears gloves—but no keys, no handkerchief, no earring—no proclamation of his sexual role. Cool, cool even in the fluctuating temperature of the bar. He is one of those electric figures in homosexual bars who grabs awed attention. He has managed to yank it away from the two waiting figures at the door.

As he passes by, the leatherman brushes Endore's hand with the gloved knuckles. The glove is cold, rough. Endore feels a distant stirring. He pulls his hand away from the somber presence. The cold black glove—warm, soft—touches Chas's hand. Chas's cock hardens.

Bill feels an ugly shudder, a threatening sexual attraction which he doesn't like.

"Il est formidable!" Lyndy breaks the spell over the men.

"Why can't we come in?" the transvestite's words pull again at the door.

"You're not wanted here. You're not properly dressed," the voice of the man at the door is sarcastic; he is now performing for others in the bar.

"Coat and ties?" the black woman derides.

How can anyone be attracted to that man in leather—masculine and roughly handsome as he is? Yes, and it's obvious he's got a gorgeous body, the leather is molded to him like skin. But he looks terrifying. Don is easing his way back toward the others. He's taking advantage of the tautened attention to shield his return. Then he sees Steve.

A few feet away, Steve waves at Don.

Steve. The great beauty of years back, everyone wanted him, Martin's most famous model. He looks terrible now, wasted. Don used to fantasize about making it with him.

Steve smiles at Don.

I used to desire him, oh, so much, Don remembers.

Steve's smile is eager.

He'd go with me now if I would resurrect his lost image, Don thinks, and feels a sigh of warmth returning.

Steve moves toward him—the smile more anxious.

With a slight flip of his head, Don walks away. *I rejected him!* he exults. Now he can move back to the others.

Oh, God! The two at the door are drag queens. Drag queens at the Rushes! Good! "Have you seen those two queens?" Don joins Endore and the others. He hurries his words, further to camouflage his bloodying in the field.

"The black one is a woman, isn't she, darling?" Martin asks Lyndy.

"Yes." The woman in the tuxedo does not look at the man who brought her in.

Did the queen only appear that tall on the ramp? Chas's words will serve as an imprecation against the two attempting invaders: "The Rushes is pulsing with 'love' tonight!" he asserts the power of his bar.

"It's the amyl nitrite," Martin cuts. "You've confused the amyl nitrite with love."

The voice of the man at the door rises in anger: "Shit, you wouldn't make out here."

"Her or me?" the black woman demands. She pushes her

large breasts. The affronting cleavage is sharper.

"Neither," the man shoots.

"Roxy makes out everywhere," the woman says.

"So does Elaine." Roxy says. Her skirt shines like black cellophane.

Elaine crosses her arms. "Not budgin."

Chas snorts: "They're disgusting." The queen on the ramp was with a black whore, the thought asserts.

They're courageous, Endore reminds himself, but does not speak the words.

"They certainly get the real men." Don remembers the "queens" and the tough "normal men" in the bars he and his friends used to brave only now and then, years ago.

"Real men go with real men," Chas controls his voice. It *is* the same queen! He transfers his anger to Don: "Haven't you been rejected enough for tonight, Don?"

"How cruel," Bill protests. He touches Don's arm. Don looks different, he notices. But how? His attention floats away and descends on a man in Levi's cutoffs. Muscular hairy legs! Striped logging socks! Climbing boots! And the round head of his cock is hanging out from under the cutoffs!

The leatherman moves farther into the bar.

"I could have gone with Steve just now," Don says, but the echo of his words snuffs out his tiny triumph.

"He'd go with anyone who would remind him of what he was," Martin says.

Endore sees Steve gliding about like a lost shadow. An avenging ghost has wounded another, he thinks.

The leatherman pauses. Near Robert.

"You won't always be young, Chas," Don erupts. Pressure clamps his temples.

"I'll survive!" Chas bolts his boots to the patched floor.

"Well, we survived, too," Don roars. "You forget that." He feels the earlier bunched words—he pushes them back; speaks others: "We fought battles, too, even if we had to hide." He remembers the subtle cruising "right under their eyes," but

"they" didn't see it. "We had secret bars, word of mouth, where we could dance," tinted memories tug. "And it was *fun!*" he insists.

"It's still . . . fun!" Chas says, but he didn't like the sound of the word. The leatherman—the mesmerizing presence—is standing near Robert. Chas feels an entangling confusion.

"No—it's all too serious," Don says. The parties. Curtains drawn. The perennial threat that one of the "cute boys" might turn out to be "vice." "Sure, the cops kept busting us, and they lied, and we were convicted, but we lived with it," Don says.

"They still bust us, man," Chas reminds him. He sees Robert finally glance at the awesome leatherman. Chas touches his knuckles where the black gloves brushed. "Maybe not in the Rushes, but lots of other places." The cop hand-cuffed *him!* I'm a top-man! he wanted to protest. "That's why we make our own ghettos. Which they *still* invade," he throws at Lyndy.

An amused smile is pasted on her lips.

In the thickening smoke the insistent forms at the door are transformed into nebulous threats.

Damn! The logger in cutoffs is trying to talk to the muscular man, Bill sees. So scratch *both* off!

Now the leatherman is looking back at him. Or at Endore? Chas saw him touch Endore too. "This is our island in the ocean," Chas tells Don.

Is that it? Endore wonders. Inside the ghettos we can pretend we've won the raging war. He wipes his hand where the glove touched. Why is he so silent about the figures at the door?

Wait! The muscular man isn't interested in the logger in shorts. Bill adds a distant possibility—two?—to his growing column; the muscular man might just—. . .

"We even went to jail," Don's voice weakens. "And even friends turned their backs on you if they discovered you'd been arrested." The stigma, the shame!

"We still go to jail!" Chas reminds him. He turns away from the two arousing, disturbing figures—the youngman and

116 ·

the leatherman. Is the gloved hand of the leatherman on his own groin? Opening the buttons there. Memories mix. His look stumbles on the two forms at the door. Don't let them come in!

"Some of our friends committed suicide," Don remembers. Eddie—always camping, doing Mae West, that feathered boa trailing. And then he was dead, wrists slashed. His friends, where now? Huddled in close groups at awful dinners, afraid to face the new soldiers.

Lyndy seems uninterested in this interlude. Or preoccupied? Endore wonders.

Don is going on: "But most of us just went on, and in style—and it *was* fun," Don pleads.

"Well, fuckeroo if that wasn't a tribute to closetry," Chas says.

Don forces the knotting words back. "Now all I see are the mean fake machos. Fake machos!" he hurls at Chas. And Endore. Yes, he included Endore. "And it's all so hostile."

"Toughened," Chas says.

"If you're not going to screw with someone he's your enemy." But Don knows it was always like that. Always. "No one wants to go home anymore, just to orgies. And everyone looks the same."

Surrender by absorption. Endore hears the muted music converted here into a sex-dirge.

Chas is becoming too cruel—and those two figures at the door, just standing there, are unnerving. Bill would go over and smile at them, yes—maybe they'd leave if someone were nice to them. Tension keeps rushing at them from all over the bar. Yet they're still standing there! Bill begins to inch away from them and the others—and toward the hairy-legged logger with his round cock on exhibit. He retreats; the logger is talking to a biker.

"We loved our difference," Don sighs. "Now everyone wants to look straight."

"But not *be* straight," Chas attacks back. "We're the *real* men now. *They* imitate *us!*" In one urgent look he captures

the magnificent display of machos. The leatherman emerges out of the sexual mass. And Robert. Chas cups his full groin, full balls, full cock.

"Goddamnit, they—you—make me feel estranged from my own," Don says. "I wish—. . . !" Pull back, not that, don't say that! He retreats. "Well, I have an open wound and I'm bleeding and no one's trying to seal my wound or stop my bleeding!"

In the real jungles, the old are sent out into the wilds to die, the young savages throw stones at them so they can't come back. Here we allow them to stay and be bloodied, Endore thinks. But not the two at the door—for any reason. Still, he remains silent.

"Because we faggots aren't bleeding anymore, not hating ourselves anymore, that's fuckin why!" Chas says.

"Oh, no? Don't you talk about self-hatred to me, Chas. You hate each other even more than we did." Don frowns. Oh, God, I hurt Steve. I'm sorry, Steve. "You, Chas, with your straps and chains and handcuffs and God knows what other precious objects of pain you call toys. Well, *children* play with toys! How do you think you get your beloved slaves to let you call them queers and cocksuckers?" His own words batter at his brain. His face is on fire, throbbing as if fists are crashing on him. His hands rise to cover his ears. "The same names they call *us* when they beat us up!" he roars.

"Don, you don't understand faggot S & M," Chas steadies his voice. "It's makebelieve—not like *that*. No one forces anyone. When the bottom-man looks up at me, he sees what he *longs* to see, a dominant faggot—a *man*, yeah, like him—standing over him, powerful."

"And when you look down at him, what do you see, Chas?" Endore hears his soft words.

"A *man* acknowledging the power of another *man!*" Chas says.

Trapped in tension, he and Endore face each other.

Chas releases words as if the intensity must be peeled

away with care. "When I confront another stud and he says he's a top-man and he won't do this or that and I know he wants me to make him do it—..." A subdued tone enters his words: "That man I told you about—shit—my first time here." His voice softens. "I still have—..." He stops, frowns. He holds his beer to his groin, to moisten it with the bottle's cold sweat. But the bottle and his hand are hot. The humidity in the bar is weighted. He moves, to locate a fuller current of artificial air. He rubs his hand on his bare chest, collecting the sweat; now again he touches his groin.

Roxy's voice pulls at the entrance. Precise. Determinedly "correct." "We'll tell you again; we're not tryin—trying—to make out here. We know we can't. Elaine and me—I—was hustlin the truckers, and a gang of thugs came at everyone—they've been at it all night, so we run—ran—here, and damned if we gonna go out there for a while yet, so allow us to enter."

"I tell you, boy, they come on us—with sticks, bottles; they called me a fag, and I'm a woman," Elaine says.

"We still don't allow trans—... women." the man at the door says.

Roxy stares into the red smoke. "What about her?" She points to Lyndy. Her finger remains aimed at the woman.

It points at him, Endore feels. "Why don't you intercede for them, Martin?" A heaviness lightens. "You're the only one who can."

Chas sidesteps as if to block Martin.

"Do they have passports?" Lyndy asks.

"Honorary ones," Endore says. A weight begins to lift.

Lyndy puts her hand on Martin's arm. "Oh, darling, don't. They're those creatures we saw on the piers earlier."

The two on the ramp, Bill knows. Does Chas know that?

"Don't?" Martin eases Lyndy's hand away. "I thought you wanted to see it all, darling."

"And be astonished," Endore reminds her.

"At the trucks that night!" Lyndy threatens the withheld part of her earlier narrative.

Martin glances down at her. "Why don't you tell them, darling?" he refuses the implied blackmail and takes a step toward the door.

"I'll wait until you return," Lyndy breathes.

"Do," Martin tosses back.

"We don't like your kind, and you give us a bad name," the man at the door tells Roxy.

"He actually said that," Elaine says.

"The same thugs were beating on guys like you," Roxy says. "Think about it."

"Actually," says Elaine, "we just got caught in the shuffle; they was really after the machos. You the guy in the limo?" she asks the tall man suddenly there.

Without looking at Elaine or Roxy, Martin whispers to the man at the door. This time without argument, the man surrenders. Martin abandons Elaine and Roxy to the Rushes.

The two are trapped in a sea of hostile stares.

"We need a drink bad," Elaine says. They make their way in, toward the bar. Men move away from them, spitting. "Just one drink," Elaine repeats, as if extending a promise, containing, trying to contain, the simmering animosity. "Just one, only one."

Roxy plants her hands on her hips, but her pose of overt defiance loosens. "Yeah, just one drink." She feels the incandescent stares, hears the muttered curses as they move through the flammable territory. "One drink."

The men turn their backs to them. A path clears before them, as if they are contagious; and it holds. Tenuously. Moving in a direct line to the bar, they do not pass Endore or Lyndy—or Martin. The cleared path still holds, bordered by angry faces, backs, bodies which may push forward at any moment. The tension is about to boil over. A man blocks their way. Roxy faces him, her painted eyes ignite, one hand rises to her hip. Other men gather behind the man blocking the transvestite. Easing her away, Elaine guides her around them in a wide loop, following a clearing curved path. The man who blocked their way pursues them there.

In the clearing, Robert does not turn away from them. He stands steadfast, and he nods to them.

They nod back.

The pursuing man retreats, slowly, bewildered by the youngman's stance.

Robert remains isolated in the abandoned area.

Then the tension ebbs. The merging bodies close the open fissures. Elaine and Roxy have made it past the most volatile area and to the bar, where they sit on discarded stools.

Endore looks at Robert. He wishes he had done what the youngman did. Had he been in the angry aisle, would he have? Now there is more to redeem, he knows; and it is possible because Martin has not gone all the way. He abandoned the black woman and the transvestite, but now they are here, like reserve dynamite—which may ignite on different fronts.

It's her, Chas knows, the queen on the piers. He confronts Lyndy: "It's your fuckin fault! If you hadn't shoved your way in, they *never* would have been able to come into the Rushes!" That kid Robert, he helped too—but he didn't know what he was doing, still has to learn. But Lyndy and Martin knew.

True, Bill knows, and his anger fans out. It now includes not only Lyndy—and Martin—but the black woman and the transvestite.

In surrogate answer—looking at Chas—Lyndy says, "I think that adorable boy is dreadfully attracted to you . . . Endore."

The face of Robert blends with another. Does he remind me of me? Endore doesn't disguise his staring at the youngman.

Robert meets his look. When he did not turn his back like the others on the two separated figures, he felt afraid, yes, but their glaring isolation—magnified—reflected his. Robert does not look away from Endore. I cried that night. He remembers the late misty afternoon when his fantasy became real; he saw the man in denim, exactly as he had conjured him when he was alone in his room and his brother was gone—or so it seemed the moment he glimpsed the man and reality over-

whelmed the fantasy. Amid the rot. Now terror and sensual excitement battle within him. With Chas he could not find the full origin of his excitement, and he pulled back from the man he knew was offering sex but not just sex, a special brand of sex.

A rough, then soft—smooth like velvet—brushing on his knuckles. Surprised, Robert looks away from Endore to see a man in black, black leather. The leather glove still touches his hand. Repelled, fascinated—attracted to the rugged man?— Robert pulls back his hand, but he does not move away. The leatherman lurks near him. To resurrect a clearer feeling, Robert locates the man in the denim shirt.

"And now that Chas is out, Endore," Lyndy continues and snaps her fingers at the word "out," "you could easily—. . ."

The outburst she counted on comes: "Who the fuck says I'm out?" Chas demands.

Bragging, bragging; he's going to start bragging again, Don thinks. The anxiety is snapping like dozens of rubber-bands stretched inside, each as if pulled by words demanding to rush out.

At the bar, the bartenders refuse to serve Elaine and Roxy.

This time with all her force, Lyndy is moving to sever the delicate balance between him and Chas. Yes, the two figures at the bar threaten her—they sit within a quarantined hollow— and she is plotting her strategy. Don't fall into her trap! Endore tries to alert Chas.

"Not sure I want someone that new," Chas inches back. It's partly true: Chas is not sure now, but not because of Robert's "newness"—that excites him—but because, reinterpreted, the signals are even cloudier. And there's the badgering presence of the leatherman, doubly powerful when he stood near Robert. Strange, though, that the leatherman isn't wearing keys or any other sign of whether he's a top- or a bottom-man. Perhaps he goes both ways. In Chas's experience, such flexible performers have been among the best.

"The youngman is quite gorgeous," Lyndy goads. "A trophy for anyone."

"He shines even in this light." Martin seems to join her strategy.

"Which is meant for us who have lost it, even inside," Endore says aloud.

"Has Michael lost his ... inner glow?" Lyndy mocks her own words.

"No," Endore says. But has he?

"The youngman is so brash, so shy," Lyndy says.

"It's his first time in a bar," Chas announces; "he said he learned about the Rushes because his brother and his friends come around to beat up on the guys cruising outside." He wants to try out the information on Endore.

"Maybe *he's* looking for queers to beat up," Don's voice is anxious.

"I'm sure he's not here for violence," Endore says. He remembers the youngman standing in the cleared aisle earlier. Now he feels sadness for him—brought here by the ramifying knowledge of violence; and that sadness floods out the remembrance of the youngman. The long eyelashes. He followed me that afternoon on the piers. The memory slides into focus.

"His brother might have been one of those boys we saw rushing at the trucks." The thought excites Lyndy.

"There are so many of them," Endore rejects.

"They're everywhere!" Bill says. "The park is a jungle. They're everywhere screaming, 'Faggots, queers, fruits!' I think it's getting worse." He intercepts trajecting gazes in the sexfield. "I believe I'll go back in again," he says as if to drown the echoing shouts.

The logger in cutoffs is alone! Bill stands next to him. The logger glances at him; eyes hold. The logger looks down at his exposed cock. Bill lets his hand fall, touching the hairy thighs, fingers spidering toward the naked head of his cock. Uncircumcised! Bill loves the uncut skin. The cock begins to grow in Bill's hands. His fingers outline the moist ring under the delicious skin. The logger moves away. Son of a bitch! Bill sees him situate himself next to another quickly interested

man, whose hand too drops to grope the exposed cock. Again the logger moves away. The bastard!—he's counting, Bill knows. He's counting contacts. Bill feels an errant hand on his own groin. Without investigating to whom it belongs, he pushes it away. Son of a bitch! He tosses his gaze into the bar again. The prostitute and the transvestite—how long can they hold out, without a drink, everyone avoiding them? The two seem to be looking in Lyndy's direction.

"You keep staring at the youngman, Endore," Lyndy says.

"I'm trying to imagine what the Rushes looks like to him," Endore says.

"A feast," Chas pronounces. "So delicious even heterosexuals are coming here now. We act out the fantasies they're afraid to even dream of. We can have sex in one day with more people than most of them have in their lives. They think they're slumming but they're sniffing out our freedom."

"Perhaps we come to watch what *we've* created and *you* call freedom," Lyndy's black lips frost the words.

"What *you've* created?" Chas snorts. "You didn't create our orgy rooms or the piers or the trucks. Or the Rushes. You didn't create them."

"Didn't they?" Endore wonders aloud.

"Try this, Chas." Lyndy's words thaw: their brutality is warmed—disguised—by an ironic tone. "We come to watch you as you wallow in the exile we've thrust on you and you don't know it."

Endore studies Martin's immutable hauteur.

It's true, it's all true! Don's thoughts shock him.

"Bullshit," Chas says. "What you call our exile we've turned into the best rush. Now *we* don't want *you*, but—look!— there *you* are!" He mimics her gesture earlier, hands out, palms up.

"So I am," Lyndy says.

"Has it occurred to you that it is *we* who slum with *you?*" Endore says to her.

"Oh, try this, Chas—*and Endore!*—like Romans we watch the beautiful captive gladiators slaughter each other for our

pleasure." Her smile is intended to palliate the words, but it cuts into her face.

Yes! Don thinks. Yes. Anger ignites. I've *got* to make out tonight. Would Steve really have gone with me?

"Are you capable of other than borrowed pleasure, darling?" Endore aims at Lyndy.

Rebounding, Lyndy turns on Chas: "I'll make a bet, Chas: If you lose the boy, you call me darling. If you win . . . you win the boy!"

"Not sure I want the kid." Chas stares at his boots.

"You do," Lyndy moves to kill. "And so does Endore. Are you afraid, Chas?"

"If I want him, I'll have him!" Chas kisses his knuckles.

"Leave him alone," Endore says.

"For you?" Chas adjusts his stance—feet apart, one farther out than the other, yes, like that, knees at a slight crook, hips prepared to thrust.

"A challenge!" Lyndy triumphs.

"I bet on Endore. No, on Chas," Martin speeds the momentum.

Chas lowers his cap so that he has to push up his chin to face Endore. They have never competed on the battlefield. The buried rivalry is untested. Endore never advances first, Chas assesses his own strategy. But the Rushes is unpredictable tonight. Pull back! "Wanna see who can get him, Endore?" Too late; the words are out. "Michael is here," he makes a vague retreat, but a warning of a conflagration on another front.

Michael's laughter, Endore remembers that increasingly. "Play your ugly games alone, Chas. Like a lonely child with your toys!" Endore turns his back on Chas.

Chas feels relief and rage. Yes, Endore pulled back, but he shoved the fight into an unexplored arena. "I'll play!" Chas says. But why doesn't he move?

"You're afraid of Endore," Lyndy slaughters.

Chas's head jerks toward her. He brings his fist to his mouth, as if to swear: "I'll make it with that kid, *my* way, and

you'll all see it!" He slaps one hand on his thigh. I should be wearing gloves, he thinks, pulling at remembered power lodged in his past. The rush of exhilaration bursts. "It's not a gentle world that kid's entered. No one knows it better than you, Endore. You entered it alone—and you're still alone, and so did I, and so am I, and so did he, and all the others now and forever, alone." He looks down at his pants, the black leather. He remembers the moisture there, that long ago time. First cold, then hot, it touched his skin.

"He was pushed here by his brother's hatred." Endore lowers his voice to exclude Lyndy and Martin from this intimacy.

"But he's staying, and he'll have to survive in it," Chas says. "I believe in the Rushes, man, and it is what it is, and you take it or leave it," he says passionately. He breaks an ample of amyl. He devours the vapor into his nostrils. This time that is not enough. He brings it to his hungry mouth and inhales it into his lungs. His voice is a murmur, a growl, barely audible—the smothered music of the Rushes pants in accompaniment to his words. The afferent chemical matches its beat. Sexual images curdle in his whirling sight. "That man I started to tell you about—the first guy, here in the Rushes. He—. . . I was so hot for him and he knew it from my hardon and he stood in front of me without a word and he started opening his pants real slow and he brought out his cock and he pissed on me." The last words fade. "He said he was baptizing me, and then—. . ."

"No, Chas," Endore breathes the words.

The coagulated images untangle in his brain as the rush of the amyl recedes. Chas looks about him as if the echo of his words surprises him. He looks down at his pants. There is no moisture there now. From under the cocked leather cap, he glares darkly at Endore: "I'll send that kid back to you, Endore—baptized in my piss!"

Don turns away from it all. He staggers toward the entrance. He can't breathe. At the door, he stands looking at the

jagged landscape. The sky is ferrous gray. Rancid air curls from the waterfront. The young hustler is outside—shirtless, his pants pushed low; waiting. I hate you! Don's mind screams. I detest you!

"Will that make you more the man?" Endore asks Chas.

"No, you less," Chas answers.

"Just make sure you play your game all the way with yourself!" Endore shoots.

Chas's sight clouds. Not the amyl, not just the amyl. His vision opens as if onto a new clarity always hidden in the Rushes. "Watch!" And he moves toward Robert.

"Will you let Chas have the boy—that hideous way?" Lyndy pretends a shudder. This time she bites a pearl with her teeth.

Chas confronts Robert. He stares nakedly at the boy. No ambiguity now! Go all the way! Chas gropes his own crotch. Hard! Then, discarding all other looks of interest, he moves between bodies and toward the back of the bar. A few steps. He stops, looks back. Waits. He locates Robert amid the twisting forms draped in dyed smoke. With the power of proffered sex, he pulls at the youngman. Yes, Robert is following.

Dodging bodies which glide to intercept him, Chas takes more steps. More. He's moved into a sparser area, to one side of the steps, so Robert can see him. Again, Robert stops. Chas hardens his grasp on his groin; the cockring tightens. He moves up the steps. Robert advances.

Extracting himself from the massing flesh within the bowels of the Rushes, the leatherman follows them.

Assertive legs spread, Chas stands at the top of the steps. Like this! he remembers, that man stood exactly like this.

Robert looks up at the form of Chas. The dying bulb taints the smoke umber behind Chas's looming form. The leatherman stands beside Robert.

Snapping it like a tiny gun, Chas cracks an ampule of amyl and holds it waiting before him. The fingers of his other hand locate the buttons on his pants.

II

Dominus vobiscum.
Et cum spiritu tuo.

8

We give You thanks for Your
great glory.

As OFTEN as he comes to prowl the
electric city. Tim is still raided by excitement and fear as he
moves like a·night animal through the battered landscape.
When he does so, he is determined to abandon even the ves-
tiges of his identity beyond the night, compressing its experi-
ences into a pastless present. The boundaries between the two
emotions are at times indistinguishable; at times one feels like
the other. Even when its scratches bloody him, he is deter-
mined never to show the fear constantly there. He conquers it
by generating it. His stance and his swagger flash toughness,
and a look of surly anger warns. That look slides at the appro-
priate time into a sexual invitation.

Tim's face has a crooked angularity which augments his
sexuality. His body has the deep outlines of a gymnast's.

He just left an apartment where he went with a man he met earlier near the Rushes. Although the waterfront is not a malehustling area, Tim can make out. Even among the abundance of free sex along the piers, in the trucks, the bars, there are men, older or not attractive, who spill out rejected.

When the turf known for hustling teems with other young bodies for sale, and there are fewer buyers than sellers, Tim will shift to the waterfront. Sometimes he goes there first, without checking out the surer territory. He carries his hustling stance like a medal into what he considers enemy turf. And he connects there. But not as often as he tells himself.

Because he comes to the area of the waterfront in order to feel outrage and rage.

He loves to watch the men who hunt there for malesex. He cherishes the anger the sight of them elicits; it purges him, soothes him. When they know or suspect he's hustling, he affronts them, and they look away, as he does—glancing at them as they move often in their strange costumes into the weird bars. When he shoots his cum later with a client, it is as if he has fired his anger like a gun at all the sights he collected.

Earlier, he asked the man he went home with for $10 more than he agreed to, "for cab fare." He said the words with a crooked ominous smile, and he got the money, as he usually does. As always, he hated the man who licked his stripped body and gave him a fierce hardon. When he came into the man's mouth—shutting his eyes, pushing his cock as if to choke the man—his fists bunched. There is always that moment in which he is sure he will batter the retreating head. But the next moment he feels a wrenching in his stomach, which weakens him, as when a blow connects. His hands remain fists for only seconds. Then they open up, exhausted as if they have done invisible battle. He feels the men who pick him up pay him to hate them, and he feels they hate him even while desiring him.

Unfair! he screams, because his only moment of importance in the crushing world is when he comes—or so he feels—and he grasps those moments that form a sextime which he

knows is short, leaving him with nothing more when it—but not he—dies. He has seen young, very young ghosts haunting the streets.

Those feelings occur each time he hustles. Tonight's fusion of excitement and fear veers toward heated terror, panic, a cumulative rage which pleads to free itself.

The night fluctuates between the last of a cool spring and the first of a panting summer. His sweat cools as he walks—his shirt unbuttoned—along the upper part of the city's main street—wide, long, a buzzing electric vein. He sees the mobs of people ignoring him and each other and the madness bursting everywhere; a tattered woman rips at imaginary figures ripping back at her, and Tim watches as if to give his fear or sorrow or anger an object. She snatches at the air, her body contracts, and then releases the tension as if for only a moment she has slain the horror. He moves on. On greenish-brown benches others sit traumatized like sacrifices to the street. The buzz is nervous.

When did tonight's new terror begin?

There are times when it is the city that makes him ache, ache with anger; so beautiful, this concrete jungle, trying to survive the raining filth, as if it knows it's dying. Other nights he focuses on the giant buildings stabbing at the sky, which seems lowered each year by a new layer of filthy clouds. Iron, steel, cement, the buildings—at times they crush him tiny; other times he searches the sharp angles of light and dark they create, shoving himself in and out of them to become a part of their ordered patterns.

But none of that explains tonight's new fear.

Did it begin when the man paid him? It has happened so often, and this time was no different; as always, the money felt warm and beautiful in his hand, not like money. Later, then. When he came? His fists bunched, and he felt closer this time to pushing them out in fury, but he did not, and so that was not different. Earlier. When he saw the men sliding for sex into the warehouses on the piers? He has seen that too often, even looks for it.

The screaming faces in the speeding car. Yes. When it rushed by, and bottles flew in his direction—but not at me, he insists, not at me—and the scream of "Faggots!" was tossed out—but not at me, not at me—he felt the tension spill. And then—. . . He pulls back.

Years ago, Tim hustled the area of the porno theaters, freaky stores, peep shows. Although he is just into his 20s, he has been pushed out by youngmen, boys, much younger than himself; they and the junky zombies and the amazonic bright-painted transvestites and women have taken over this turf. As if to locate an anger buried deeper than tonight, he walks that broken street, lights a smashed spectrum of colors. He sees the hustling teenage boys, and he feels old.

He traverses the city to the hustling bar he often frequents. Only hustlers there and those who buy them. Outside, other youngmen lurk almost to the edge of the river. But Tim doesn't enter the bar. He feels pulled back to the area of the Rushes tonight, as if it—or what occurred there—has magnetized him.

But he pauses outside the hustling bar. A flashy, not-yet-drunk man approaches him. "I know you're selling it, but where can I go for just love?"

The question enrages Tim further. "I dunno!" he yells.

At the corner, he descends the concrete stairs into the subterranean city. The roar of the trains is ominous thunder. The walls along the slanted walk are scrawled with wordless curses. It is late, the hours of fear. People hurry close to the walls, as if for shelter from those who prowl the violated maze. One man clings to the wall as if pinioned by an invisible betrayer. The urine-scented tunnel pulls ahead of Tim. He concentrates on the sound of his feet. He is returning to the area of the Rushes. Astonished, he realizes he has a hardon.

In the train, he sits in the uremic light. The train crawls through the cadaver of the city. He does not blink as the lights from each station—and he's counting stops—shoot like bursts of lightning into his eyes.

He changes trains. Menace clings to the yellowing foul

tunnels. Inside another car, he touches his groin, the hardon has not relented. He toughens his look. Fourteen stations—and he's back almost to the waterfront.

The men he comes to despise are out in hordes tonight—some in jackets and leather, others shirtless and in shorts, variously courting the weather which is in limbo. The genitals of some are outlined by tight pants, or even exposed under cutoffs. Without moving his eyes, Tim continues along the street. Clusters of men appraise him, admiring.

The mist from the subterranean trains emerges through iron holes into the street, as if from a hell seething below. The heat shakes off a gust of wind. It scatters trash and old leaves against the edges of a small park, shoving angry green grass against the grime.

The hot-cool air fans Tim's body; his sweat turns cool, evaporating, then hot, sticking.

Against the gray night-sky, the abandoned warehouses along the piers cut ugly black patches. Tim will take the long way to the Rushes, telling himself the watered breeze will cool him further. But his eyes attempt to penetrate the darkness, to pull into his vision the sexhunting forms within the rotted gut of the piers. Still, the smeared rage finds no clear form within the marred landscape.

Near skeletal buildings, plastic bags overflow with packed trash. He kicks at a bag, to push it away into the watery curb, which is smoothed by debris. He pulls back in horror. He almost stepped on an old, tattered tramp lying on the street, a discarded heap.

Tim stares at it—him—watching for its breathing. Is it dead or drunk? The man's chest rises and falls. Tim feels like crying, but his anger chokes the tears. He begins to run, slows, stops; swaggers.

Near the meat trucks, two men kiss, naked cocks crossed like weapons, hard against each other. Tim inhales the bunched anger. He opens his mouth to taste it. As he approaches the Rushes, he realizes he is panting.

Faggots! Queers! The echoing words badger his mind. It

wasn't at him the men in the speeding car were yelling; they were yelling at the older guy he was talking to; they could tell he himself was a hustler, maybe even one of them—not a queer. Or maybe they were yelling at the goodlooking guy nearby.

The memory is shaken. To shelter himself from the shower of glass, he shoved his body against the wall of the Rushes, and it touched the other man's by accident. Anger rushed like an orgasm. When the man moved away, it was as if he had snatched a part of him, severed it brutally away. Soon after that, he met the man he went home with. He poured orgasmic rage into his mouth.

He recreates the scene: Pressed against the wall to avoid the crashing bottle, he had to thrust himself next to the handsome man he saw earlier. They looked at each other as they both faced the wall. Was it then that tonight's new tension grew?—to be so close to one of the men he comes here to despise; the goodlooking arrogant sexhunters he hates in a way very different from the way he hates those who pay him. When he shot earlier into the mouth of the man who paid him, he poured his anger at the sudden memory of the man who had stood next to him against the wall.

Tim has found the source of the pressurized fury.

He stands on the street looking into the Rushes. At the open door, a middleaged man stares into the street. Tim knows: That man can't make out in that bar. Thumbs hooked into them, Tim pushes his pants lower on his hips, exposing more of his lean torso. The eyes of the middleaged man drill into him.

Then the man turns away from Tim and back toward the Rushes.

9

Cause us to be numbered in
the flock You have chosen.

As OFTEN as he comes to the Rushes,
Bill is still amazed that the unexpected remains possible. Now
the unexpected is not in the transmogrification of the early-
night macho into the late evening "queen"; certainly it is no
longer in the recurrent presence of the haughty ballet dancer
in full leather regalia—"a flaming masochist"; that causes no
stir. A movie star, a rock star, a politician—they elicit only
cursory interest now. The permutations of possibilities—whom
one finally goes with after all the ambushes and surprises—
become the norm.

The presence of Lyndy qualifies, yes, but even that was
pure only during the suspenseful moments before her enter-
ing; men here might have seen her only an hour earlier at a
sparkling disco or in an exclusive restaurant—might even have

been in her court; and so while hating her presence here, they "accept" her. With the entrance of the transvestite and the black prostitute, the unexpected has occurred. Its sustained acknowledgment is a low simmering of rage; one degree may cause it to stir again. The paradox is that Lyndy's accepted presence may be its primary control—that, and that young-man's curious extending toward them.

Bill has never been threatened by transvestites, and certainly not by women. His enjoyment in assaulting the rigid macho posturing asserts that by implication. But the dark light of the Rushes has a strange capacity to illumine a more secret dark.

Oh, he wishes they weren't here—he faced that—and especially now, now when the Rushes is about to become a total world with its own rules. Before Last Call, a collective intensity charges through, uniting enemies and lovers in a brutal, but mutually condoned, code. When the time comes to connect, or die a sexual death, all else, and everyone else, will be tossed aside. Cruelty is allowed, friendship abdicates to sex. Joy, disaster, triumph are all defined in terms of "making out." Last night's success has no reality. If the earlier moments of this night have been a purgatory, not making out will turn it into a hell.

Bill stands in the midst of the churning. He has just dismissed two unattractive men—he marvels that one is relentlessly pursued by those one doesn't want. Tonight the memory of Luke has wafted his thoughts; Endore's words have bruised those remembrances. He has stopped his strict lineup of prospects: they've scattered about the bar, and he's forgotten which of two cowboys—or was it a construction worker?—did not work out. Some of his good prospects have faded into the darkness in back. I will not go there, Bill promises himself again.

But he allows his look to brush the dark area—and slide away. As he often does, he lets his eyes wander toward the figures drawn on the walls. Where is a favored panel in which men kneel before the erect naked figure— . . . ? He's annoyed

that, instead, his eyes fell on one he dislikes—a beautiful man is kneeling—crouching—before others, one man is flogging him. Where is the panel he's looking for? It's not here! God, the memory of Luke has suffused his thoughts tonight—the drawing he's looking for was one he pointed out to Luke as particularly sexy— ...But where was it? No, wait, the panel he's looking for *is* in the Rushes. There. The muscular nude figure, the barest trace of pubic hair visible through the torn shorts, the flushed genitals an outline— ...Oh, is that Chas standing at the top of the stairs at the back of the bar?—he seems to be staring down intently at— ...More bodies joining the shadows block Bill's view.

The Rushes has been changing, and he is not sure he welcomes that. Still the best cruising bar—men meet, kiss or not, grope or not, and go home—it has become for some, not all, a proscribed sacred territory; a sexual rite begins and ends here. It used to be only a few adventurers who huddled in the back shadows, and then only on flesh-crammed nights. Now the numbers, and the activity, in the back part of the bar are growing.

God, look at that tall man!—he's stripped down to a leather jock strap and boots, and he's heading for the vortex of shadows at the back. Others will be shedding clothes later to similar abbreviations—usually black leather. So "artificial." Bill dismisses the tall man.... Is that Endore on the stairs now? He's—... Bill's attention is yanked away by a man walking by wearing a ripped shirt. Bill's eyes follow him back to— ...No, impossible, it can't be Endore at the top of the stairs, the man there is kissing—... Again Bill's eyes are grasped by the man in the ripped shirt. Bill follows him until he determines he's not really interested. Now Bill sees Don at the entrance. Is he about to leave? Or to pull back, tugged by the power of the bar.

I hate you! Don yells in silence at the youngman outside. But he waits at the door. Damn him, so sure of his attractiveness—he even assumed a cocky pose for me, goddamn him if he thinks I have to pay!

Poor Don. Who is he looking at outside? Bill wonders. The space about the transvestite and the woman is still empty; animosity still quivers at the edges of the hollow. I should go to them and show all those machos. That kid did. But what the hell *are* those two doing here? They know they're not wanted. His resentment shoves into anger.

Again he flings his gaze toward the panels on the wall. Lucky! His eyes fell on his favorite panel—the lone figure in ecstasy or asleep. The lower portion is undrawn. Sometimes Bill imagines a head burrowed between the man's legs, imagines the angle of the oval thighs, calves rounded at the crook of the leg, the cock dormant ready to be aroused—... Other times he imagines someone just watching the dormant figure. Sometimes there seems to be the suggestion of another man bending as if to raise the prone body from deep sleep. Bill lets his eyes glide away dreamily. Don's still at the door.

But maybe he's not a hustler, Don thinks, maybe he really likes a mature man who—... He's been out there so long. Does he get rejected too? Maybe he's not a hustler. So attractive. Don faces the youngman again.

Bill looks away from Don. So strange tonight, the way he keeps his head lowered when they talk to him. Is his face puffy? he tries to remember an earlier fleeting impression. Where did he go, those past days, or however long he was gone: did he say?

Harsh voices rise from the back of the bar.

That *is* Chas standing at the top of the steps. And Endore? It *is* Endore. Has the tension between them finally erupted? Bill's line of vision is obscured. Is the man in total leather there too? The muscular back of the man in the white tank top blocks Bill's view. The man removes his shirt, and Bill's cock stirs. He'll just watch the broad flexing back for a few moments. He'd like to move the man just a little to the right, better highlights. His hand floats to his own groin. He feels himself nudged. The kid—Robert? was that his name?—is pushing his way out of the bar. When Bill looks again, the

exposed muscular back has moved away. Damn! But a new cowboy has maneuvered next to him.

"Hi, Tex," Bill is hopeful.

"Howarya?"

Pretty good tone. "Just in the city?"

"Yes—just drove my truck."

In a cab. Bad fake, quickly apparent. Waving, Bill glides away. There's the bared muscular back again. And the raised voices from the back: ". . . —made me believe—. . ."

"You sonofabitch! You made me believe you wouldn't interfere!" Chas shouts at Endore. They stand on the top step. Like a dark sentinel, the leatherman waits below

Beyond the two men and the trapezoid of soiled light over one pool table, bodies coagulate in the smoky arteries. Red lights darken like drying blood. Its outlet the retral part of the bar, electric sex sizzles beyond the shadowed scrim, pulling others in.

"I said I wasn't playing your ugly games. But you weren't playing," Endore says.

"What did you say to the kid?" Chas demands.

Endore walks down. For the first time he's aware that the leatherman has remained standing there.

Following. Chas reaches out as if to force Endore around. His hand stops just before it touches his shoulder, pauses there, then drops. "You wanted to humiliate me." He's aware—as he has been throughout—of the black-gloved waiting presence. So near.

Endore faces Chas: "You wanted to humiliate him."

"To bring him out," Chas says.

"Down," Endore says.

"It's what he wanted," Chas insists.

"It's what *you* wanted," Endore says.

What *I* wanted! The words strike, ricochet, strike again. Chas's fists clench. The reverberating words clarify; he misunderstood—Endore meant what he, Chas, wanted from the kid, not from—. . .

The moments of intense attention about the two men are passing. Others listen only cursorily. As the sexual tension in the bar crackles, these altercations are not rare. All attention is sacrificed to the sexual ferocity to connect.

"Shit—you, so proud of not approaching anyone!" Chas hurls at Endore.

"You said yourself that's nothing to be proud of. Now I agree." Endore pulls his hand away to avoid the touch of the leatherman's glove.

Even the men whose interest in the altercation has waned are shoved in again by Chas's yelled words: "What the fuck did you say to him?"

"I offered him what he wanted—not what you wanted," Endore lowers his voice.

"And what do *you* want, Endore? Huh?" Chas pauses. He lets his hands fall—to invite the touch of the leatherman's glove again. It comes. It feels rough. "Yet the kid ran away from you, Endore!" he shouts.

Over the strange softened shouts of the music. Chas's forced laughter pursues Endore. No, it's not laughter—it's the sound of rage like laughter. Endore is startled by the discovery: In that sound of anger, there is that similar break. He has never heard it until now in Chas.

Chas allows the gloved touch to continue; his knuckles and the cold black leather fuse. His eyes connect with the leatherman's. The two face each other. The smooth blackness of the leatherman's uniform is solid in contrast to Chas's, broken by patches of exposed flesh, the miniature pyramidal studs, the metallic network of cycle chain-links on his waist, about his cap. The dark glove warms on Chas's hand. To preserve the feeling, he eases his hand away.

Eyes clamped on the leatherman's, Chas touches his keys—on his left side. The leatherman nods. Confirming the exploratory invitation, Chas touches his keys again and nods back. Now he has to move away from the man—for now—because too much is unfinished between him and Endore which will mar every connection. He has to know what he said to Robert.

That knowledge may bandage the deep wound rent by the mysterious rejection. As he stood looking up at him, Robert was dazzled by male sexual power—Chas was sure of that. *Baptism!* the word pulsated in Chas's mind as he waited, boots spread, at the top of the stairs. The leatherman remained there, a goading witness. Baptism! My warm piss will soak his pants, and then pounding fists will—. . . No, that memory belongs to another night; the two are united ineluctably now. Tonight, it was him and the leatherman, no, the leatherman and Robert, no, Robert and him. And Endore. Suddenly Endore was there speaking to Robert—but Chas saw only the moving lips. He felt encased in black glass drowning the words and trapping echoes. Robert moved away with Endore, flesh blocked Chas's view, he stood alone, the leatherman judged him, then Robert ran out.

In the midst of the bar, Chas inhales, devouring the odor of male flesh and leather. A hand gropes his groin. He gropes back, a rough squeeze, the suggestion of pain, to purify the act of "sissy-love." He *has* to know what happened between Endore and Robert. Or will it remain one of so many unsolved mysteries buried with so many others in the Rushes?

Chas shakes away the heavy mood. His knuckles feel cold now. He sees Endore winding ahead through the crammed bodies.

Hands grope, bodies grind as Endore nears the bar. Michael is sitting there. Endore begins to move toward him. Did he see me with Robert? Many bodies separated them. I can't go to him now. He does this: He orders three beers. Now he enters the forbidden circle about Elaine and Roxy, and he presents each with a beer. In astonished gratitude, Elaine and Roxy thank him. He feels hostile stares from the men nearby. He thinks of Robert's earlier brave act. Endore waits for moments with the two female figures. Then nodding at them, he moves away. He has broken the contagious circle. Slowly, other men begin filling the gap.

"How did you take the boy away from him, darling?" Lyndy reaches out to touch him as he moves by.

Remembering the cold touch of the leather. Endore pulls his hand back.

"Clearly Chas lost, but did you win?" Lyndy asks. "The boy ran out."

"Chas did not lose—there was nothing to 'win,' " Endore says.

This section of the bar is thinning as the packs on the sidelines disband to hunt in more fertile territory.

Chas is here. He addresses Lyndy and Martin: "How about that? Our grand aloof Endore—never approaches anyone, remember?—he broke his own rules, the first time, man, and the kid ran out on him!"

"And on you," Lyndy accuses Chas. "You lost in our bet . . . darling," she reminds him.

"Hey, the night isn't over," Chas warns. "Might be able to do better. Surprise even you! Surprise even Endore!" His voice is breathless. Now he feels outside the black glass which encased him at the top of the steps. "There's still Mike!" His surprise takes shape.

"Michael," Martin corrects him. "You know Endore always insists."

"He's still here, spreading his angelic blessings, one assumes; didn't we see him earlier on the piers, Martin?" Lyndy asks.

"We've all been there, even you, Lyndy," Endore says.

"Oh, why are you so upset, darling?" Lyndy pouts. "Because the boy ran out? Or because of Michael?"

"You taught Michael real good, Endore," Chas shifts his assault.

He's chosen the wound. "What was learned or taught blurs," Endore says.

"I'll help you remember! Or find out!" Chas promises.

"What is between you and Chas, Endore?" Lyndy's voice is a lazy purr.

"What is between you and Martin?" Endore shoves the question back.

"Mutual contempt's between *them,*" Chas spits the words at Lyndy and Martin.

"Is that what's between you and Endore?" Martin asks.

Lyndy hardly turns toward Martin. Her words are slow. Each pause underscores an implication. "No, Martin, darling, I think they respect each other."

Martin's eyes shift to the bar. Lyndy follows their direction. To Elaine and Roxy.

"Would you like to meet them, darling?" Martin asks her.

Lyndy's fingers float toward the double strands of pearls, but they do not touch them.

She tried to pay Martin back for bringing the two in to taunt her vaguely, but she miscalculated in her move, Endore realizes.

"Martin ran away that night at the trucks," she drops a part of the withheld narrative.

Prematurely. "Oh, do tell them." Martin turns his back on her. "Tell them the rest, too, darling. Shall I get you another drink, in the meantime?"

"Yes!"

Martin moves toward the bar, and toward the transvestite and the woman.

Chas holds his breath. He wants to engulf Endore in anger—to let the animosity of years flood, but there is now the diffusing threat of the transvestite.

The three are trapped in a net of silence and tension.

The isolative boundaries about Elaine and Roxy have wavered, restored intermittently. Martin is speaking to the two.

Bill looks at Martin across the bar—the shirtless muscular man has been churned into the mass somewhere—and he turns away from Elaine and Roxy. Another construction worker is cruising him—cute; but at that very moment Bill spots a tough-looking man in—. . . mixed clothes—an army fatigue cap, a brown leather vest, logger's shirt. Feast or famine, Bill thinks. On the one hand, the construction worker has ex-

pressed overt interest, but the tough-looking man next to him is so—. . . real, in a spectacularly unreal way! Bill decides to gamble. He turns his back on the "sure" construction worker and smiles an invitation at the man in hybrid uniform.

"I like to get fucked by a big stud," the rough-looking man is direct.

Bill blinks. "Well, I think we're barking up the wrong tree," he gasps. With a conciliatory smile, he returns to the construction worker. Too late. It's the man's turn to reject him. Oh, good, Bill thinks as he watches the construction worker begin to cruise the logger with his cock showing out of the cutoffs. The logger walks away after a few moments; he counted one more, Bill thinks in annoyance. . . . Ridiculous! A man in black chaps is not wearing anything under them; the exposed dual ovals of his ass are being explored by probing hands.

Bill slides aimlessly through the bodies, pushing away whatever hand searches his groin, allowing an occasional special one on his buttocks. He feels he should go to the transvestite and the black woman, confront his vacillating feelings. He saw what Endore did, and admired it. But each time he begins to move in their direction, he's pulled back, and—. . . Oh, look! Martin is actually ushering the two over to Lyndy. Still, he cannot bring himself to join them.

"They're here, darling," Endore says to Lyndy.

"*Ah, bon!*" Lyndy faces the two figures.

Even in the red-hued light, the bright assaulting fabrics, the blinking sequins, the resplendently cheap jewelry assert themselves brazenly.

Martin holds out a fresh drink to Lyndy. She touches it with her lips for a moment, as if in an undecided toast.

Recognizing him from the earlier moments at the bar, Elaine and Roxy smile at Endore; he nods back. But he is aware of—and he does not welcome it, knows that pursuing demons are being unleashed—a resurgence of resentment at their presence in the Rushes. Different from what he feels toward Lyndy? It's difficult to know, his feelings toward her

have developed over a vicissitude of encounters. His gesture in buying Elaine and Roxy a beer, was that in premature penance for resurfacing doubts?

As if sensing his doubts, Roxy looks away from him.

"They wanted to meet you, darling," Martin tells Lyndy. "Roxy admires your designs. And this is Elaine."

A smile lashes Lyndy's face. Her hands flirt with the necklace.

"Oh, and did you tell them, darling? About the incident at the trucks, I mean," Martin taunts her attempt at blackmail.

"No," she answers, kissing the glass. "I didn't have to."

She is still withholding the implied blackmail, its power defused for now. She will recharge it, Endore is sure.

Chas searches out the leatherman, as if to grasp for threatened identification. The interlude with Endore will fester in suspension. For now they may have to become allied. But it is all too splintered. They all saw him buy beers for the transvestite and the woman, but it's obvious he's not at ease now.

Endore's body tenses at Roxy. Perhaps if it were earlier, he defends his resentment of them, and Lyndy. These moments approaching are only for the faithful, the initiated in the carnal rites. He is glad Robert left. The memory of the boy's sadness flowing to anger recurs. He looks toward the entrance. Don is there.

Don moves from the tempting figure outside. He sees Chas turn away from the transvestite and the black woman. And Endore, too! After all he's written. Finally they're all machos, Don thinks. He touches his face. Why should he be concerned? They haven't even noticed, that's how clearly they see me. Though he's relieved, he thinks that with bitterness.

Yet I coaxed Martin to let them in, and I sealed the gap about them at the bar, Endore defends himself. For their sakes? His own? When Robert stood blocking the hostility, it seemed natural. He says to Roxy, "It's refreshing to see drag." And knows he's stumbled.

"It's what I wear," Roxy tells him.

Elaine recognizes Chas. Does Roxy know it's the guy on the piers?

Lyndy studies the two as if they were on private exhibition for her.

It *is* her, Chas recognizes Roxy. She stood on the ramp looking down at him; she's so much shorter now. I won't run this time! Chas promises himself. He searches out his psychic anchor—the leatherman.

Our eyes are made up the same, Roxy thinks, looking at Lyndy.

"I adore your gowns!" Lyndy exults. "So 'new feminism'— so right for the Rushes!" The outlined eyes shift her words to Chas.

Pretending to admire them, she's trying to thwart whatever power they may have, if any, over her. Endore sees Bill; he's hesitating to come back.

Roxy's voice becomes very precise. She is choosing her most impressive tones and words: "I try to keep up with the current world. I enroll in courses and everything, and I must say that I do love your clothes—uh, dresses—uh, gowns. They make such a statement. I am so glad you have admired our— . . . wardrobe." She looks down at her slit skirt

She's trying to win her over. Endore feels saddened. He has seen that look on Lyndy's face, impassive features, a gash curved into a masquerading smile.

"Très chic," the woman's curved lips utter.

"Ah, merci, merci!" Roxy shows off.

"You speak French so well," Lyndy moves.

"Oh, real good," Elaine offers, "she been teaching me!"

"I studied it, yes," Roxy says. "It's real important to extend your—uh—. . ."

Lyndy shoots the words like rapid fire: *"C'est un raffinement nécessaire, n'est-ce pas?"*

"Je—. . . Oui, oui. Uh. *oui—* . . . You know, one time, I—. . ."

"Quand les nuances d'une langue s'avèrent insuffisantes, on peut les chercher dans une autre."

"Moi—... You know, I used to—..."

"C'est l'essence de la vraie communication."

"Ah, certainly-*ment,* we was—..."

"Si on est assez sot pour faire semblant de chercher la communication. Eh bien, vous êtes donc certainement d'accord que quand—..."

Roxy looks around as if for protection from the slaughter.

Why don't I stop the attack? Because I *want* them to leave? Allowing the enemy to slaughter the enemy? Enemy! The word has formed. Endore feels trapped. Lyndy has annihilated Roxy's pose of gentility. She has weakened her at least for now for any attack he or Martin or Chas may mount against her through them. Through them? His thoughts accuse, shaping dangerously.

"Et si on—..." Lyndy is about to continue.

Elaine thrusts herself between her and Roxy. *"Lay! Plum! Day! May! Tant!"* Elaine shoots each mangled word at Lyndy, ending her tirade.

Did my silence align me with Lyndy? the doubt rips Endore.

"Elaine was a model, you know," Roxy still struggles.

The defiance and the courage with which she invaded the macho territory have withered before Lyndy's accusative power, Endore understands.

"Were you?" Lyndy withdraws for now. Her gaze flashes her triumph at the men.

"Not the kind you thinkin," Elaine says. "Live-model art." She sat naked in a plastic cage with other women. The cage rotated. Men in booths around them put in quarters. A peephole would open onto the displayed flesh for a few minutes, more for more quarters. "We pretended to be doin things to ourselves, and men in the booths jerked off and yelled at us—..." She frowns at the memory. "Yelled at us," she says with anger. Pussies, cunts! the men yelled. Their faces were squashed, ugly against the peepholes.

"What did they yell?" Lyndy prods.

She's collecting wounds, Endore thinks.

"Ugly names." Elaine will not pronounce them.

"She punched out three guys in a row before they could stop her," Roxy announces. "Just rushed into one booth after another and pulled them out for calling her filthy names. That's why she ain't—is not—there no more."

"You're a truly liberated woman," Lyndy derides.

"She sure is," Roxy says. They met the night Elaine was fired, almost arrested, but she ran wrapped in whatever she could find. Roxy was hustling that corner. Elaine thought she was a woman. Roxy gave her her elegant red coat to cover herself.

I pretended I thought she was a woman, Elaine remembers that night. Roxy was so grateful.

Chas stares into his precious country, drawing strength from it. But the sexual plenitude does not assuage him now. His anger at Endore resurges. I'll pay that bastard back. Tonight. If only he knew exactly what happened between Endore and Robert—if only the transvestite and the two women and Martin left—then his strategy against Endore would be pure.

Don is back. Endore touches his arm. Don is aware that his own body jerked, resentful of the pitying touch.

"I can see you in chains," Lyndy says to Elaine.

Another assault is shaping, Endore knows. Martin brought them here to confront her, and she's flaunting proving him wrong—without having to release the blackmail. Martin is impassive.

Roxy frowns at Lyndy: "Elaine's not into that S 'n' M, people think she is, cause she's so sexy and gorgeous, but she isn't—ain't—isn't; she's real gentle, aren't you, hon? The only time she'll punch anyone out is if they do her mean."

"Or if they do *you* mean," Elaine threatens. "What do you mean, chains?" she growls at Lyndy.

"Not real chains," Lyndy says. "I was thinking of new designs."

"She designs her clothes on naked black models. She calls them her savages," Martin ambushes her.

Lyndy's tongue moistens the frozen smile.

"Savages!" Elaine exclaims.

"Whose bodies she covers," Endore feeds Elaine ammunition. "It's *her* art." His self-questioning abates.

"Bodies are alive!" Elaine aims at Lyndy.

Yes! Chas thinks.

"Yeah!" Roxy approves. Too instantly bloodied, she did not feel the assault till now.

"Oh, Chas would agree!" Lyndy pulls him in. "But—look—he can't even face you."

She's trying to shift the battle away from her, Endore realizes; and Chas will help her clumsily. It worked:

"Don't turn your back to me," Roxy says to Chas. "I'm one of you!"

"Not one of me," Chas rejects. He looks at the nearest panel on the walls. Blurred!

"Hey, well, look who's here!" Roxy recognizes Chas. "We met on the piers earlier, remember? You ran away." She slides next to him. The black of her vinyl blends with the black of his leather; the sequins on one shine like the bradded studs on the other. "See, I was right—we *are* dressed alike! Just like I said before you ran away on the piers. We even wear earrings, both of us."

"*One* earring!" Chas points to his, on the left. He pulls away from her. He drinks from his beer, to push back the nausea threatening him at her touch. "Leather and drag don't mix!"

"We mix when we fuck on the piers!" Elaine says.

"And when the thugs beat us up!" Roxy asserts. "When they call us *all* faggots! So we have to ... love ... each other because *they* hate us so much, all of us."

"Amen," Elaine shakes her head.

How strange that word ... love ... sounds now, Endore realizes. So difficult to pronounce. Roxy had to pause to form it, and she looked down when she did.

Don is glad for the two avenging presences affronting the machos. Including Endore. Look at him, so quiet, just stand-

ing there. Don pushes the increasing antagonism: "Endore here," he identifies him to Roxy, "has written in his columns that you're the real sexual radicals, that you assault our sexual bigotries most clearly—..."

I believe it, Endore knows; I do believe it.

Roxy studies Endore.

I believe it. But she will pass judgment on me anyhow, Endore knows. He looks away. The artificial currents of air part the smoke ahead. In one of the panels on the wall a man pushes another to his knees. The clouds of smoke shift. Now the man is helping the other up. Another panel: Jacketed men stripping another. The last panel: The tangled signs. The annihilation of order, or of disorder? He thinks of the photographic paintings he saw earlier at the exhibit tonight. The inevitable question is, he writes uncertainly in his mind, for his column, whether after the disorder of violence—... He revises: ...—after the order of violence, the disorder—...

But Roxy releases him without a word.

Bill is about to approach. I can't. I hate them. He turns away.

"Sick," Chas says aloud.

"Me?" Roxy's eyes grow enormous.

"Don't you call her sick," Elaine says harshly.

"Let him! I know they hate me; you saw it—..." Roxy says.

Endore detects triumph in her voice. No, it isn't there, he rejects.

"Why'd you bring us in?" Roxy whirls toward Martin.

"You wanted to come in," Martin shrugs.

Endore wants to align himself with the transvestite—so much courage there, and in Robert's gesture toward them—and to align himself against Chas's cruel charge. But there is a tone in Roxy's voice now—as if she's welcomed the accusation. She has come to court our hatred, not discover and redeem it, the unwelcome thought ambushes Endore. Is he disguising his fealty to the Rushes?—and to Chas?—by thinking so. We were only too anxious to oblige with our own despicable courtship

of hatred of her; and Martin's "power" to bring them in was assigned, spurious; allowed. Had we really not wanted them—and Lyndy?—to come in, Martin's power would have bowed.

Roxy confronts Endore: "I know who you are, sure. You're the guy who writes about loving women but fucks only with men."

Lyndy's look on Endore is cold on his hot skin. I can never reach Roxy, no, he knows, and while surrendering to the sorrowing knowledge, wants to protest it.

"You call your black models savages," Roxy moves on to Lyndy, "only because they're alive—and you're the manikin in your sexless drag!"

Lyndy's fingers flirt with the pearls. Her reaction is in suspension.

Chas faces Roxy for the first time, acknowledging her and her anger. Somewhere else, perhaps, he might explore it, even accept it, but in the hallowed macho country of the Rushes?

Lyndy sips her drink. The men are looking at her. Then she laughs. *Tu es drôle. C'était fatal avec eux.* By veiling her insult to Roxy, she has thwarted further attack.

And Roxy pulls back.

Finally she is more threatened by women than by men, Endore discovers.

"Look at me!" Roxy stands in front of Chas. "You know why my drag makes you uncomfortable—why you had to run away from me?" her withheld rampage continues. "Because yours is just as gay as mine."

Chas pushes away the flicker of understanding he felt earlier for the transvestite's anger.

"There's some truth in that—..." Don stumbles.

Chas flings at Roxy: "Wrong! You're accusing everyone, huh? What about you? You hate being queer so much you want to be a straight woman."

"I feel like a woman!" Roxy defends. Then the tone of entreaty is swept away: "So don't call me a queer!" she shouts. "Cause you're the fuckin queers!"

It is as if she, and Chas, had been waiting for the word,

eager for it, Endore thinks. It is what made the mutual ravaging possible.

"Oh, hon, don't use that ugly word, baby," Elaine says to Roxy.

Anger trembles in the bar.

"I hate them as mucn as they hate me!" Roxy curses the men about her.

Anger rushes at her from the bar.

"Aw, you know that ain't true," Elaine asserts. Loudly. She wants the enraged men to hear, those near them, before the wave of anger sweeps others in. She has to placate the menacing faces. "Not true," she repeats. She's proffering a truce. "We've talked about it, babe, remember? You're always saying we shouldn't hurt each other, cause them others hate us all so, and we gotta—...", It's working. Sheltering her, she's leading 'Roxy past the mined field. Elaine's eyes implore the staring men: Wait, wait! And it's working: "No one's queer, baby, you always saying that, babe, no one's queer." She is evoking the dormant mutuality of outcasts—and it's worked. The angered buzzing dies. The two sides release each other.

But after the slaughter, will anything change? Endore sees Elaine and Roxy leaving the Rushes. A certain silence holds— and then it's pushed away by voices, laughter.

"How touching," Lyndy says, "the black whore and the white drag queen." Then her words tumble: "We'll photograph my models on the piers, Martin." Her words crackle. "Men in leather and chains in the background." Her hands slash as if draping the cruel fashions on her black models. "Vinyl, much vinyl! Bold new fashions in tribute to it all. Oh, you *must* get me into the Rack, Martin, I want to see it all— and I'll use chains, keys in my designs, whips—..."

"This time for women," Endore says. "And they'll wear your hatred of them." What he has discovered in himself during the questioning of his fealties and vaunted attitudes—Endore will ferret out its implications no matter how ugly; but he knows this: Elaine and Roxy should have "belonged" here—as outcasts among outcasts.

154 ·

Lyndy touches her cheek. Her look penetrates Endore. Her fingers tangle on the necklace. "And my models." she continues in the fevered voice. "will stand—... 'Like clothed corpses. Life always in the background. and in the foreground. fashionable death.' It wasn't Plato who said *that,* was it. Endore? Oh. I believe it was *you* who wrote it about *us!*" She tosses at Martin: "And I was *not* astonished!"

Martin glances down at the small form of the woman on the bar stool. "Weren't you. darling. astonished? For a moment or so I thought you might have been. But then it becomes so difficult in our time. to be astonished. One can only keep trying. But *do* let go of your necklace. Oh. look. you've broken a strand of it."

Lyndy stares down in astonishment at the pearls about to cascade onto the patchy floor. Her fist chokes their flow.

"You can let go. darling." Martin says. "I'm sure they're your cheap ones."

Her grasp loosens. tightens. Loosens. Tightens.

"Don't you believe Martin, Lyndy?" Endore prods. "Why *don't* you let go?"

Lyndy's fist opens. Like a feeble bullet, one pearl pelts the sawdusted floor. Then her fist clasps the remaining pearls of the broken strand and she thrusts it and them into a pocket of the velvet tuxedo.

"I'll find the one that fell, darling." Don bends toward the floor.

"Leave it!" Lyndy's voice is peremptory.

Chas's boot brushes the littered floor, as if threatening to smother the fallen pearl in dirty sawdust.

10

We bless You We adore You.
We glorify You.

As OFTEN as he comes to the Rushes,
Don is still surprised by his inability to leave even after the
first mangling of the night. No matter how often he goes to the
door for the "breath of fresh air" he hopes will pull him out,
no matter how often he restricts himself to "one more drink
and ten more minutes with dear friends," no matter how often
he insists he will not cruise, just "perhaps peek in at the boys,"
no matter how often he reminds himself that if he stays he will
wake up to despair, no matter how often he recalls a previous
evening's vow never to come back, never, to the Rushes, the
Rushes will clutch him. He will remain trapped until the night
is dead.

Wondering, Where are the boys letting their hair down
and camping? and answering himself, They've been replaced

by the armies of machos, he will plunge into the arena of cruising, and he will be bloodied.

The connective miracle he screams for—... Tonight the scream is taking another form.

The fatal minutes before Last Call will soon occur. All around him men are connecting, leaving in pairs or threesomes, and the sight lacerates him. They have abandoned him again. He watches men kissing, and he watches the beautiful, unattainable men all around: the Adonic muscular man, the mahogany man—still here. Even the sinister man in leather. And Chas like a lean version of the men in those awful panels on the walls. And Bill, a tiger plundering the bar. And Endore waiting hungrily to be hunted. All so desirable, so sexual. Damn them!

The withheld words surge to the edge of his throat. He looks at Martin and Lyndy, and he pulls the words back. Only one shapes and he's not even sure whether or not he spoke it aloud: *"I!"*

"What?" Bill is back. He studies Don's face.

"Nothing." Don realizes he spoke. I have to be careful. Stop drinking. He moves away from Bill's stare.

After the encounter with Elaine and Roxy, and her febrile oration following, Lyndy seems removed. She makes a wisp of a touch over the remaining strand of pearls, the long one. The loosed pearl lies, unextraordinary, on the sawdusted floor.

Lyndy will strike, Endore knows.

Don assaults Bill: "Do transvestites upset you? I saw you staying away." He is proud of his own reaction.

"She looked so strange, in her costume," Bill hears himself. He detects an iron mood in the others. Chas's rigid back is to Endore. Lyndy and Martin are somber. "Home from the wars," he tries to lighten the mood. Here, he will get a distant perspective, again. "The cowboy over there—..."

"He's *not* a cowboy!" Don interrupts. Oh, God, they have choices. I would go with anyone, he thinks. Steve. I'll go with Steve. Where is he? Probably drunk at the bar. They'll put him in a cab, if anyone cares.

"Of course I'd prefer the muscular man," Bill says. "I'd lick his body from his toes to—..." His graphic words are meant to assault Lyndy again; increasingly he wants to tear the bonds of civility between them.

But there is no reaction. Now her fingers rest listless on the isolated strand of pearls.

"But he's not enough like—..." Bill's voice became serious.

Luke, Endore supplies the suspended name.

"...—what I want tonight. Luke was a wonderful cowboy." Bill tries to sound flippant. "I bought him his first contruction helmet, he loved it." He's studying Endore, to detect any spark of judgment.

Don looks at his watch. "Oh, God, it won't be long before Last Call."

"It's still a while before Last Call," Endore soothes him.

But *he's* begun to look into the bar, Don notices. He'll make out, yes—although he does go home alone more often than the others, but out of choice, Don thinks.

"Last Call announces the last drink before the hunters are released from the pretense of drinking," Martin tells Lyndy. Even he seems aware of the pall of silence over her, a palpable brooding. She stares into the bar.

A new rhythm is moving through the Rushes. There is a greater silence as if in acknowledgment of the increasing seriousness of the balletic rites. The bass notes of the throttled music are steady beats. Like fleshed ghosts, men move in the red limbo of sex, pulled toward and separated by the same invisible flux.

"Oh, I hate those minutes before Last Call!" Don's voice is strident. "You feel trapped, tired."

"It's the best time," Chas breaks his own silence. Sometimes he will sacrifice a "heavy conquest" to remain for those sacred moments. "The time when the sexual ... *savages* ... prowl the jungle."

Even those words, aimed at her, have not broken the electric silence of the woman.

Yes, Chas loves the moments when sexual mettle is tested.

Yet one single incident may shake the structure of the hunt's well-ordered anarchy. The incident with Robert, still sealed—and the moment when he felt a flashing unity with Roxy; those disturb. He tilts his beer, the bottle is empty.

Two men walk by. One is dressed in the brown-shirted uniform of the German SS, another in the black uniform of a Nazi. Both men are heavy, balding, tubby, red-faced. Only their uniforms get them into the Rushes.

"Disgusting!" Don says. "How dare they wear that uniform? Don't they know they put homosexuals in concentration camps?"

Endore and Bill turn away from the two men.

For now, this area of the Rushes is Chas's headquarters, from which he will evaluate the "prime meat" in the battleground. Right now, his attention focuses on a man fresh in the arena. No shirt, belts crisscrossed over a hard hairless chest. Keys on the right. A proud masochist. Chas likes that. But his attention is magnetized repeatedly toward the leatherman. And Michael.

"After Last Call, the white lights crash, and everything is exposed," Martin tells Lyndy. He seems to be prying at her silence.

Lyndy glances at him.

"Will you be, Martin, exposed?" Endore asks. "I assume you'll stay till Last Call."

"Of course." Martin retains the ambiguity.

"I've got some sure ones," Bill evaluates. Anxiety pricks his voice. It will soon be that time, and there's always the chance, always, that all connections may fail. "The logger is a mess. Out! One cowboy is a cowgirl! Out! The construction worker—possibly, just possibly—but the waist's a little thick. Did you see the ridiculous man with the naked ass? And *that* one—ugh! Oh, look, the bitch! He's talking to that other guy who was cruising me earlier. There's one I like a lot, but I can't tell what he'd be—..."

"Why don't you tell him what you *want* him to be?" Endore cuts the mean evaluation. Bill is becoming cruel, discarding coldly. He even looks different, harder. But Endore's

reaction is only a congealing of the hostility he has kept in abeyance all night.

"I could, I suppose," Bill snaps. He always felt Endore sided with Luke, although he and Endore are the real friends. He tries to dissipate Endore's accusative look. "I did whatever Luke wanted."

"If he'd be what you wanted to own," Endore says.

"Own!" Bill is indignant. "I gave myself completely—and gave him total freedom."

"And let him know it, like a kind master," Endore says, astonished by the rush of his anger.

Chas eyes Bill. The firm ass. I'd mount him like a neighing pony, he thinks.

"Luke was always saying you'd understand, but I never expected you to side with him like this, Endore," Bill says. "You *know* Luke controlled our affair."

"Yes," Endore relents.

With his boot, Chas teases the fallen pearl, pushing it even closer to the litter. He glances up at Lyndy.

She remains silent, not reacting.

The black man Don solicited earlier is walking out with the blond youngman who was at the bar. Don looks away from them. "Do you realize the beauty in the tank top is still here?" he asks.

The shirtless muscular man has located himself in the clearer area of availability.

"He probably hasn't turned down enough people," Bill says, considering it, yes, but also thwarting Endore's possible interest.

"Or no one's dared to ask him," Endore says.

"Luke said sometimes people would look at him all night, and no one asked him home. He said he felt so isolated," Bill says. "He was always using that word. Isolated. Especially when he couldn't get hard any more." Bill is no longer attempting to assault Lyndy with his candor, she seems hardly to be listening; he is releasing evoked memories. "He did get hard once more." Bill frowns; he remembers the dry hot tongue. "But it was wrong," he smashes the memory.

160 ·

"Stop thinking about Luke," Don says. It is irritating him dangerously to hear about Bill's lover. *I* never had one. But I arranged so many affairs. And what did that get me? "Just remember how he used you."

"He said *I* used *him*," Bill says in wonder. "Yet I did everything he wanted, to arouse him." He assaults Endore's judging vision of what occurred between them: "I even let myself be strapped in one of those contraptions they have at the Rack. Yes! Did he tell you *that*, Endore?" He regrets the words.

"It *was* you I saw," Chas says. "Strung on that rack, your feet in the stirrups. That guy was pushing his fist into your ass." He feels his cock stretch.

"Chas, you are—..." But Bill has trapped himself.

Endore looks at Lyndy. Her hand is glued to the remaining strand of pearls, as if she were evaluating her tearing of the other strand.

"I did it for Luke!" Bill releases. Luke stood a few feet away, staring. "It hurt! But he kept nodding, yes, encouraging me. A man was sucking him while he watched me with those sad—mean!—eyes of his. Then he ran out. Later at home, he kept crying. Maybe because he hadn't been able to get hard.... Maybe because—... He cried a lot, especially for such a macho man," Bill says in amazement. "And then—..." But he withholds the worst moments, he's smothered by their intimacy. "You *did* understand him, Endore, didn't you?"

Luke cried that night, and he clung to Endore. "No," Endore refuses, "I didn't understand him." Suddenly Luke said, "Bill wants me to hurt him, in weird ways, and he says it's because *I* want that; and he calls it ... love." Endore eased Luke away, seeing another truth, another possible truth.

"What I did that night at the Rack, I did it for Luke," Bill says.

"Out of ... love." That was the last night Endore was with Michael.

"Why else?" Bill wonders aloud. He plunges back into the bar.

Bill's words have made it easy—essential—that Endore face

Michael at last, now, after all the fake "attempts." His eyes explore the bar. But Michael has left. No, he's standing alone against another post in another section of the Rushes. Endore glances at Chas. Chas looks at him and then toward Michael.

Before any new untruthful "reason" may intercept his determination, Endore approaches the intimate stranger, who, seeing him near, waits for him this time too.

"How are you, Michael?" Endore asks him. The banal words, the ease with which he spoke them—they render the moment surreal. The blond youngman—reddish-blond—is perhaps handsomer than Endore remembers. In so short a time, the boyish features have found sharper definition.

"Okay. You?" Michael's words are as banal, as easy, unreal.

Endore hears crash behind them the sourceless laughter. Does Michael laugh like that? Is the joyous sound he remembers invaded now?

"Christ, it's easy," Michael is amazed, and a touch of the discarded boyishness returns to his face. "I've wanted and dreaded talking to you, almost every day, and now it's so damn easy." He laughs, a short laughter.

The expectation of joy, even at this moment, is still there. "We moved at the same time," Endore says. "*I* moved," he corrects, determined to avoid subterfuge.

"I would have," Michael makes it easy for him.

He understood me so well, and yet he was wrong, Endore insists. "I almost followed you into the piers, earlier." He wants to find out whether it was him. "But the traffic—..." A note of accusation punctures.

"Yeah, I was there earlier."

Now the banality of the approach cannot shelter them.

Rehearsed for days, weeks now, the unspoken accusation, reinforced by memory, rushes out of Michael: "When I first said I loved you—...!"

"You said it so quickly, so easily, you said it the very first time," Endore thwarts the certain assault.

"I felt it that quickly, that easily—*and* the first time," Mi-

chael's words slide from anger into benign memory, bruised again by accusation. "I did feel it—but you told me there was no such thing."

"No, no! I said. Let's not brand it, just experience it," Endore tells him. Accusing each other, they may see their respective truths, solve the mystery of their coming together, the mystery of their breaking apart.

The tone of accusation grips Michael's voice: "When I first saw you with someone else—. . ."

"I had warned you, I had told you; I didn't lie or hide—. . ."

". . . —I cried, and—. . ."

"I held you."

". . . —you convinced me we had to protect each other against possessiveness."

"I believed it, I believe it. I was determined not to surrender my life, nor allow you to surrender yours to an imprisoning concept of 'fidelity' as ownership." And to guard against pain, Endore reminds himself; against myths which wound when exposed as myths. Yet he knows he tried and was pulled by warring lovers—the Rushes and Michael. When he questioned, Why not both? he found no negative answer. But there was another battling lover, the most possessive and powerful—his aloneness, the vulnerable isolation; and that lover joined forces with the Rushes.

"I even asked you about the others you were with, I wanted to please you," Michael reminds, "to let you know that you *were* free."

Granted freedom. "While you let me know—with your unhappiness—that you felt I was . . . 'unfaithful.' " It's coming, Endore knows, Michael's judgment. "And you told me about the ones *you* were with." He hears his words with astonishment. It is *he* who has rendered the judgment.

"And *you* couldn't cope with it! After all your bullshit about selfish 'fidelity,' *you* couldn't cope with it."

"I would have," Endore knows. He had discovered the hated attitudes like venom injected too deeply, too early, in

him, too. If Luke hadn't come over that night, if I hadn't seen myself in him, and Bill in—... "If only you hadn't wanted pain!" he hurls.

"Because I thought you missed that world, and I loved you that much!"

"Is that true?"

"Find out!" Michael's voice is angry. "I'm not blaming you for anything, Endore! Damnit, stop trying to change the jungle you understand so well!" Michael squeezes through the flesh in the bar.

Is that, then, all? All that will be revealed of what occurred between them? These fragments of unclear accusations and judgments, like splintered pieces of a mirror reflecting different shades and hues, not even shapes; and even the tint and outlines of those glassy splinters may be reinterpreted, over and over, by memory. Or will there be more clarity? Or more mystery.

How long has the leatherman been standing next to him? How much did he hear? Endore looks away from him. Michael is resorbed into the thickening mass. From this distance Lyndy and Martin look like spectators at a slaughter. Endore feels his anger engulfing them in a wave which roars beyond them.

Chas studies Endore, back with them. "How's Michael?" He acknowledges the undertones of his question by not taunting with the shortened name.

"I've got to have sex tonight!" Don says aloud. He looks at his watch.

He said that before. Yes, the night he called from "out of town." In that urgent tone. No, he said it earlier when Endore saw him at—... Cruising, attentive bodies thwart Endore's remembrance.

"It'll be Last Call soon and I'm still alone. All night long I've tried to connect." Again, the shout threatens to rage out.

"You shouldn't feel you have to connect, that's what's cruel, Don," Endore says. Tonight he senses a much greater

pain than usual in the troubled man who is becoming an alcoholic.

Lyndy's head makes a slight tilt toward Endore. Her fingers press open on her chest, covering the pearls. When her silence is broken, it will crash, Endore knows.

Don confronts Endore: "I *need* to make out, *you* can always make out."

"No one can—always; we all know the horror of ending up alone when we don't want to," he tries to soothe Don. But Endore's attention is pulled by the gorgeous flotsam of flesh in the smoky sea of the Rushes. Yes, he wants sex tonight.

"I need someone *tonight.*" Don's face is contorted with urgency.

A momentary substitute for salvation, Endore knows. Ahead, the resplendent, lewd carnality lures again.

Look at him, so "compassionate," Don feels anger focusing on his good friend. So desirable—and he's not that much younger than me. And Chas, all that boasting! Bill! If he doesn't get what he wants tonight, he'll start fresh and young tomorrow. But for Don the pain of each night cuts closer to a core each time, so close to it now, so close to screaming.

Endore. Chas. Martin. Don. And Bill is back. They all turn to look at Lyndy. She has pulled out one of the pearls from her pocket. She bites it hard. She touches it with her tongue, now with a finger.

"They *are* the real ones, Martin," she breaks her long silence. She tosses that pearl on the floor with the other. Now her voice is eerie as she releases the blackmail with which she tantalized Martin earlier. She can now discard the ugly information like garbage.

"The night we went to the trucks, Martin waited in the Jaguar, and after I had seen the shadows locked in sex, I moved across the street to witness it all." She strokes the remaining pearls about her neck. "A carload of those boys rushed into the trucks, I got into the car with Martin. The boys drove off yelling names, men staggered out, and one man—

bleeding—came up to the window on Martin's side." Her fingers soothe the pearls. "The man pushed his bloody face against the glass and he was yelling to be let in, and Martin drove off, and then he stopped and cleaned the bloody prints the hands had left on the windshield. That's all." She pauses. Now, for her, it comes: "Except that later, at Marissa's party, Martin couldn't stop trembling, it was the first time I have ever seen him tremble."

Don wishes he could reject the evoked image of the bloodied face. "How cruel of you to run away!" he accuses Martin.

"Perhaps," Martin tosses aside. "And perhaps the man was one of those who raided the trucks." It is the first time he has even seemed to want to explain anything.

"Left behind by the ones who drove away?" Endore pursues.

"Perhaps," Martin says.

"Then why did you tremble?" Bill asks him. "You're always so cool, so cold, so in control."

"Oh," Lyndy finishes, "but that time *he* was astonished. By the scent of sexual blood."

11

As it was in the beginning,
is now....

As OFTEN as he comes to the Rushes,
Chas is still awed by the resplendent sexual animal the bar
becomes near Last Call. Raunchy sweating currents rush
through amyl-injected veins of red smoke. Groaning music
comes. Flesh and leather—his eyes select the two—crunch into
one sensual body. You make out now—the only release the
grasping animal allows now—or you offer up the evening to
aloneness. The bar clutches by reminding that no matter how
many connections have been sundered, redemption is possi-
ble; one surpassing contact may atone for all the broken ones.
Only when the lights crash after Last Call is shouted will the
death of the evening be acknowledged in the Rushes.

As he stands in the curdled silence which followed Lyndy's
narrative, Chas feels a growing sexual hunger. He evaluates

his prospects. The leatherman wears no insignia, so he will go either way. Even machos who wear their signals on the left side, proclaiming dominance, will shift for a good top-man; it happens often to Chas, and he enjoys vying for the dominant role, and winning. By touching his own keys, on his left, Chas asserted himself as a top-man; the leatherman affirmed it with his nod. And there is Michael. True, he has received no clear invitation to invite, nor has he felt the requisite hardon, but he has been aroused by his presence in the past, and they have not been in proximity tonight. Having him would erase the defeat with Robert—that still stings. But conquering Michael would involve an astounding configuration—the evening hints of possibilities. And it would force him and Endore into combat. Oh, and there is Bill, ripe tonight. Or one of so many others who may yet give him a magical hard cock.

He wants the sex to be heavy; a masculine slave kneeling before him, tongue lapping the black boots, buttocks squirming at the hint of his belt, which he will slide along the other's naked back, tantalizing with it and with his cock. Images bombard Chas's brain, he holds an ampule to his nose, to retain them longer and more tightly. And then, no longer wearing pants, just the black chaps, he will wrap the belt about the other's neck, after dangling the tip over his mouth, and pull the head against the naked groin and force the eager head to drink, and shift it artfully back against the crack of his buttocks, the knot of flesh there, forcing the tongue to explore the opening, and he'll wrap a part of the belt about his fist and slap at the flesh with the other part, awakening the raw flesh, stinging, yes, but not cutting, no, indulging only the charade just one degree before real pain, and the epithets of macho love-contempt will bless. And then tying—. . . He feels his cock growing under the clinging pants, the cockring clasping. The imagined figure with him has altered among his choices, the leatherman, Michael, Bill, and—. . . Strange that the fantasy did not span out to Robert. . . . Or a three-way, the resurgence of the amyl provokes. Two mouths on his cock, and a hard

thick cock juicy in his hand, yeah, as he reaches to pectorals, squeezing, pinching, biting the nipples.

Don breaks Chas's revery, and the entranced silence since Lyndy's narrative: "Those damn lights are going to go on in a few minutes," he repeats obsessively, as if to hold the lights back with his warning tone. "There's a man over there—my age. He looked at me. I'm not attracted to him at all, but if I close my eyes—..." He realizes he's thinking aloud. He clamps his hand over his watch, to stop time.

"Be alone!" Endore hears his voice become blunt toward Don for the first time this evening. The Rushes is flaying the vestigial compassion the earlier part of the evening allowed.

Don welcomes the tone. He would like to arouse anger so that his own may be flushed out. "You talk about aloneness as if it were your lover!"

"One not to be betrayed." Lyndy uttered the unexpected words.

Endore glances at her; a whisper of unwanted ... empathy.

Without a word of parting now, Bill and Chas invade the heavy pit.

A man pushes his back against Chas's groin. Attractive, but not what Chas wants, no, not macho enough, but okay for a moment's "charge." Chas's probing finger discovers split pants. He shoves another finger in, another. The man allows it. Chas digs into the smooth, smooth, oiled flesh. He bunches his third and fourth fingers and tries to force them in in one rough shove. The man jerks. Chas pulls out his fingers and moves on.

"If you got a big cock, I'll go with you," an ordinary man offers Chas.

He's the type who hasn't much to lose, and so, aggressive. "I got the biggest *you'd* see," Chas boasts. "But you won't see it," he discards.

He passes Bill. He hears Bill's Southern drawl; he's talking to a tall man. "I like a man who knows he's a—..."

Seeing Chas, Bill stops his words. True to the rules of the sexhunt, the two pretend not to know each other—any outside gesture may break a connection. Bill isn't as turned off as usual by Chas's clothes. Tonight they show off his sexy body.

"Whore! Don't you *ever* let *me* see you *here* again!" The shrill voice of a man raids the stagnant air from somewhere deep within the crunch of flesh.

"You fucking bitch! You're nothing but a wasted tramp, give up!" another voice screeches.

"Good enough for *you* to get all hot over *me!*"

Hearing the shrieking voices, Chas feels outraged. These strident outbursts occur as the tension knots toward Last Call. Chas loathes those moments. They scratch out rancid effeminacy, and they jar the ritual, which, in the arena, should be as silent as possible now, the exhortations and verbalized explorations like prayers. He sees the heated, shouting men ahead: A drunken man in leather—chains and keys askew on his left side, handkerchief dangling, the uniform in ugly disarray—faces a lanky, shirtless man; earlier he looked good, now he's haggard. Get the fuck out! Chas issues a silent curse as he prowls his kingdom, nodding to the many he has been with.

The voices of the angered men regurgitate. Lashing, they invoke the harshest curse in the Rushes—effeminacy—while personifying it in cruel paradox: *"Cunt!* You just—. . . !"

Another fresh wound peeled, Endore thinks, hearing the distant fury. Throughout the Rushes, this very moment contains a myriad separate moments—lives.

"The precious minutes before Last Call," Martin intones.

His façade is intact. He will not allow Lyndy and the victory of his anger. Or do they admire each other only in mutual ambush?—a game which joins them, bored, together? Endore wonders.

"Now even the sleeping beauties will awake," Martin is explaining the sexual hunt to Lyndy, "and even the ones who kept hoping for someone better, surrender to tonight's reality. You see, darling, when the men who have desired each other all night wait too long to signal an invitation, it becomes a

contest to see who will look away first. Then the exact moment of rejection becomes as important as the exact moment of approach was. Oh, there, see, he moved too slowly, the other left—victorious; they'll both end up alone or with someone they did not prefer—but, look, a stalemate! Ah, the backs are about to turn. Desire denied converts both hunter and hunted into enemies for life. Fragile connections—. . ."

"And yet they *do* connect." Lyndy's eyes are wide.

"Miraculously we manage, over and over and over," Endore says.

"All of them in heat," Martin spits. Now he passes his judgment: "So chic and beautiful away from the Rushes. And so vile and hungry here."

So chic, so beautiful. And so despised. The screams outside remind us, Endore knows. We cruise and fuck away the knowledge of the stalking hatred. Whipped by strobe lights, young warriors desert the battle for sequined disco graves. In bars we numb it away.

"Chas has moved toward Michael." Martin announces.

But also near the leatherman. Endore makes the important adjustment. Don't prove me right with Chas, he sends an urgent silent message to Michael. He shifts his gaze to the drawings. The artist meant to leave the last panel unfinished because he didn't understand the meaning of his creation; he pulled away from it, Endore has a sudden clarity. His look is drawn away. Chas is moving next to—. . . The shiny black back of the leatherman obtrudes.

About the bar, bodies are increasingly bared, shirts are open or removed, pants pushed to the edge of pubic hair, deep oblique muscles. In the carnal arena an erotic army of exposed soldiers is gathering. Terror of rejection wars with the desire to connect. Lovers are potential enemies. Against the walls, on the beer crates, on stools, against the posts and pool tables, men pose now, fingers looped, hips loose and forward, cigarettes drooping, boots always, always asserting, shoulders hunched. Alike. While seeming never to look, they look constantly, masking fear with disdain.

At the bar a man slides down. his head buried in another's groin. Like a spark flying from a conflagration onto waiting tinder. the synergetic sexuality from the dark back of the bar crackles forward. Another form is crouching on his knees. A man pushes against the back of another. Knots of men throughout kiss. hands anxious. A few bodies have stripped down to shorts. jockstraps. elaborate leather pouches bradded with silver studs. Red-dyed flesh, oiled, sweating, gleams.

The shiny back of the leatherman slides to one side, and Endore sees Michael and Chas. But before he can determine whether they're talking, Bill's wandering form blocks his visual vantage. Bill looks lost.

All night he's felt Endore judging his relationship with Luke. The tension he's been feeling—that's what's been intruding in his cruising. By confronting it, he will clear it away so his style will uncramp. He moves back to where Endore stands with Don, Martin, Lyndy. "I've got three lined up!" he announces.

"Oh, Christ, the fatuous bragging!" Don says. His sweating body is cold. The artificial air chills him hotly.

"The problem is that of the people I really want, nobody's really dominant." Bill wants to pull out a definite accusation to rebut. Without a plan, he's just stabbing. "They seem to be, but they're not."

"Boundaries blur," Endore says.

Chas is back, and there's a new cockiness about him.

He spoke to Michael. Or to the leatherman; Endore adjusts his evaluation.

"Not with us, the boundaries didn't blur; Luke was the dominant one," Bill says.

Anger seeps into Don's words. "Does it matter!" The words he longs to shout bunch inside, bile.

"Yes! It *matters.*" Bill is irritated by Don, and he is ignoring Lyndy and Martin.

"Amen, it matters!" Chas pronounces.

"It certainly mattered when Luke tried to change it; that's why it ended, and it was *his* fault!" Bill thrusts at Endore.

"I thought it was because he couldn't get hard anymore," Don says. The unspewed words taste like vomit, yes. He pushes it back with the last of his new drink.

"He did get hard again—once—the same night he ran out of the Rack. Later." The memory spills out: "He tried to express desire for me the way I did for him. He began kissing my body, licking it, licking me all over, sucking me, rimming me, I don't know what got into him, he wasn't supposed to do that, *he* was the dominant one, I wanted him to stop, kept telling him to, but he was too aroused by then. He came!"

The image of Luke licking Bill's body—the two beautiful men; and Bill pushed him away!—it lodges in Don's mind like a needle.

Too late to stop them, the words flow out of Bill: "But then *I* couldn't get hard." He waits for Endore to absolve him.

Endore says nothing.

Bill's voice is frigid. "I. Did. Love. Luke."

"Did *you* love Michael, Endore?" Chas faces him.

His body is so close to Endore's that Endore can feel his breath.

Assaulted by that closeness—no matter how tense—between the two men—their chests bared!—Don knows he has to break it: "Goddamnit, don't!" he almost shouts, and his hand drops like a knife between the two men. It's because of my face, my bruised face!

Endore hears the ambiguous command like an alert of toppling control.

"I thought you were really going to be angry at each other, I thought any moment you'd—. . ." Don tries to explain away his strange action. So beautiful, Don thinks. The two men are so beautiful.

Feeling released from Chas's powerful clutch, Endore looks into the sea of bodies in which Michael and the leather-man swim.

"I have. To have. Sex. Tonight." Don squeezes out the words.

Yes. Endore remembers. The same words. The same des-

perate tone. On the piers, the last time he saw him before the night-call. Endore was surprised to see Don there and left. Looking back, he saw Don inching into the arteries of darkness in the warehouses. Oh, no, the thought begins to form.

Don's face is grim. The words which invaded his mind earlier reshape: A wish. I wish—... *I wish!* A curse. I want—... *I want!* No, don't. He forces the horror away. I love Endore. He closes his eyes, wanting to shut his ears, too, his senses, his feelings, to disconnect them. He hears the echo of each of their earlier words about sexual choices, like traversing bullets in his brain.

I wish—... He opens his eyes. Now Bill is close to Chas; no, closer to Endore. Don's mind screams, Stay apart or I'll shout the words! "Bastards—. . ." The word escaped.

"Don, what is the matter?" Bill asks him softly.

"You just leave me alone, you!" Don says. His hand begins a pushing gesture. Instead, both hands cover his face.

"Why do you keep hiding your face?"

Did someone really say it? Yes, it was Bill. Don can't believe the blunt words. "I'm not, I—. . ."

The thought struck Bill with such abrupt clarity that he verbalized it automatically· "Oh, God, Don, did you have your face lifted? You were gone all that time, and—. . ."

No! A sustained moan implodes in Don's mind. *No!*

Oh, God, it isn't that, Endore knows. I should have known. My God! That afternoon on the piers! He wants to shout to Bill to stop.

Chas! Martin! Lyndy! Bill! They're all staring at his face. And Endore is too! *No!* Don covers his face again. "Bastard!" he yells at Bill. "Bastard!"

Bill tries to pull back; he didn't want to hurt Don. "There's nothing wrong with it, Don," he tries to placate. "I'm really sorry. You do look so much better, really. I'm sure you'll look great when you heal, it's the puffiness that's still—. . ."

"They beat me!" Don howls. He tears Endore's hand away from his shoulder. "On the piers! I had to have stitches!"

"Oh, Don, I'm sorry, really so very, very sorry; you should have told us," Bill pleads.

"Beat me with clenched fists!" Don clenches his own. "Kicking me when I fell. 'Faggot! Queer!' They kept yelling and kicking. I followed the little bastard, thinking he really wanted me, the way he kept looking at me, signaling to me, following me around. And they ambushed me! Five, six, I don't know how many. They robbed me—but that wasn't enough. They kept kicking." The memory floods. Earlier that same afternoon, he had attempted to join a cluster of sex-pressed bodies and was pushed to the filthy floor of the warehouse. He ran. Playing with his own groin, the handsome boy stood in a gash of light. Don followed him into the darkness. Then the young savages captured him in a terrible circle of thrusting feet and fists. "I just wanted to have sex with him," Don sighs. His voice grows stiller. He lay there bleeding, trying not to move so they would think they had killed him. Even after they left, he just lay there, knowing that even if he called the police and they came, they would act as if *he* were the guilty one.

"The bastards," Chas feels a powerful anger at the murderous assaulters. "The fuckin bastards.'

"The bastards," Endore echoes.

Lyndy's eyes badger Martin to remember the bleeding face at the window of his Jaguar.

She didn't care about the man, no, Endore notices her look; she cares only that she has a weapon against Martin, that he may—*may*—have felt . . . something!

Only when he opened his eyes and saw Endore—so hurt—and Chas—fierce—and Bill—shocked—staring at him in disbelief, only when Don saw Lyndy and Martin watching him in fascination, only when his eyesight blurred and he realized, I'm not sweating, I'm crying—only when he was aware of others near him staring—only then did Don know that he was shouting, is shouting out the accumulated words:

"I wish the cops would rush in and arrest everyone like

they did us. I wish they would padlock the Rushes and all these places. Goddamnit, we couldn't even dance, not even touch—and look what's going on right in this bar! I hate all of you—Bill, Chas, Endore—I hate you!" Then he yells at no one: "Arrest them! Arrest them all!"

12

Cleanse my heart and
my lips.

AS OFTEN as he comes to the Rushes,
Endore is still amazed to uncover a nuance missed before in
the erotic cartoon figures on the walls. To avoid the avalanche
of Don's words and the wake of resentful silence, he looked at
the panels. The contrasting vagueness and sharpness in the
primitive line drawings have a new possible explanation.
Whether this clarity will survive into another night—others
have not—for now Endore is sure that another artist tried to
restore the original drawings, but selectively. He inserted or
expunged only certain expressions, clarified or blurred only
certain attitudes. Yet he too pulled away from definite mean-
ing and left the last panel blank—only inserting the vague
sketch, or refusing to restore it.

Endore remembers the photographic paintings he saw earlier tonight. The artist painted blood over beautiful settings—arranged, ordered. He did not allow them to bleed in disordered ugliness. How would that artist depict the Rushes stripped of the rage of emotions? The disemboweled stools, the overturned crates, the sawdust in jigsaw puzzle patches, the ampules of amyl like dead insects. No, Endore cannot "see" the painting. Then he locates Lyndy's pearls on the floor, and the painting shapes. Endore realizes then the brutality of the earlier-evening's exhibition. The artist proffered purification through beautified—beatific—violence; he omitted the overwhelming factor of feelings, emotions, the pained disorder that must precede and follow his perfect frozen violence. Those paintings were as cruel in their implications as the architectonic sterility of Martin's work—both praising order through an immolation of feeling. Like Martin himself. And Lyndy.

Again Endore looks at the bloated muscular men drawn on the walls. He searches the faces from which emotion has been excised. Crushed too long by ancestral hatred against them, is that what the real men standing against the drawings long to become, in defense—but can't? Do I? he questions.

He hears that new laughter rising from a red-shaded depth within the Rushes. Tense, he waits to listen to the break. His clarity about the drawings, the paintings at the exhibit earlier, the incidents of the night have roused a sudden expectation of discovery. The laughter holds, almost stopped. Is the "hollow" stasis the intersection of desperate hope to become insensate—to be bludgeoned feelingless—and the reality of intensive vulnerability? If so, which of the two components survives longer?

In couples or alone, men leave the Rushes; squads, perhaps fresher, replace them. There is a late-night flow to the Rushes, by those who cherish the crucial last minutes of the hunt. Eyes, staring eyes, are palpable presences throughout.

Endore has learned to turn his back on the sexhunt, to walk out in triumph over the radiating power of the Rushes;

but there is a certain time—different for each man but usually before Last Call—when a certain stirring demands fulfillment or sexual death for the night. Handsome and desirable as he is, Endore is not immune to the series of missed connections that lead to a sentence of sexual aloneness for the night.

Although in his columns he has praised the abstract beauty of the choreographed hunt—"the solo dancers join the corps in shifting patterns of elegant geometry"—when he and others are caught in its bloodiness, he sees its horror.

Like now. Don's face is carved by tears and pain. His body trembles as if caught in a fatal chill.

Endore puts his hand on Don's trembling shoulders. This time Don does not thrust it away.

"I didn't mean that." Don looks about him in surprise.

"Of course not, we know that," Endore says.

He meant it, Chas thinks. Without glancing at Don, he walks away—"to get another beer"—to push down the vomitous anger. And to assess the territory.

Bill turns to say something kind to Don. But the pain-racked face makes him turn away. I wish he wouldn't come back. He too moves away.

Don inches toward the exit. The man he saw earlier—about his age, carefully arranged—moves from a deeper part of the bar, as if to approach him. Nearer to the exit—he doesn't want to look out, to see whether the hustler is still there—Don waits. The man approaches him. Don smiles a grateful but uncertain welcome.

Let it work, Endore thinks.

"He's back," Lyndy says. "The beautiful youngman who ran out earlier is back. Look, Martin."

Near Don talking to the man, Robert stands at the entrance.

Ahead, approaching with fresh beer in hand, Chas stops.

Robert searches the bar.

For me? For Chas? Endore's body tenses.

"Chas may still win—or lose again," Lyndy resurrects the battle.

"Is it important that he call you darling?" Endore postpones the reality of the youngman's return.

"I so want to be loved," Lyndy says. Because she has drained the word of all meaning, she can use it easily.

"Have you chosen yet whom you will be pursued by, Endore?" Martin stabs.

Rage bursts. "When will *you* finally choose, Martin?"

"I choose not to choose," Martin answers. "There is no greater power over the beautiful than to withhold desire from them."

"What do you feel, to watch it all at a distance, Martin?" Endore pursues. He feels an inner trembling.

"Nothing," Martin answers.

"Are you afraid your vaunted power will not survive the battles?" Endore has crossed the boundary of their hostile truce.

"It does, that's all that matters," Martin says.

"Even if you have to slum among your own." Endore declares open war.

"Did that hurt, darling?" Lyndy acknowledges the declaration.

"Not at all," Martin says. " 'My own'—as you put it, is me, just me. I."

"Oh, I like that," Lyndy joins. *"Moi aussi."*

"Then why did you tremble after you saw the bloodied man at your car window?"

Lyndy waits for his answer.

"There was a dreadful chill at Marissa's that night," Martin says.

Lyndy applauds, releasing him from her earlier judgment of feeling.

Robert locates Endore. Chas still waits.

"In all the encounters with you," Endore says, "the bouts with you at rancid parties and dinners and sterile exhibitions, in all that time, I've waited for one single moment of revelation about you. Epiphany. When one detects and understands,

180 ·

perhaps, the psychic wound. But that moment hasn't come. Not in either of you."

"Ah, sad," Lyndy says.

"Until tonight," Endore says.

"I'm breathless to hear your epiphany," Lyndy jibes, but her hand brings an invisible pearl to her lips.

"The revelation is that there is no revelation," Endore says. "Your core is nothing."

Lyndy applauds, this time one slow clap follows another, dead applause. "I adore your epiphany of us, Endore. No pain, no psychic wound."

"Gorgeous!" Martin's hands join in the dead applause.

"But just one question, Endore," Lyndy says. "Did the epiphany about our nothingness reveal anything about you?" She is evoking the malign attraction that has bound them for years.

Did it?

Endore looks away from her, and the question.

Robert glances at Martin and Lyndy and then at Endore.

Chas locates Michael and the leatherman, as if he's determining foes, choosing allies, evaluating reserves.

"I came back to ask you why you told me to leave after you got me away from Chas," Robert has walked up to Endore. He pushed out the rehearsed words.

"Oh, yes," Lyndy sighs.

Endore will not allow her to listen. He moves away from them, the youngman follows. In a thinning area of the bar—as the men rush inward to clash and fuse—Endore is aware of Chas's clenching look. Robert continues the prepared words:

"You came over, man, and I was with Chas," he is trying to find meaning in the sequence he has recreated over and over since he left, "and you said I was—. . ."

"I said you were beautiful," Endore repeats, to emphasize, "because I knew Chas was making you feel ugly." And he's a master at it, like me, once. "I told you you didn't have to feel dirty."

Robert abandons the rehearsed words, searches for others.

Endore feels caught in a web of looks—Chas's, Lyndy's, Martin's. And Michael's. The leatherman has returned to stand near Michael. Endore feels a coldness like that when the black glove touched him earlier. Has it touched Michael?

"And you are beautiful," Endore says to Robert, "and very brave, when you stood with the transvestite and the black woman."

"They felt alone, and I felt alone," Robert says. "I did feel ugly, with Chas, but turned-on too—he was talking weird shit, and my head was fucked like when my brother talks about queers and it all seems mean and I know he's wrong, but it makes *me* feel guilty and dirty, and that's how I felt with Chas—and I'm glad you came over, man." His words struggle to order the confusion. "Then you kissed me."

Kissing away—. . . Endore tries to remember.

"It wasn't ugly then," Robert says.

"No, it wasn't ugly," Endore says.

"Then why did you hide from Chas when you kissed me? It *wasn't* ugly."

"I was afraid to be vulnerable before him."

"Something between you?"

"No."

"Then why did you tell me to leave?"

Endore can't answer. He knew then, when they kissed.

"You're the first guy I ever kissed," Robert prods him.

"It was a first time for me, too," Endore says. The first time he approached anyone.

"I saw you on the piers first."

"I remember." In the warehouse the slender figure watched. It was an afternoon when the sexual nerve chafed insatiable and Endore moved from man to man along the crush of rubble. In a diagonal of light, Robert stood—so close for that moment that Endore could see the thick eyelashes; he looked out of place there too, because his clothes were care-less. He followed Endore. Then he disappeared.

"I kept hiding from you, you kept making out with differ-

ent guys," Robert seems to accuse. "I didn't do anything. I never have, I went home and I cried, fuck yeah, I cried wishing I'd made it with you."

On the rubbish? On dank boards? Stairs like blackened teeth? In the cadaverous warehouse? Pier filth? Ensnaring wires? Oxidized metal? Endore looks at the boy's face, the angles which will mature into those of a handsome man—the way Michael's have already. He looks at the beautiful body with the natural muscles hardening, the exposed flesh under his shirt traced by definition, and he desires this youngman. His tight body would fit into mine. His furry crotch, the hairless chest, the—probably—surprisingly hairy legs, the eager cock would press against my crotch, chest, legs, cock. Our mouths will kiss, then slide between each other's legs.

"Can we make it?" Robert asks Endore.

He's not afraid to ask, so easy for him; he's not afraid to feel. "Yes," Endore says.

"Every night I imagined it would happen, and it will. I love you," Robert says.

"Don't say that!" The terrified words bolt out of Endore's lips. "There's no such—. . ." He hears his voice, his tone—and echoes: There's no such thing, Michael!

A few feet away, Chas dismisses a man trying to approach him.

Assuring that Chas is watching—to make up for the covert act earlier—Endore kisses Robert on the lips. The youngman's lips part, the tongues touch. Then Endore eases Robert away.

Robert frowns. "We are gonna make it, aren't we?"

"No!" Endore says, and now he knows and can answer why he told him to leave: "Because you threaten the cynicism by which I survive," he says angrily. "And it was threatened once before." And now by memories, of Michael. And he is here in the jungle I prepared him for without wanting to, and you'd inherit it too.

"Then all you wanted was for me not to go with Chas, huh? There *is* something between you."

"No," Endore says.

"I could still go with him," Robert threatens.

Chas holds out his beer in an unfinished toast.

"I'm sure you won't go with Chas." Endore's voice is unsure. "Because you know it doesn't have to be ugly—and you know he can't give you what you know now you want. But somebody else can."

"Not you?"

"Not me. Not Chas." It's too late, he thinks.

Robert erupts, "Then fuck you—you're as fucked as Chas in your own way, as fucked as my brother in his. Fuck you!" he shouts.

Chas takes a step toward the youngman.

Tense, Robert waits.

Against the wall, the leatherman watches.

Chas takes another step.

He won't go with Chas, he won't go with Chas, Endore thinks.

Robert walks out of the Rushes.

He left. He left Chas. And me, Endore thinks. He left us both.

Feeling abandoned in hostile currents of the Rushes, Endore moves back to the safety of the trenches.

Before Lyndy and Martin, Chas confronts him. "The kid told you to fuck off!" he triumphs. "Endore even kissed the kid, did you see him?" He wants the others to acknowledge that, as if he does not—does not want to—believe it. "Did you see him? And the kid told him to fuck off! He came back to tell him to fuck off!"

"I told him to leave," Endore says.

"Shit, we heard him tell you to fuck off." The strength in Chas's voice wanes.

"You didn't hear it all," Endore says. "He walked out on both of us, Chas. He won't grovel at your boots, nor—. . ."

"Nor yours!" Chas thwarts a further accusation.

"Nor mine," Endore agrees. "Some of us are scarred beyond healing. But that kid isn't yet." Is Michael? "You wanted his initiation to be brutal. Like yours."

"I wanted it to be *honest!*" Chas contradicts. His hands

form fists. They begin to hurt. He unclenches them, feeling the warmth flowing into the strangled fingers. He remembers the touch of the leatherman's glove.

"We can't leave him—them—the same brutal battles," Endore says. "We can't leave them our ugliness."

"Ugliness! Whatever you call it, we'll leave him—them—what is *ours*. Only ours." Chas stands in defiance before Endore. "Yeah, the piers, the trucks! And the Rushes! And the Rack! The places we've made for ourselves."

"The places they pushed us into and we've converted into our own," Endore says.

"The same now," Chas says. "Ours. In them we live more in one night than they do all their lives." He indicts Lyndy with a glance.

"But if we leave them only that—..." Endore begins, and imagines a new generation for whom sex exists only in clusters in filthy orgy rooms, its anxious sextime over, so quickly, at 35, a deathtime confirmed by posted notices in bars, baths, orgy rooms. "If we leave them only that—..." he repeats.

"The bountiful sex you've praised, written about, remember?" Chas prods.

"Yes—that—which we've earned," Endore says. "But if there's nothing more than what we have now, we're doomed and we doom them."

"Doom," Lyndy pronounces. "What a curious word."

"You really think you 'saved' that kid from me!" Chas derides.

" 'Saved,' too, has a curious ring, a certain obsolescence," Martin says.

"And from myself," Endore says. "But not ... saved—..." That word—like ... love, so difficult to pronounce, even in one's thoughts. "... —just ... more choices." Yes, choices. "And if then he chooses your piss or to grovel at your boots, so be it." Yet *those* words flow out easily.

"We may be doomed, but we're alive!" Chas stares at the mysterious presence Endore has always been for him, from the beginning, throughout the years, now, always.

Alive! The word reverberates.

"Listen!" Chas says passionately. "Listen. When you're still walking the piers, a faggot all alone looking for sex, and it's Sunday morning, you know you're alive, man. Alive. Because you know you've been through the greatest adventure. And you're alive! Still alive! Despite the punks and all the yells of 'Queer!' and all the raids—despite all their shit, the shit we live with, we're alive! That's the only victory we have, man, and that's what makes being a faggot special. That you can survive all that—for an excitement like no other, and you're always on the edge, and that's when you're most alive, when you know you're *still* alive, and tomorrow, too, because tomorrow it all starts again, our only continuity. That's the joy that only we faggots have. Because in between the busts and the headbashings and the screams for our blood—before whatever it is that finally takes us over—getting drunk or going crazy or, yeah, killing ourselves or just dying—we're alive, and they can't even feel, not even pain, but *we* do, pain and relief when it's over, and you call it S & M and that's okay. But we *feel,* and they're dead—having to come here to sniff at our world, breathe our sweat. So where the fuck is it all more honest even when it's brutal!"

"Only in our jungle, where we flaunt our defiant survival," Endore answers.

Chas exhales in triumph. Excitement roars. The Rushes stretches its limbs—alive! "And *that's* what we'll leave the ones who come after us—because it's righteous, and that's what we *owe* them!"

Endore frowns. His words just spoken echo as if out of a hypnotic trance created by Chas. Clearing it, he shakes his head, to shed the acquiescing words, but they're insistent, they cling—and others are equally insistent, clinging too: "There's got to be more," he says emphatically.

Chas feels betrayed.

"All that, too," Endore says. "Yes, that's uniquely ours now, to leave, yes, that, yes, but with less pain at least, at least less guilt. At least that. And goddamnit more, too. There's got to be more. That and more! *And not the fucking cruelty!"*

The two men strain toward each other.

"Bravo!" Lyndy applauds. A requiem for the living!"

Chas faces her. Outlined in the dark black paint, her eyes narrow with hatred. Chas rubs his armpits, wiping up the sweat there. He brings his moistened hands right up to her face, her nose. "Smell it, you shit!" he yells at her. "Smell the fuckin sweat, you slumming shit!" he demands.

She reaches out and grasps his wrists. He thrusts her hands away. He turns to Endore:

"Look at the Rushes, man. Would you trade it for anything else?"

13

All of you take and
eat of this:
For this is My Body.

As OFTEN as he comes to the Rushes,
Chas has never felt his view of it as alternately threatened and
strengthened as he has tonight. Not threatened by Lyndy, not
anymore; after he thrust her hands away, the pasted smile
returned to her face, and he ignored her. Nor in his view
threatened by the memory of Elaine and Roxy—that is reced-
ing, he assures himself. The matter with Robert still burns,
yes, but there may be'redemption for that. It is Endore who
provides the threat, and, just now, the strength.

Always before when they moved into the arena, they
staked out separate areas and waged different campaigns.
That acknowledged their respective power. Often verbalized,
the ambiguous rivalry between them has never been tried.
The unnamed stakes are so high that neither has wanted to

test them. When Endore approached Robert, a crucial barricade collapsed, however mysterious the full tactic involved may still be for Chas. Yet Chas goaded Endore into an acknowledgment of mutual love—implied—for the Rushes, a love they may share. Glimpsing an extorted victory, Chas felt outraged by Endore's sudden betrayal—as Chas saw it. So Chas withdrew his question about total fealty to the Rushes.

Now he thrusts his look into the field, where the stronger combatants relish the final moments of this night's battle, now that safe early "victors"—and deserters—have moved out and the wounded begin to stagger. He, Endore, Michael, the leatherman form two potential flanks which may shift before the night is over.

Yes, Chas's implied demand of total devotion to the Rushes was premature, not enough open allegiance had been exposed in Endore to support it. Endore's silence confirmed that. Chas will wait. If he pushes, Endore's resurgent momentum might engulf him.

Looking at the leatherman, Endore feels again a heated charge which he does not welcome. He searches out Don, he's still talking to the man his age. Insisting the hot stirring abate, he looks again at the leatherman, and feels again the jabbing heat. He tries to locate Michael. Instead he sees Bill.

Bill turns away. Behind him in a wall drawing, crouching figures gather at the feet of an exposed body. Steve walks past Bill. Steve is drunk again. Bill remembers him from the "body" magazines he used to pore over. How often he stared, aroused, at photographs of Steve's perfect body, each striation a badge of beauty. Now look at him, a prematurely aging ghost. He should stay away and let people remember his photographs and not him, Bill thinks. But now his attention returns to what has developed in these latter moments, a most interesting, and interested, prospect. He and the man nearby have cruised each other within a narrowing circumference.

Goodlooking, grand body, Bill evaluates the man. But the clothes are *wrong!* Plain boots *and* khaki pants *and* a striped shirt *and* an awful fatigue cap—*not molded!* So wrong! Yet *he's*

so right. But let's hear him talk. "Hawrya?" Bill assaults. In his mind, he removes the man's cap. There! Now he replaces it with a cowboy hat. Better.

"Gettin along, getting along."

The voice is fine—but watch the "*g*s." "Leaving soon?" Bill asks. Leave the vest on, substitute the boots.

"Figure I might, yeah."

He hasn't lost his macho stance, good. But, oh, those *clothes!* Well, the shirt comes off. The vest is good, getting better now that the shirt is gone. He removes the khaki pants and substitutes a—. . . jockstrap! Wow! Cowboy hat and boots, brown vest, jockstrap!

"Can you get into macho fantasy?" Bill decides to go all the way.

"Uh, well, I guess," the man is unsure.

Oh, oh. "I bet you could! You look so—so—macho, and, well, dominant." I'll teach you, he thinks. I'll tell you exactly how to do it.

Already the man is altering his stance to conform to Bill's words.

"Let's go to my place, then," Bill says. "We'll share a cab, I like things always to be equal, it's the only way."

"All right. Yeah, sure."

All right! So easy! Bill feels relief. The night's tension—no matter how intense—is always dissipated by a good contact. This was one of those nights when it did work out well, yes, after all the jerky abortive starts. He chose correctly, although—. . . although—. . . Well, yes, he would have preferred the shirtless muscular man. But! "I have some clothes I'm sure will fit you," Bill tells the man. "They belonged to—. . ." He pauses. He tries to remember Luke's face and can't. Instead he remembers the spooky crucifix. Well, *that's* gone!

Without looking at them, he walks with his trophy past all the others he cruised earlier or who cruised him—the cowboys, the biker—was it another one?—the construction worker— two?—the man in mixed uniform, and—oh, good, the bastard will see me—the man in the cutoffs, his cock *and* balls dangling

out now. Sweet revenge. "Pardon me, sir," Bill snips at him, "but I believe your *brains* are pouring out of your pants!" He nods to Endore and Chas. He pretends not to see Don talking to an older man at the door.

Bill says to the man he's going home with, "I bet I could get to like you. A lot. I always get a feeling. You know, I guess maybe it's silly, but I *still* believe in love."

Seeing Bill leave, Chas spits. Okay, another time. He brings his fist to his lips. He glides toward Michael. Pauses. He's wanted to talk to him all night. Earlier, he almost did, but the glance from Michael was too brief. It's longer this time—but still no definite clue. Chas moves on. To the leatherman. Pauses. The dude is as macho as they make them—and hot for me. Chas knows. He remembers Robert's face when he looked down the steps at him. Chas approaches the leatherman.

Endore sees him. He feels relief. It has to do with himself and Michael. Chas is talking to the leatherman. Or is he? Didn't it work? After a few minutes with the leatherman, Chas is returning to where Endore stands with the others. Whatever occurred with the leatherman, Chas is exultant.

Ignoring others who approach him, the leatherman waits, tall, brooding, awesome.

Now! Chas faces Endore. The same close proximity of the earlier severed moment: a continuation, yes. Chas squeezes a popper to his nose. Then he lets it fall. It touches one of Lyndy's abandoned pearls. Chas separates it with his shiny boot, shoving the ampule aside in the sawdust. Swaying sensually, he removes his vest. The perspiration gleams red on his chest. Gathered, the moisture streaks erratically and lodges, hot, in his groin. He waves his hand in a sweeping arc as if to embrace the Rushes. The sexual implosion, the first, the best one of this popper, bunches sexual heat. His cock strains. He touches the sweaty groin, and then brings his hand to his lips, kissing it, licking it.

"The fuckin Rushes is seething. And naked," he says.

Endore looks into the bar. Yes. The sexual currents are

flowing with power out of the retral shadows. Glued by sweat, more bodies caress, mouths kiss. Another head bends, a body arcs. More flesh is bared.

"Powerful, man!" Chas blesses the Rushes. The erection hardens. "Dozens of hard cocks throbbing together at the Rushes right now. All is sex now. Feel the fucking excitement growing!" Yes, he will now move to conquer the massive threat of this night, particularly this night, emanating from Endore against him. In approaching Robert—the first time he ever made an initial solicitation—Endore abandoned his role as verbal antagonist; he questioned Chas with action. Yet Endore's questioning wavered earlier before Chas's onslaught to elicit an acknowledgment of mutual faith to the Rushes and its life.

Now Chas has to pursue the part that wavered in Endore. Conquering it will provide a transfusion for strength, and for their love of the Rushes; and that new strength will wash away the vulnerability—did they detect it?—of Chas's earlier confession and, if not erode, temper the mysterious humiliation radiating about the encounter with Robert. Its possible meanings permeate this night.

"Its power is undeniable." Endore feels the bar's heat.

"But you try to resist it," Chas begins his renewed strategy.

"Only to keep from being a total animal in it," Endore says.

Whatever form it took, Chas's encounter with the leatherman has emboldened him.

"But you *are*. You are a sexual animal," Chas pursues. "Like the fucking rest of us. You belong here—and no matter how hard you try to write it away, you come here because that's what you are and where you can be that. Smell the male sweat, the poppers, the odor of cum, and look at the beautiful writhing bodies that lasted the night with hard cocks."

Endore breathes in the sweet rancidity of the Rushes.

"This is all we have, you and me," Chas makes a daring move to extort the verdict he needs. "You and me, Endore, we're alike!"

Waves of dark sensuality seem to toss Endore within the sea of flesh. He will have sex tonight. He sees the panels—even out of sequence, they depict a journey to disorder. "You're wrong. Chas: we're not alike," he pushes away.

Chas winces. Rejection. He'll fight! He pops another ampule of amyl. The odor invades the air. He lets it waft chemical sex as he did earlier when he stood at the top of the stairs. Robert looked up.

Lyndy and Martin reject the sexual fumes.

Chas holds the chemical burnt offering to Endore.

Endore breathes the crushed ampule. The afferent charge rushes erotic redness and images of denuded flesh. He continues to breathe from it. A blackness funnels, almost closing his vision, but funneling open again; and within the sensual whirlpool he sees the leatherman, and then Chas—the top-stripped animal body.

Chas holds the ampule to his own nose, siphoning the vestiges of the chemical's charge. He drops the crushed ampule on the filthy floor, and he steps on it, squashing it on the sawdust as if to seal the act of communion between him and Endore.

He pulls Endore against his body. Endore allows the pull. Chas tries to pry Endore's lips with his tongue. Endore's lips seal. Chas's hungry tongue licks Endore's face, cheeks, ears, chin, mouth, then moves down to the exposed triangle of flesh at Endore's chest. Then his head rises, and his lips wait for Endore's to move. Endore shoves his mouth against Chas's. Their tongues hunt each other's wetness. The sweaty chests slide against each other. The hard groins kiss.

Martin looks away. Lyndy's hand reaches up as if to turn his head to face the men.

Endore pushes Chas away.

Out of the clearing blur of sexuality, the faces of Lyndy and Martin emerge staring.

"You're right, there's no difference between us," Endore says darkly to Chas.

Victorious, Chas smiles.

"Who are you going with tonight, Chas!" Endore demands.

Michael. Chas pauses. "The guy in black leather," Chas's voice is a sexual growl. "I got it all set up, hot and ready."

Not Michael. They will not have to fight for him. "We want the same man, Chas!" Endore hears his words.

"How appropriate!" Lyndy's voice is hungry.

"Of course," Martin understands.

Ambush! Chas's voice is quiet: "That guy in leather's a heavy bottom-man, he's into heavy humiliation." Chas's voice is lower: "You're not into that anymore."

Lyndy licks her dried lips.

Endore feels hatred, desire, anger, pity. "There's no difference between us, Chas, remember? We're both animals in the sex jungle!"

"He's into heavy masochist stuff." Chas's voice is firm.

Endore's is cold, like Lyndy's, like Martin's: "You've made it clear."

In the redness, the leatherman's dark clothes gleam as if bloodied.

"I can understand, with that kid," Chas's whisper attempts to expel Lyndy and Martin. "I'm not even sure I would have gone through with it, with him. That other guy—my first time here—I punched him out, Endore, after he—. . ." Yes, that long ago time: Chas looked down at his pants, the man's piss continued to wet them, it soaked his hard cock. After moments, Chas's fierce fists shot out at the man's face.

Lyndy taunts: "You sound afraid. But look how formidable you are, in your shiny black boots, your cocked cap, your keys and handcuffs—and your *sweat!* And Endore isn't even wearing the uniform."

"That uniform is worn in a look," Endore says.

"I'll go with you, Endore."

Endore jerks back from Chas's words. When the two men kissed, it was an acknowledgment of desire, yes, always there, but not a promise of fulfillment; more, a kissing away of any

possibility of fulfillment. "Don't, Chas!" Endore says—for himself, for Chas—but desire clutches them.

"Of course!" Lyndy says triumphantly.

"Stay out of this!" Chas turns to her. "I mean it." Anger carves every word. "You can watch the last moments, yes, like the tourist you are, but stay out!" Then he turns to Martin: "And you, too, Martin, just watch like an honorary tourist for as long as we *let* you. But don't say one more fuckin word to me, either of you."

Lyndy and Martin wait.

"I want to Endore," Chas says. "I still have the pants I was wearing when that guy pissed on me years ago. You said earlier to play my game fully with myself, that's what you meant. This *is* myself, too. I've always wanted that other side too." He feels freedom, a sad freedom.

"No, Chas," Endore says.

"I want to."

"No."

No! Chas shakes his head. No! He breathes deeply. No! He sheds a trance. No! He grasps for anger. No! "No!" he says aloud, echoing and answering Endore, as if that one resonating word will restore his previous world. And it does, but cracked. "All right, then!" The softness drains. "All right, let's play for that dude! You'll lose, Endore!"

Chas moves to the leatherman.

"What a sly hypocrite you are, Endore," Lyndy says.

"I mean everything I say," Endore says.

"You'll gamble your power again?" Martin asks.

"Chas is formidable, look at how he's displaying himself, now that he's a proud ... 'top-man'—again! Are you so sure you can take him away from Chas?" Lyndy prods. "You offered the youngman more of what he wanted, one assumes, but—..."

"I'll offer this man more of what *he* wants," Endore's voice is colder. "Because I have a deeper knowledge of our contempt than Chas. I long ago faced what the 'top-man' sees

when he looks down at the groveling masochist. He sees himself."

Chas is talking heatedly to the leatherman. The bare chest shines.

"That's the knowledge you turn away from in terror, Martin," Endore pursues him. "The bloody face you drove away from, yours and the other's, reflected in the window of your Jaguar."

Martin lashes: "Oh, tomorrow, Endore, if you 'win' tonight, will you write a column about how we're destroying ourselves and each other in rituals of self-hatred?"

"Yes! And I'll know it from the *inside!*"

He moves away from them, toward Chas, toward the leatherman.

From the thinning bar, Michael watches Endore and Chas flanking the tall dark figure in leather.

"I've come to say good night." Don stands by Lyndy and Martin. "And, Lyndy, I want to apologize for the shameful way the men in this bar have treated you, a lady."

"Good night, darling." Lyndy offers her cheek for Don to kiss. He does, and she dismisses him. Martin nods to Don. Don moves away. The man his age waits for him.

Lyndy and Martin see Chas's lips move, then Endore's. Forced laughter leaps. From Chas. From Endore. The leatherman is quiet. Lyndy and Martin watch the raging battle from the distance. The three men are dark figures burning in the dusty fire of the Rushes.

"*Last Call!*" the bartender's voice booms.

"Ah! And soon the lights will crash!" Lyndy anticipates.

Endore hears Chas's ugly words. They tumble. He hears his own words crash against them in cruel power. He hears Chas's guttural laughter. No, it's his own! He can hear it for the first time. He listens in fascination. It breaks in the middle, like Chas's; and he knows, Yes, the origin of that crack in the laughter is a contradiction as simple as that of intimate love and intimate hate, and in the clash lies a buried scream. He

feels the pain of the touched nerve. Then the laughter resumes, and fades. Was it Chas laughing? Or himself? Is it his and Chas's laughter he's been listening to all along, seeking out the meaning of their shattered sound?

The ferocious blandishments to win the leatherman rush out of the two warring men.

The leatherman turns his back to Chas, choosing Endore.

"Michael!" Chas calls loudly for Endore to hear. Chas moves toward the bar and the youngman there.

From across the battlefield, Endore sees the blond youngman he knew so well and the dark man he knows even better. Michael nods to Chas—and, his hand tight on Michael's shoulder, Chas turns to face Endore.

Endore moves away from the leatherman. He walks up to Michael and Chas. "That man is yours, Chas," he says. "You've won him—all in black leather and eager to grovel for love."

"I pulled you down, Endore," Chas says, but with no note of victory. "I pulled you back in."

"I was never out of any of it," Endore says.

Michael catches the words.

A sorrowful knowledge unites us now, Chas, Endore knows, and it will separate us irrevocably. This is the moment of our greatest intimacy.

The two men face each other. Long moments. Longer. They stretch them longer.

Endore turns toward Michael, and Chas moves back to the leatherman.

"Would you have gone with that man?" Michael asks Endore.

"Would you have gone with Chas?" Endore counters.

Neither answers.

"Last Call!" the summons is repeated.

White brutal lights crash on the Rushes. Black shadows collapse on the floor.

Debris from the night's battles lies among the sawdust like

the aftermath of a storm. The taped music is strangled. Shadows, forms of men now, adjusting their clothes, abandon the back of the bar; they do not look at each other. A few men conjoin, these last moments. Others are leaving alone, dazed. The plain and the beautiful, one tattered army now, straggle into the destroyed night.

"Ah!" Lyndy sighs in amazement.

The man he's with frowns at Don in the glaring light. Don tries to hide his face. "I just remembered, I'm meeting some-one else," the man tells Don, abandoning him to a vortex of terror.

Alone in the ruthless light, Don looks about him. The shirtless muscular man is alone too! Is it possible? Don's eyes plead. The beautiful muscular man looks at him. The tip end of acknowledged recognition? Then he turns away from Don. As if rendered too nakedly vulnerable, the muscular man puts on his white tank top before walking out alone.

"Good night ... *darling,*" Lyndy calls out to Chas as he walks by with the leatherman.

Chas stops before her and Martin. He waits. He looks at them. He waits longer. "You can try and try and you'll see it all," he tells Lyndy. "But you'll *never* be one of us—and that's what you want, because we're *alive,* and you're dead!" Roxy, she said something like that, Chas remembers now. Yes, it was the queen in vinyl and sequins who said that first.

Lyndy pulls back. At her throat, her hands seem to dis-cover anew that one strand of pearls is missing.

"And you, Martin, you'll *always* be one of us," Chas says.

The cold eyes of the man freeze on him.

Chas leaves the Rushes with the leatherman.

"Tonight!" Lyndy's voice destroys the quivering moments. "Tonight, Martin, you'll take me to the Rack. Won't you, dar-ling? Oh, *you* can get me in." She slides off the stool, looping the remaining strand of her necklace about her hand, releas-ing it, looping it again.

"Perhaps there we can astonish you at last," Martin says.

Hatred blazes between them.

The bar is emptying now. The bartenders have begun to clear the wreckage. Lagging casualties sway. A man is trying to rouse Steve, folded over on the bar. A few other men still linger.

Still at the door, Don sees Endore talking to Michael, the beautiful youngman. Endore could still have him, and yet—. . . Does Endore really prefer aloneness? Is it possible he does? *I don't hate you, Endore. I love you.*

"No, I wasn't going with Chas," Michael tells Endore.

Endore wants to believe that. Has to believe it. That incident between him and Michael, the same night Luke left Bill— memory seems to be soothing it. What was it, really? Did Michael really insist—. . . ask for—. . . suggest—. . . only hint— . . . *What!* "I'm glad," he says simply.

His eyes glide along the exposed walls of the Rushes. It is the first time Endore has seen—remembers seeing—the panels in this damning light. Impressions—which may fade or become permanent this night of revelation—bombard him. There *is* a central figure which recurs from panel to panel, and—this astonishes him—there is a definite sequence of events, like recorded stations, but they are scrambled, not in order. The "last" panel—the recurring man now pinioned in ecstasy or pain against the trunk of a tree, the uniformed men assaulting his flesh or stripping the remnants of his clothes— depicts a final pornographic immolation, willing or forced. Now Endore is sure there are 14 drawn panels, and one more, left blank. He looks at the vortex of scrawls entangling flushed organs: the vague, ghostly image there. The artist saw no meaning in the scattered procession to violence. He pulled back by leaving the summary panel undrawn. Endore knows— and now he too pulls back from the impact of the panels. Illumined, cracks in the walls slash the drawn figures like bolts of lightning.

"You're damned to see it all so clearly," Michael says. "All the worst in our world. And still need it. Even love it. Chas

needs it as much—but he'll never see it. But you'll both always need the Rushes."

"Before long, that may be true, for you," Endore says wearily.

"Then I'll have to live with it. In it," Michael tells him. "As well as I can. As well as you do." He waits. "And even if there is no . . . love, I'll pretend—like you—that there can be."

Dazed men pull out of the bar. Some stagger out, drunk—pretending gaiety or slurring anger at this night's waste, which has only now connected into a barren vista of other wasted nights of empty hunting.

Michael's hand reaches out to touch Endore's shoulder, and then it retreats. He walks away.

Dark silhouettes against the darker night, Martin and Lyndy stand framed by the door. "Endore, are you coming with us?" Martin calls out.

Lyndy loops one arm through Martin's. "Of course he is." She holds out the other arm extended for Endore to take.

Looking at Lyndy—hating her—and at Martin—hating him—Endore takes a step toward them. He stops. He looks down. Smashed beer cans, mangled cigarette butts, empty bottles of butyl nitrite, worms of ampules, cum-smeared tissues and handkerchiefs, dirtied sawdust—and two pearls—lie dead on the floor. He looks up at Lyndy and Martin and shakes his head: No. And knows his fascination with their inability to feel—with their dead living—is over: I do not belong with you.

Anger smirches Lyndy's face for one instant. Then she laughs her tiny laughter. She drops her extended arm to her side and links the other one more tightly through Martin's.

The woman and the tall man walk into the wreckage of the night.

14

And this deign to regard
with gracious and kindly
attention.

As OFTEN as he comes to the Rushes, Endore is seldom more aware of its power than when the bar abandons its casualties to the wasted street. Squads of men linger outside. Some still hope for a connection, made those last moments, that will save them from aloneness—tonight—or from the deeper caverns of the sexhunt. In their uniforms of defiant masculinity—slightly tarnished now—they exude a collective desperate beauty, a desperate sexuality, dozens and dozens of men waiting, just waiting. Eyes searching, they stand alone, lean against smirched walls. No matter how cruel the Rushes may have been, it protected them from a vaster cruelty outside.

Now the mass of men begins to separate.

Endore looks at the sprawling waterfront.

A desolate scenery of gray and black shadows is almost extinguished toward the edge of the water, the end of the land, before total darkness.

A breeze pushes at the sweaty heat. It stirs the rotten exhalations from the piers—a psychic poison. The warehouses cut giant gravestones into the electric orange scrim created by the streetlights.

Within the hypnotized night, the lingering men outside the Rushes stir. Behind them, the Rushes—unsated—gathers its energy to pull them back tomorrow. Now men move into the aisles between the meat trucks or toward the blotting darkness of the piers. Feet will further crush the blight. Along the spilling blocks, dark doorways and walls will shelter other waiting bodies.

In the scarred apartment building across from the trucks, dim lights frame denuded men inviting floating forms below.

Hot vapor coats the streets. Reflections of broken light quiver on the oiled grime gleaming like vinyl.

The black arrogant limousine purrs in the sullied light. The tiny form of Lyndy, smaller from this distance, so much smaller, bends toward the lowered black window of the car. Her darkened lips instruct the chauffeur. Then she crosses the street to join the tall imposing form of Martin.

He will attempt to get her into the Rack, Endore knows.

Unable to face Endore among the stragglers choosing among the trucks, the piers, the Rack, Don hides in the declined entrance to a locked building. Earlier, he was relieved to find that the shirtless youngman was gone from the street; he did not want even to glimpse the taunting presence. In the clasped shadows behind him now, three or four bodies toss in slow sexual convulsions. Don looks away.

Next to the Rushes, a new life has begun to thrive.

Taxis, private cars, motorcycles converge. Squads of men come on foot. Most but not all are dressed in leather and metal, some in authoritarian uniforms. Even bared flesh is decorated with linked chains, intertwined black belts, studded crossed straps, cut whips. In the Rushes, there was not the

cumulative black austerity coalescing here. The black, en-chained leather uniforms have assumed the solemnity of the sacramental vestments of officiants at a rite.

Under the rotting iron skeleton of a rusted fire ladder out-side, the men will move up the leprous corridor, past the tough guards blocking out "undesirables"—"Strict Dress Code No Fats Femmes Over35s," the posted sign warns—and into the maw of the created ruins of the Rack. Some of the men have waited all night, waking for these moments. Whetted or still unsatisfied, others return from earlier encounters. Resus-citated after the hiatus in the hunt between Last Call and now, some men move from the dormant Rushes and to the Rack. It flanks the Rushes like an inevitable extension, separated only by a decaying wall, a partition which may one day topple, joining the two in irresistible power.

Endore watches the mass gathering across the street. More cabs and cars arrive, depositing men. Some will change inside into their decorated leather. There is an awed traumatized seriousness. Endore has not been there since before he met Michael. He's aware of its pulling emanations, this hot, cool night. He looks away from the procession of leather and silver. He sees a familiar form. It is. No, it isn't—. . .

Robert is standing alone across the street. Endore does not take a step toward the youngman. Instead, he slides into a cove of darker night. No more is possible between him and Robert. There was a beginning, a middle, and an end. An end. What happened—like what happened between him and Mi-chael—will continue only in memory, that real.

The hustler is back! Don saw the young figure from where he still waits to escape from Endore's sight. After a groaning convolution, one body untangled itself from the sexual knot in the shadows behind him. Two others joined, pulled by the sighs, the slide of flesh on flesh. Don doesn't dare look back. Doesn't dare be lured. No, it isn't the hustler, he realizes with relief; it's the boy in the bar. They look so much alike.

The violent scraping of brakes on the wet pavement—a car stops. Alerted to the recurrent battering violence sweeping the

waterfront this first hot night, men on the street tense. The car stops only for a moment. It does not spill out the angry plunderers, only a shirtless youngman. Tim does not wave back at the driver of the car. He still holds, warming it, allowing it to warm him, the money his second client of the night just paid him. Holding his breath, Tim watches the stark dark-leathered men ascending the steps to the Rack.

Across the street, Robert waits. He has not seen Endore. Gauging the youngman's interest, figures lean against the wall, cruising him.

Endore recognizes Tim. He remembers the face mellowed by terror when the invaders flung their curses at them and he and the youngman touched against the wall. The long eyelashes. No, Robert's. The youngman next to him, too, had—. . . Grasping, the possible connective meaning, he looks at the two youngmen.

Frozen on opposite corners, Robert and Tim stare at each other.

The shirtless hustler *is* back, Don knows. And he's running—. . .

Tim runs across the street.

. . .—toward the youngman Endore and Chas talked to in the bar.

Robert starts to dash away. He stops, waits. He faces Tim.

From the distance, Endore hears exacerbated words, and he understands the confrontation.

"What the fuck you doin here?" Tim asks Robert.

"I was just—. . . Walking. I—. . ." Robert wavers.

Figures slide into the muddy maze of trucks.

"Were you in that queer bar? That Rushes?"

"Hell, no!" Robert denies. Then: "Yeah! But I didn't know who—. . . You said—. . ."

"You *were* in that queer bar, my own little brother in a fucking queer bar!" Tim rails as if he's been wounded.

More men are entering the Rack, more menacing black and silver. The emaciated bulb over the entrance creates a shredded veil through which they pass.

"I told you, I was just walking past." Then Robert's words bolt out: "Yeah, Tim, I was in that qu—... in that bar, yeah!"

The hypnotized night is violated by the sound of their voices.

Tim tries to hide the money he just hustled. It's crushed in his fist.

Robert understands: "That's how you get your bread; all this time you were lying about—..." But he's relieved. Listening to Tim so many nights when he came back late, Robert would lie on his bed and hate himself for allowing the aroused voice of his brother to narrate his violent encounters with "queers." Later, excitement at war with fear, Robert would sever the described figures from the violence, converting them into sexual fantasies. It was out of those that "Endore" arose.

"Don't call me a liar, cocksucker!"

Robert winces.

Tim withdraws. "I'm really sorry I said that, but, look man, that word don't mean nothing unless you're a fag."

From the piers, as if rising out of the vaporescence on the streets, other men are transferring to the Rack to avoid the damning dawn.

Tim's voice is firm: "I asked you: What were you doin hangin out with the fags?"

"What do *you* do for the bread you were hiding?" Robert questions back.

"Nothin! I just take 'em. And if you go for bread and don't do nothin', that don't make you nothin!"

They're going to go home together, those two beautiful boys. If it weren't for that affronting possibility, Don would feel a spark of triumph. He outlasted the bunched men, did not try to join. He can't see Endore now. Still, he waits. They seem angry, though, the two youngmen. There's so much anger, he thinks. Was there always this much and I don't remember it?

"Why're you staring at me like that?—like I'm the one who was in that Rushes. Not me, man! No, man, not me!" Tim stares along the block.

· 205

The footsteps of the men moving toward the Rack are muted.

Tim turns to Robert; his voice is forced: "Hey, I bet you were tryin to hustle up some bucks of your own, huh? That's it, huh? But you can't hustle inside that bar, see, I coulda told you that, there they just go with each other, not for bread; in there, they're all faggots! And in that other weird place they're going to now," he says with deep anger. He wipes his sweating body. He wishes now the cruising men nearby would disappear, not hear even the snatches of their talk. He feels their eyes. "I hate them," he blurts. "Drink my piss!" he says to one of the men glancing at them.

Robert pulls back. The memory of Chas's body standing on the top of the steps stamps itself over the image of his brother. "I'm queer," Robert hears his own words.

"What!"

"I'm queer." The words are firmer now.

Tim looks about as if someone might have heard. "Don't you ever say that again, hear?" He grabs Robert.

Endore watches—hearing only a word, a phrase—the rise and fall of their voices; and reading, certain he can read, wanting to read, the movements: Robert's stance is firming, Tim's is shaken. Endore touches his lips, as if to seal in the past—and touch—the earlier contact with the youngman. Had there been anything more possible? He glances at the men drawn like ionized particles to the magnet of the Rack. He feels a deadly excitement. No, no more was possible.

Robert pushes his brother away. "You face it—because I have—that I'm queer! I went to the piers first because you told me—without knowing it—that it was easy, and then I went to the trucks because you told me about them, too. But I didn't make out."

"See!" Tim clutches.

"Because I was afraid—of people like the ones you said you ran around with, beating guys."

"Shut up, I'm warnin you!"

"You listen!" Robert demands.

Tim starts to walk away.

Don emerges out of the shadowy decline. He watches the shirtless youngman swaggering away, like a young animal, Don thinks. He glances around. He can't see Endore. Just the gliding forms like ghosts of sleepwalkers. Now the youngman who was in the bar is following the other. Angry. Yes, Don thinks, there's more anger now.

Robert reaches Tim. They're nearer the trucks now. There's the crunch of steps, the pervasive odor of amyl. Naked men in several muted frames of light in the building stand like aroused statues.

Robert forces Tim around.

"Don't ever touch me, you little punk," Tim rages.

"Then listen to me, because there's a lot I gotta tell you. You made me feel dirty, but tonight—. . ."

"Dirty like the fags who go where you went," Tim hurls.

"*You* go there too," Robert reminds him. "Man," he says in a quiet voice, controlling each word, watching Tim's reaction, "you can hustle somewhere else, the guy at the door told me, better places, and if that's what you want, so what? But why do you come here, if you hate it so much?"

"Cause it makes me feel good—angry; and that's what I wanna feel!" Tim says. He feels the waning heat, heavy. The waterfront looks uglier than he's ever seen it. "Fuck, it's so hot tonight, I'm sweating. Look." He blots perspiration from his forehead. But a cool breath of a breeze is blessing the night.

Tim shakes his head, a desolate move. "The only moments I got," he says aloud. "All I got is now," he says. "All I got is now," he echoes himself.

"Tim—. . ." Robert tries to soothe, but he doesn't know what to say. Tim looks so tired, more tired than he's ever seen him. He feels as if tonight Tim is younger than him.

Tim touches his lips. "Sometimes I wish I could shout and have everyone listen, but no one does. The only people who see me are the ones who pay me."

"*I'll* listen, Tim. But if that's true, why do you want to hurt them?"

"Shut up, you don't understand. It's only for *then* that they want me." His own thoughts tangle. He tries to remember the straight dark lines buildings make against the sky on windy days when he sits by the river. Sometimes that makes sense, sometimes it doesn't. "I'm telling you why I hustle—if you'll just listen. It's cause I don't know what words I wanna shout. I never have hit no one—..."

"I'm glad, man," Robert says. "I'm really, really glad."

"I...—just rob guys."

The sound of footsteps, slow, searching, disembodied; yet no one is visible nearby—until the tapping of hurried heels scarifies the night.

Martin and Lyndy are rushing down the steps of the Rack and into the street.

They were refused entrance, Endore knows. She was shut out. She was left out. He sees the tiny figures summon the waiting limousine.

Before the chauffeur can get out, Lyndy opens the door. Inside the car, she shuts the door with a crack like a shot. The limousine moves away. Martin waits on the street. Then he snaps his fingers at a cab which has just surrendered more men to the Rack.

She was shut out. Her greatest defeat of the night, Endore knows. She is damned to reach out and be blocked by the blackened window of her limousine.

Tim glares at the disdainful mechanical animal of the limousine as it moves without a sound past him. "But I'm *gonna* hit someone one day—..." he finishes.

"But the person you hit won't be the one who made you hurt," Robert pleads.

Tim looks about. "Look at it all, man, so fuckin ugly. Rotting; and, Christ, smell it rot." His hand sweeps as if to cut down the crumbling buildings, clear away the broken streets, push back the metal-stained water.

Robert senses Tim's blinded rage. "I wish I could help you, and I will, if you let me—..." It's as if, always, Tim was younger, Robert realizes now.

"You can by—... by—..." Tim clenches his teeth. "Just stay away from fags, that's all."

"Not that, and I won't even listen to you if you talk about hurting people who aren't hurting you and feel hurt, like you."

Confusions clot in Tim's mind.

Endore has moved closer along the street. He can see the two young forms. The endless battles, he thinks. The invisible ones, and the open ones. Unending. How deeply they've wounded us. He looks toward the entrance to the Rack. Some of the same men at the Rushes, but hardened even more now in their black leather, linger to enter. There are fewer outside now. Inside, the pit will be grinding. The varied tensions of the night will overflow in violent rushes.

"I'm grateful to you for bringing me here, Tim," Robert tries to absolve whatever his brother feels of guilt, "because I know where I belong."

"In those filthy trucks with the blood from meat? You seen the butchers in the daytime, man? You seen the chunks of meat like—like—..." Tim's voice is weary. "And on those piers where everything is rotten? In that bar, with those weird guys? You belong there?"

"You're here too," Robert's voice is gentle, reminding again.

"So I can *hate* them! You really want all that?"

"I don't know," Robert says. "Maybe. And maybe something else. But whatever it is, wherever it is, it'll be *me* there, and it won't be ugly, Tim, like it is for you, like it was for—..." The memory of Chas is blurred. He remembers Endore. "I kissed a guy in there. No, he kissed me first, and then I kissed him."

"I'll kill the fucker!" Tim rages.

"It was beautiful. I told him to fuck off!" the memory of anger cuts.

"You see, you're not queer!"

Within the aisles of the trucks abandoned like the corpses of huge animals, men roam, finding other bodies.

"Just because he wouldn't go with me. He was scared. Like you, Tim."

"Scared? What do you mean, *scared?*"

"Just that if you faced—. . ."

"You little queer!" The word shot out of Tim. He reaches out in terror as if to clutch back the fatal word.

The orange glow from the piers is like weakening fire.

"Man, you're my little bro'. I love you, little asshole." Tim punches playfully at Robert's stomach. "Who made you tough so you'd never be afraid of nothing, huh?"

"We're all afraid sometimes."

"No! . . . Remember how I showed you how to fight? And took care of you. I mean, man, I really love you," Tim says.

In a window of the building across the street, two men kiss.

"Not dirty or nothing." Tim rips his gaze from the window. "I mean, I just *love* you."

"You actually had to explain that?" Robert says. "Look, I remember real good how you took care of me, and I love you, too, a lot, and I'll listen whenever you want—whenever you feel like hitting on someone, I'll listen instead, man, I swear. But I can't if you want to hurt me."

"Not you! *Them!*" Tim points to the cruising men.

"I'm one of them, Tim!" Robert yells at him.

"No. You're just mixed up." Tim pushes with his hands, to shove it all away, all that's been spoken, seen. "You heard me tell you about those places," he says firmly, "and it's natural you'd be curious, wanna find out for yourself. I'm sorry I told you—. . ."

"I found out about myself long ago, man, it's just that you made me feel it was dirty, because *you* feel it is, and it isn't."

"You go home now," Tim orders.

"And you'll stay, huh?" Robert challenges. "Find someone to pay you, or someone to rob, or—. . ." He feels afraid for his brother. "Please don't, Tim. It won't make it better, it won't. You just add more hurt and it comes back. Don't, man, okay? Okay?"

Don waits against a wall near the trucks. Behind him, the shadows of men have lost even their outlines.

"Didn't you hear me?" Tim's voice is rigid. "I said, go home."

"No. Before tonight is over, I'm gonna make it. With a guy. Really make it, together, and it'll be good, and I won't feel guilty. Not dirty either, Tim; and it'll be with someone I want and who wants me." He remembers his lips on Endore's. He searches out the memory. It's coated with love now, soothing. I wish he hadn't been so afraid. Afraid and angry, he thinks.

Endore sees the squared shoulders of Robert. What occurred between Robert and his brother, he'll never know exactly—another of tonight's fragments. But he can deduce. And hope. And for Michael. The youngman's brother? He remembers him rushing after the raiding car long ago this evening and proclaiming his . . . masculinity.

"If I see you here again, I'll beat the fuck out of you!" Tim threatens Robert. He has to end this encounter. He feels bombarded by invisible threats. The waterfront is smothering him.

"No, you won't, Tim," Robert says. "Because you're as gay as I am."

Tim's angered fist almost connects with Robert's face. But Robert swayed.

Endore sees Robert walk away from the waterfront. The fake uncertain swagger is gone.

"He . . . ain't . . . queer," Tim whispers. Now he adjusts himself, arranging his hair. He slings his shirt over his shoulder.

Don takes a few steps away from the trucks.

Tim's tough-sexual stance is returning. Then it shatters. Too heavy. He's tired. He touches his wet forehead.

Endore moves across the street.

Tim sees him, recognizes him.

They both hear the screeching brakes of a car. They push against the nearest wall. Other men on the street move for

shelter. But the car merely stopped to release more leathered men to the Rack. Laughing, they seem to welcome the fear their arrival aroused. Don moved back into the shadows.

For the second time tonight, Endore and Tim stand touching, pressed against the wall. Neither moves, feeling welcome warmth where their bodies touch. Again, Endore sees the sad, pleading, long-lashed eyes of Robert's brother. Tim's lips open. His mouth inches toward Endore's. Then Tim's eyes squeeze shut, his teeth and lips clench, his hands tangle into fists, wringing out the vulnerability, converting it into the need to wound.

Endore feels the tension in the trembling body next to him. Once more he looks at Tim, and then he moves away.

As if forcing each part of his body to respond, Tim adopts his tough pose again. First the shoulders, slouched: then the legs, spread. The head tilts—...

Endore sees Don on the other side of the street.

Don was about to cross, but seeing Endore, he lowered his head, avoiding him.

Endore passes the lowered entrance to the darkened building where Don waited earlier. He hears beckoning sexsounds. He pauses. He looks back toward the Rack. A shirtless man wearing black chaps and leather cap pauses there. A tall man in leather stands near him. The two move past the weakened light over the entrance to the Rack.

Don walks toward Tim. But he turns back. Endore has stopped. Help me! Don wants to call back to him. Instead, he moves along the street toward Tim. Help me! But now he's standing next to Tim, who waited.

Keep moving. Don walks past Tim. Keep moving. Tim's eyes follow him. Don moves farther away, faster. Don't turn back! He turns the dark corner.

Don's going home, Endore thinks in relief.

Out of Endore's sight. Don waits. He hears distant footsteps. Endore's. Now he hears closer ones. The youngman's. Don leans his head back and looks at the shut sky. We used to be able to see the stars, he thinks

Pulling at Don with his inviting look, Tim walks by slowly. Don follows him into the darkness of a sealed building. Don can hear the sound of Endore's footsteps again.

On the moist pavement, the footsteps move back along, not away from, the savaged waterfront.

15

As often as you shall
do these things,
in memory of Me shall
you do them.

IN A LIGHT like cold fire, two naked men
crawl on the wooden floor. Chains dangle from their wrists,
studded belts are crisscrossed like distorted harnesses on their
torsos, black cockrings and straps contain their flushed geni-
tals. The odor of urine, dead cum, stale sweat, the putrid va-
porescence of amyl and butyl nitrite saturate the torpid air. A
leathered man wearing dark sunglasses in this dark dusk holds
a chain looped to metallic collars about the necks of the crawl-
ing men. Each time he tugs, they grovel at the boots and
crotch of whatever dominant-stanced man he indicates. With
a black belt, the man strikes the bared buttocks. His thrust
spittle forms sequins on the lubricated flesh.

In the large barren room, slabs of wood slant in fallen

diagonals. They create the atmosphere of a collapsing subterranean world. Muted here too, its origin invisible, music groans, as if the panting of the Rushes is transducing through the shared membrane of walls. Here, the redness has been further bled to dark.

Like mangled traceries of unframed pornography, men bunched against the walls masturbate each other and themselves, suck, kiss, rim, fuçk. Within the clasped shadows, sudden fissions occur in the carnified masses, a body separates along the reddened lubricity to find another mass of flesh. Smaller rooms open into deeper darkness.

Silent processions of men, some leathered or uniformed, others in iron-, chain-, or leather-decorated nudity wander about, pause to stare at, or coagulate in carnal rites.

Garbage has been allowed to accumulate—or imported, in homage to rot, a welcome extended to the effluvia from the piers: crumpled mired papers, oxidized smashed cans, shreds of spóiled underwear. Melding, separating, reshaping, men often spit on the floor in rehearsed contempt.

Whack! The sound of a belt or a whip flailing, comes muffled but assertive from a bottom room.

A gash in the floor connects to a wooden ladder leading to two other large rooms in the lower depths. As they descend, figures swallowed by the throttled light appear to burn in dying flames.

Face smeared with contempt, a man teases with the tip of his cowboy boot the writhing ass of another man on the floor. On an army cot, its flattened mattress redolent of nights of sex and sweat, a naked man is pinioned by two cop-uniformed men, one at the head of the emaciated cot, another at its feet. A third man holds his boot over the face of the supine man, his tongue laps the sole. Another boot grinds into his groin. Releasing one hand, the pinioned man forces the boot down harder onto his own genitals.

Whack! The demanding lash summons.

Several cubicles contain toilets, exhumed props in the de-

cay of fantasy. Men sit crouching, blowing whoever stands before them, a clot of bodies pushes in to share the anxious arcking mouth.

In a tenebrous corner, a man in split handcuffs leans against a wall. A tiny ring punctures his right nipple, a small chain dangles from it. His face is ecstatic as men take turns twisting his nipples like screws.

A man in leather mounts a harnessed man. a silver bit between his teeth. Each time his head jerks like that of a bolting horse. the black-gloved man on him thrashes at the bared flesh. Then he lunges into it with his cock and pulls back on the bit.

Whack! The flailing commands steady attention.

Not a word is spoken here. The sounds are of mouths on flesh, flesh on flesh, of crunching feet on the imported debris, of assaults on flesh—sighs, moans, groans, gasps—and the harsh punctuation of a belt cracking beneath these rooms.

Whack!

As intent as students over an operating table, men gather to watch a naked man, bound at the wrists and feet to a leather distortion of a childhood swing; it is attached by heavy chains to the low ceiling. Between the legs of those watching, other men crawl—one wrapped in chair.s—sucking, licking, rimming, groping. The feet of the bound man are cupped by metal stirrups at two ends of the hanging incurvated hide. His bent legs are spread so wide that his ass opens in a round hollow.

Random cocks take turns penetrating his hole. Probing fingers open it wider. A grotesque dildo is crammed into it. Now a shirtless man wearing leather chaps and boots and a black cowboy hat begins pushing his fist into the begging ass. His tattooed forearm—a menacing panther running the length of it—strains to shove farther. The strapped man is covered with sweat like red dye. His face is delirious. But his cock is soft.

Now the leathered-cowboy's fist is swallowed by the

starved ass. It widens to receive the muscular thighs of the tattooed panther. The bound man gasps. The face of the leathered cowboy is stoical. Other intense eyes watch, faces press closer to observe the anus violated by the fist, a portion of the wrist. The arm rams midway to the elbow, the snarling panther disappears into the ass.

In a soundless howl, the strapped man's mouth opens, issuing silence.

Throughout the room, other similar contraptions are occupied. Men straddle the faces of the eager, bound men leaning back. Men move their cocks and fists from hole to hole. Before an empty leather sling, a tall man holds up a prepared fist coated with melting lard, summoning a willing hole and alerting the witnessing men who will now shift like wandering acolytes along with the crawling figures into a transferred ceremonial circle. The fist gleams in the strangled light, which is the color of drying blood. A man is now being strapped to the sling.

Down the wooden ladder. Red silhouettes of naked and leathered men glide within the lower depths of the cardinal sea, past the imported garbage like flotage.

Shackles, chains on the walls, manacles restrain men in anxious surrender. Even when there is for this moment no visible source of pain—no violative fist or belt or instrument, even then, they moan and writhe in soft motions of deep hurt, as if it were being inflicted by an absent torturer.

In a tub a man lies nude. A circle of thighs and exposed cocks surrounds him. Men urinate on him, jerk off, spit on him. The sweating, growling man in the tub slurps at the mixture of urine, cum, spittle. A hand shoves his head against the stained porcelain. The thirsty tongue laps at the dripping liquid. A circle of men wait for their turn to grovel in the tub or to thrust their liquid contempt into it.

Like a slavemaster, the man leading the naked men by metal collars pulls back the chains before Endore.

Endore stands in the midst of the carnage at the Rack.

The man before him tugs at the collars of the two naked men. They open Endore's pants. The mouths devour his genitals. Endore's cock does not harden. He has moved with cold excitement through the vicissitudes of the decay—the death—of fantasy; has floated, now shirtless, past crawling, licking, clutching masses of bodies in this rubicund twilight of mangled sex, has shifted from mouth to mouth, pushing his cock in. But it has not hardened. Not once. Here, he will not reciprocate. He knew that when a man attempted to kiss him and he turned away, sheltering the touch of Robert's lips. And Chas's. Now he pushes the collared heads away.

Whack! the sound pulls from the lower room.

Endore moves through the frozen fire. Shadows wrestle in the corridors.

Whack! the slap of flesh lures.

Why am I here? Thoughts rush to protect him. The sexhunt, endemically ours, its unique joy and opulent profligacy, yes, earned, outlaw defiance against repression, yes, that, converted, full, unique, ours, envied by others attempting imitation, yes. But he knows that that is not here at the Rack, and that the Rack is the inevitable extension of the Rushes—and that what he loves and has vaunted in the sexhunt is not in the nightly deaths of mean bars nor in the charade of filth and pain. No, the Rack is permeated by the punishment *for* sex. He sees this clearly and with anger: This is what they have done to us! And he sees this as clearly but with sorrow: And this is what we do now to ourselves in ritual reenactment of *their* hatred, and we masquerade it all as masculine strength.

It is only charade, a part of him argues, only a charade, a willing charade, all willing.

But he knows the psychic bleeding is as real as the rancidity that coats these ugly rooms; and, recognizing with equal clarity his own part in the hateful ritual, he knows that later, oh, yes, later, he will bear reliable witness to it all, and to his contribution to it.

Now he will surrender to the onslaught of the Rack

He faces a growing cluster of men, five at first, then seven, now ten, more. They fuse into a grinding mass of sexflesh. It throbs, moans, sighs. Like a great wounded beast devouring itself or licking its own wounds. Coming or dying.

Which!

Whack!

Pulled by powerful undercurrents, he enters the third large room of the Rack.

At the back is an elevated platform. The outstretched hands of a naked man are shackled to a horizontal board supported by two upright ones. The man's slender body is beautiful. The muscles are taut, bold. His booted feet are shackled to a lower horizontal board. On the platform a man pops a series of crushed ampules of amyl nitrite to the nose of the strapped man.

The back of the tied man is turned to the room and to the spectators gathering for this central spectacle.

A man kneels licking the boots of the bound man.

Black chaps, black boots, black shirt, black cap, black gloves—all leather—a tall man stands before the back of the nude figure. The leathered man grasps a long black belt. He flails it with a snapping *Whack!* at the fetid air—another summoning sound. The naked man tenses in anticipation of the nearing assault. More men join to watch the promised ritual. Their faces are drained of expression.

Endore pulls away, to leave. He turns his back to the cruel spectacle about to begin. Untangling from the darkness ahead, a man nude except for thick silver-studded belts forming an "X" across his body, approaches Endore. The man holds out a vial of liquid amyl as an offering. Endore brings the pure liquid to his own nose. He inhales the strong vapor in long, long breaths, clutching each in his lungs. Now he sucks the odor through his mouth. The naked man with belts crisscrossing his body begins to slide down.

Before the naked figure on the platform, the leathered man cracks the belt behind him in the air.

Whack!

He is still tantalizing, only that—but each time, the forward lashing of the belt reaches closer to the eager flesh. The buttocks of the naked man gird. The leathered man unleashes the belt again. It cracks—

Whack!

—still not touching, but this time the tip breathed on the flesh. Still the man in leather is prolonging the anticipation of the strapped man, who growls in pained expectation.

More men are gathering for the rite. Now crawling manacled figures explore the booted legs, the indifferent groins.

The black-leathered man arches his long feline body.

The amyl clasps Endore. The beating of his heart pounds in his head.

Whack!

The tip of the belt stings.

In one sudden motion the leathered man brings the belt back and lashes it in brutal surprise across the back of the bound man, who growls in deep, pained, deep pleasure.

Whack!

Endore turned at the same time that the head of the naked bound man jerked in ecstatic hurt to one side and in that moment Endore saw the face of Chas and Chas's body being thrashed by the leatherman. No! It isn't Chas! It's someone else! Not Chas! It isn't Chas, it isn't Chas it isn't Chas it isn't Chas. No!

The head of the strapped man turns again.

Whack!

The head turns to the other side.

Whack!

The roaring amyl rushes Endore.

Whack!

At the same time that Endore saw the man with studded belts across his body slide down before him to his knees, at the same time that he felt a mouth sucking his unhardened cock, at the same time that he throttled a scream lodging in his

throat, at the same time that he closed his eyes to blind himself to the carnage—at the same time, Endore saw the head of the strapped man twisting to one side, then the other, and to one side it was Chas's, and to the other it became his own, then Chas's, then his own, Chas's, his own, Chas's—and then it was a stranger's! It's someone else, not Chas, not me! Endore told himself—and felt the lash of the belt on his own raw flesh and saw himself lashing the same belt across the twisting naked body.

Outside on the street, dawn is exposing the plundered battlefield along the waterfront.

Distant bells, announcing Sunday, resonate across the blighted streets.

The beginning glare of the rising sun purifies the water only for these translucent moments. Endore's hand rises to clear his eyesight from the lambent sheen of dawning light. Because through blinking eyes he thought he saw in the distance the luminous form of Robert moving away from the waterfront just as he had earlier, but farther away now, much farther, farther; and Endore thinks now: There *is* hope!

A car speeds past. Its angered motor announces the return of the night's plunderers for a final act of violence. A block ahead, the car stops before the parked trucks, its motor left running. Alerted, men scramble out of the trucks escaping past five young bodies rushing with iron pipes into the maze.

"Queer cocksucker faggot!"

Speeding away, the car abandons a horrible reality.

Beautiful, slender, naked, a man emerges out of the maze of the invaded trucks, and he walks to the very edge of the street. For moments he looks straight ahead in astonishment or horror. Then blood oozes from his head, runs down his chest, covers his groin, flows down his legs, gathers at his feet, and rushes into the filthy gutter. The man collapses.

Soon Endore will run to help the man, as others are already doing. But for this moment he cannot move.

His hand is still raised as when he tried to filter the shim-

mering dawn to see more clearly the luminous figure he thought was Robert's. But now his hand moves instead to cover his eyes. Even that motion stops. His palm pushes outward, as if attempting this time to thrust away the terrible sights and the memories of this long night—except one, except one, except one memory.

Still raised, Endore's hand pauses as if in a benediction impossible to complete. Then it falls to his side in a fist.

Selected Grove Press Paperbacks